She needs
a convenient
marriage with no
complications—
especially not love.
But then
_he_ walks in . . .

"I want you."

"You wouldn't be standing here if not for my bridal settlement."

"What do you want me to say?" Lord McKinney said, his words a growling rush. "That I'm not in need of funds? Yes, you have the money my family desperately needs. But you also fill my thoughts. I ache for you."

Their gazes locked, clung. Cleo searched his face, both reveling in and frightened from his stark declaration.

"I don't want you to say anything," she whispered. "I-I don't care."

"Do you want me to profess my love?"

She choked and jerked as though slapped. "N-no! I would not believe you if you did."

At his decidedly relieved look, she rolled her eyes. Apparently he believed in the sentiment of love as much as she did.

Desperate to end this, she shoved past him, but he grabbed her arm and turned her back around. "You feel something for me. I know it."

His mouth took hers completely, roughly. He crushed her against him, trapping her hands between them. His lips devoured hers. She moaned, sagging against him, sinking into his kiss, drowning in the deliciousness of the moment.

By Sophie Jordan

Sophie Jordan

Lessons From A Scandalous Bride
Forgotten Princesses

AVON
An Imprint of HarperCollinsPublishers

AVON BOOKS
An Imprint of HarperCollins*Publishers*
10 East 53rd Street
New York, New York 10022-5299

First Avon Books mass market printing: August 2012

For Sarah MacLean—
a brilliant writer and excellent friend.
I relish our every phone call.

Lessons from a Scandalous Bride

Chapter One

The late-evening sea air swept through the open window. Cleo inhaled greedily, glad for the fresh gust of salty wind. The cottage was stale, rank from too many bodies and the ripe, coppery tang of blood drifting downstairs. She shook a strand of hair away from where it dangled in her eyes and readjusted the sleeping toddler in arms that had long since gone numb.

She knew from experience that it would be days before the stench faded. And even then she would still smell it. The odor of death never completely vanished from her senses.

Heavy footsteps sounded on the plank stairs and she moved the sleeping toddler from her arms. Quickly, gently, she laid Bess on one of several pallets lining the floor before the stove.

A total of fourteen children slept on the ground floor. More crowded than usual. The youngest four usually slept in the loft with Cleo's mother and stepfather while the rest of them bedded down on the first floor each night. The pallets were always cleared away each morning like a bad dream erased and forgotten.

Except Cleo could never forget. It was a wretched existence. Even though she knew nothing but this life, Cleo knew this. She felt it, absorbed this awareness of her squalid surroundings with every sip of breath. Pulling the threadbare blanket up over Bess, she swung around as Mrs. Dubbins reached the bottom floor.

Cleo rose to face their neighbor expectantly, her heart a tight, twisting mass in her chest. Mrs. Dubbins had helped with her mother every time, too many times for Cleo to count . . . which made her a regular fixture in their home.

"How is she?" Her hands fisted at her sides.

Mrs. Dubbins shook her gray-streaked head, the weathered lines of her face drawn and tight. "She can't do this again."

Cleo nodded jerkily. They were the same words Mrs. Dubbins had advised last time. The last five times. Still, he didn't listen. Didn't care. Didn't stop.

Her eyes ached, but no tears burned there. She stared with dry eyes. She was past weeping. Tears

would not help. Nothing could be done. Her stepfather would never change.

As if the thought conjured him, the thud of his
boots shook the stairs. She looked up, watching as
he descended. His large frame ate up all the space
in the small cottage.

Cleo gazed at his ruddy, thick-boned face, carefully schooling her features to reveal none of the
loathing she felt for this man. He'd been handsome once. She could see the evidence in the swol-
len features of his face, the nose bulbous from too
much drink and hard living.

Her mother claimed that he'd been charming
once, too, a catch. Which made it all the more
incomprehensible that he'd ever wanted Cleo's
mother—an unwed mother, ruined and reviled—
living off the charity of relations. And yet wanted
her he had. Even with a four-year-old Cleo in tow.

She saw nothing appealing about him as he
stopped before her, his boots sliding to a halt.

"See to this," he said, holding out the small
blanket-wrapped bundle.

A familiar command.

With a single nod, she took the still warm
bundle and brought it close to her body, waiting
as he fished the halfpenny from his pocket. With
great reluctance he handed it to her.

She knew if he could, he'd simply toss the body

into the sea, but people would know. Ceremony and ritual were everything. Such an act would bring the wrath of their neighbors upon them. He'd do the bare minimum and see that the babe was laid to rest on consecrated soil.

With a murmured farewell to Mrs. Dubbins, Cleo collected her cloak from the hook by the door and set out into the night.

She held the bundle close. She always did— always felt an overwhelming compulsion to hug the little one. She felt the need to give something to the child who, even gone from this earth, had never had anything—and never would. Not even a proper burial.

The waves crashed against the sea wall as she walked a steady line on the broken path in her worn-thin slippers. Leaving the row of cottages behind, she made her way toward the end of town. As the small spire came into view, she muttered a quick prayer over the child, the sibling she would never know.

She opened the squeaky gate into the still churchyard. A single light shone in the window of the caretaker's cottage. The place was smaller than her home.

She knocked briskly upon the door of splintered and cracking wood, shivering inside her cloak. It always felt wrong doing this. A sacrilege. Not that she had any choice in the matter.

All warmth had faded from the small bundle in her arms. She peeled back the cloth to take a glimpse. She had to do this. She did so each time. It was all she could do—give the lost babe a final glimpse, acknowledgement that its life mattered.

It was a boy this time. His little nose tiny as a button. His small lips wrinkled blue with death. She brushed a finger against the tiny curve of his cheek, surprisingly smooth. Cold as marble. She blinked. Suddenly her eyes didn't feel so dry.

"You deserved better than this," she lowered her head and said so softly she could scarcely hear herself.

The door opened, flooding her in a burst of light. She lifted her head and dropped her hand from the tender, nearly translucent cheek, shielding her dead brother with the blanket again.

Training her features into her usual mask of impassivity, she lifted her chin a notch and faced the caretaker. "Good evening, Mr. Hollis."

"Ah, got another one there, do you?"

Cleo nodded, hugging the body close as she endured Hollis's rot-toothed smile. It made her ill that he always appeared happy to see her on these occasions she knocked at his door. As if this was a social call and not the grim, heart-wrenching task that had fallen to her yet again.

"Yes, and I'd appreciate it if you would bury him alongside the others."

The others. Three stillborns. And eight-month-old Rosie, two-year-old James, three-year-old Lottie, and seven-year-old Helen. It seemed only right that they had each other in death.

Her family was a regular factory of death. Truthfully, it was the same with many of the families in her small fishing village. Children left the world as easily as they entered it.

"Well, give it here, love." Hollis took the babe from her. She clung for only a moment, thinking of the cold grave awaiting it. No ceremony or rites for the lost life. The halfpenny was barely enough to cover the meager burial on consecrated soil; it couldn't pay for the reverend's time.

Hollis's pasty-cold fingers brushed the back of her hand in a deliberate, lingering stroke. She slithered free, releasing the brother she would never know into the caretaker's grasping hands.

He held the cloth-wrapped bundle with little care, like a small sack of grain tucked beneath his arm. She clenched her jaw and looked away, backing from the door, feeling the need to flee. Run. Only there was nowhere to go except home. And she knew what awaited her there.

"See you next time," he called.

She froze for the barest moment. A chill scraped her spine because she knew he wasn't mistaken. He'd see her again. She'd be back. The next time. Her mother would give birth again. Another would die. Perhaps even her mother.

She spun around and rushed into the night. The caretaker's grating chuckle followed her as she fled the churchyard, doing her best not to glance at the chalky-faced tombs and headstones. The baby left behind would receive no such marker. A wooden cross was all to be expected, lost to wind and time before the season passed into the next. The fact that he'd been born at all would be wiped from memory.

Except she would remember. She'd always remember.

Every life. Every death. They were etched upon her soul.

As she neared home, she noticed the dark shape of a carriage in front of her house. Unusual, given the late hour.

She entered warily, hoping she was not walking in upon a lender harassing her stepfather. Not tonight of all nights. Even more surprising than the carriage out front was the sight of her mother sitting in a chair near the grate, wrapped in a blanket, her face leeched of all color.

Cleo rushed to her side, heedless of the others in the room. "Mama, why are you not abed?"

Each birth took its toll. She doubted this one was any different. She pressed the back of her hand to her mother's clammy brow. "I'm getting you back in bed." She cast a glare over her shoulder at her stepfather. "What could you have been thinking—"

"Please, Cleopatra," her mother interjected, using that dreadful name.

"Watch your tongue, girl," her stepfather blustered, his face ruddier than usual as he glowered down at her. He tossed a self-conscious glance at their guest, doubtlessly trying to look manly and dominant in his presence. "You'll not speak to me that way. Not beneath my own roof, hear me?"

Cleo rolled her eyes, undaunted. He never did more than raise his voice at her. For the obvious reason—he feared she would leave. He needed her. When her mother fell ill—which was frequently—she managed the household. As long as he wanted the children tended, clothes washed, and his meals on the table every day, he dared not offend. He needed her and he knew it.

"Come, Mama." She slid an arm beneath her mother's arm, determined to help her back up the stairs. Roger didn't require her presence while he entertained his guest.

Her mother seized hold of her wrist, the fragile fingers around her surprisingly strong. "We have a guest."

With a sigh, Cleo straightened and turned, following her mother's stare. Her gaze collided with the stranger. He looked like a gentleman, if his manner of attire were any indication. Most of the men in her village made their living on the sea and went about without a jacket and cravat.

"Who are you?" she asked with no thought to civility. Her mother had just given birth to a stillborn child. This was an ill-timed visit to say the least. Civility could be cast aside.

Her mother's eyes, still glassy from the pain of her ordeal, shone anxiously. "Your father sent him."

Cleo blinked again, pulling back as if physically struck. "My father?"

Her mother nodded swiftly. Something that dangerously resembled a smile graced her bloodless lips. "I always knew he'd come for you."

"Did you? Interesting, as I've never thought that to be likely at all." Truthfully, she'd never thought about it. Ever. Dreaming of her father rescuing her was as useless as dreaming of a knight in shining armor riding into her life. "Nor did I know you were harboring such hopes."

"I'd always hoped. For you . . ." Her mother's

voice faded, the implication clear. She never thought her lover would claim her . . . just their illegitimate child.

"Miss Hadley," the stranger began. "Your father has hired me—"

"Miss what?" she interrupted, swinging around and pinning her attention on the stranger.

"Miss Hadley."

At her incomprehensible blink, he elaborated, "You are the daughter of Jack Hadley." He nodded at her, clearly encouraging this bit of information to sink in.

"I'm his illegitimate daughter," she clarified with emphasis. "And since he never saw fit to acknowledge me, I've never borne his name."

For a moment, the gentleman looked prepared to argue, but instead he inclined his head in seeming acquiescence. "Mr. Hadley," he announced in a conciliatory tone, "wishes me to fetch you home—"

"Home," she bit out, glaring at her father's errand man. "I don't have a home with Jack Hadley. I never have." He saw to that.

"Cleopatra," Mama swiftly intervened. There was actual color in her cheeks now. "You must go. Your father is a very wealthy man. He can do wonderful things for you." In a fervent whisper, she added, "He wants you." As though that was everything. The only thing that mattered. *To be wanted*.

She stared, aghast, at her mother. "You wish me to go?"

"For a chance at a better life? Yes." Her mother nodded, and Cleo realized yes, of course, her mother would wish her to leave. To seize the future she'd always wanted for herself. At least Cleo would have what she never could possess.

She swallowed against the sudden lump in her throat. "I can't leave you."

Her mother's clammy hands gripped hers tightly. "You must."

She shook her head. "I won't go—"

"You haven't a choice," her stepfather intoned, and for the first time she noticed the small bag of coins clutched tightly in his hand. "It's already been agreed."

She pointed to the money. "What's that?"

He waved at her father's man as if that were ex-planation enough. And it was.

"You sold me?" she demanded.

Her mother gasped. "It's not like that. He's your father!"

"Stop saying that. I've never even met the man."

Roger jostled the bag of coins. "Call it whatever you like, but this will keep us for nigh on a year."

She stared, unable to form speech as his words

sunk in. Her mother, her brothers and sisters . . . none would go without. None would suffer a hungry belly for a year.

Her gaze slid over the room, colliding with several pairs of eyes peering out from beneath blankets. Apparently their voices had woken them. Their pallets were only feet away, but usually they slept through all manner of noise: their mother giving birth, Roger crashing around in one of his drunken binges.

It seemed almost fate that Bess would choose that moment to wake and peer at Cleo with her soulful, too-old eyes. Her mop of brown curls fell into her eyes. She shook the hair back to better see Cleo. Cleo knew that it would be a bear to untangle in the morning. The lump in her throat thickened. She didn't want to lose Bess to the churchyard. Or any of them.

"I'll go," she said numbly, staring at Bess as she spoke. Without blinking, she motioned to the sack of coins Roger clutched and added, "For twice that amount."

If she was doing this, she would make it count.

Her mother gasped as if she had just asked for the moon, but Cleo didn't care. If her father wanted her, he would have to pay. It was only a token of what he owed her mother for abandoning her all those years ago.

Their guest stared at her with a steady, un-flinching gaze.

Cleo lifted her chin, feeling very much like a businessman negotiating the agreement of a life-time. She held his stare, determined that he see not the slightest chink in her armor.

With a nod, he reached inside his jacket and withdrew another pouch. He'd come prepared. "Very well."

Her stepfather made a hissing sound between his teeth and extended his grasping hand. "Gor, Cleo! Aren't you the cunning minx?"

Her mother beamed, clapping her hands to-gether with happiness. Cleo bent down and hugged her, surprised at the strength in which her mother hugged her back.

"Take care of yourself. Find happiness," Mama whispered against her hair.

And Cleo heard what she wasn't saying. *Don't make my mistakes.*

She nodded tightly, confident that she'd never let a man drag her through the misery her mother endured.

"Go fetch your things," Mama instructed.

She scanned the room, her gaze settling on the small faces peering at her from their pallets. She'd miss them, but she was doing this for them. For all of them.

Perhaps if she played her cards right, she could provide for them well into the future. She could land them into proper schools away from this village. Away from their father. Perhaps she could secure a future for them.

"I'm ready," she announced, not imagining she would have a need for her only other dress. It already bore too many patches to count. There was nothing she needed to bring with her. Again, the forlorn faces of her siblings drew her eye. Not yet at least. "Let us go."

With a final farewell to her mother, she turned and left the cottage, determined never to set foot inside again.

Chapter Two

Eleven months later . . .

Logan McKinney stormed down the corridor and burst through the drawing-room doors.

His sister blinked up at him from the letter she penned at the dainty rosewood desk. "Feel better?"

"No," he growled, dropping down onto an equally dainty settee much too small for his frame. The furniture groaned in protest, earning him a frown from Fiona. He glared back.

Nothing could make him feel better. Not if he had to abide another moment in this fog-ridden, overpopulated city. The only thing that made this visit tolerable was spending time with Fiona. She scarcely visited since she'd married. He supposed he understood. As was customary in his family, children soon followed the wedding vows. Three babies in five years made travel to the Highlands difficult.

Fiona set down her quill and pointed to the still shivering drawing-room doors. "Might I remind you that this isn't McKinney Castle, with its five-hundred-year-old oaken doors?"

"Aye, puny English wood."

His sister arched a carrot-colored eyebrow. "Might I remind you that I'm English now?"

He waved a broad hand. "Speak not such sacrilege. You're not English. You've simply married an Englishman—a fine man even by that account, I'll grant you, but an Englishman nonetheless."

If possible, his sister cocked that eyebrow higher and leveled him a reproving glare.

"Don't give me that look, Fiona Rosalie," he said. "I'm still three years yer elder."

"And I'm married with three children and a fourth on the way. Until you've accomplished as much, you'll not be chiding me, dear brother."

He sank a little lower in his seat, suddenly feeling like a lad again dressed down by his mother for one of his many boyhood mischiefs. With her snapping amber eyes, Fiona was the very image of Mary McKinney.

"May I remind you," she continued, her faint brogue thickening, "that you're here to find a bride? An English bride? Unless you know of any Scottish heiresses?"

Smug wench. She knew there were no Scottish heiresses to fit his pressing financial needs. He snorted. "Reminder unnecessary. You remind me every chance you get."

She thinned her lips until they practically disappeared and shook her head in disapproval. Holding out her hand, she began counting off on each of her fingers. "Abigail's come-out is in one year. Josie's in four. And Simon needs funds for university next year. I'm also certain Niall would like to join him there soon. He is the most scholarly among us, after all . . . and only at the tender age of fourteen. Or did you not wish your brothers to take their studies beyond what the governess can provide?"

Logan scowled. "I'm well aware of the situation. This is what brought me to your doorstep, after all."

She nodded, sending the carroty sausage curl draped artfully over her shoulder bouncing. Since she'd married, his sister had become quite the fashionable lady. Her husband, the owner of a shipping line, provided her with a beyond-comfortable existence. "Now. Shall you get about the business of finding a dowered bride instead of finding fault with every candidate thrust before you? Honestly, Logan, you're running out of choices."

He bit back the retort that burned on his tongue. Every heiress he had met was as appealing as Nan's day-old porridge. All were vapid girls who pelted him with silly questions about his castle in the Highlands.

Is there a drawbridge? La! And a tower? I always imagined myself a princess in a tower.

If he could find a bride who at least made his pulse race, then he could perhaps overlook a less than scintillating personality. Or simply a lass with something more substantial than feathers in her head would be palatable. If he had to live with the female for the rest of his life, could she not at least possess some aspect he found desirable? Was that asking too much?

Fiona stared at him, waiting, her expression one of forbearance.

Logan gave a terse nod and sighed. His desires bore no significance. He had a duty. And little time in which to perform it. He'd tried to find a bride he wanted. Now he simply must select the bride he needed.

Using her husband's connections, Fiona had

gone out of her way to see he was properly introduced to the *ton*. He couldn't blame her for being so vexed with him.

Her features softened. "Logan, perhaps you need to simply adjust your . . ." her nose wrinkled as she grasped for the right word, "expectations?"

He shook his head. His sister married for love. He knew she felt guilty that he could not consider his own heart in the matter of matrimony. But then he'd never been a romantic. When he'd considered marriage—a rarity, to be sure—it had always been with practicality in mind. A female he respected . . . who would be a good mother to their children. He'd never wished for more than that. No point in getting sentimental now.

"What is tonight's agenda?" he asked, clapping his hands once and forcing an air of efficiency.

He'd suffer marriage to an Englishwoman he felt nothing for just as he'd survived everything else in his life. The deaths of his parents and eldest brother. The sudden obligation of finding himself The McKinney, responsible for countless lives.

After all that, he could easily stomach wedding a woman for whom he cared nothing.

With a considering look, Fiona murmured, "You and Alexander are attending the opera with Mr. Hamilton. Alexander bumped into him at his club. They attended school together as boys. Mr. Hamilton was kind enough to invite us to join him for the evening."

"You're not joining us?"

"There are only two additional seats."

Logan eyed her as she patted her barely budding middle. Shrouded beneath her gown, the bulge was beyond notice except when she called attention to it. "Alexander shall merely explain that I was not feeling quite myself, but he decided to bring his delightful brother-in-law instead."

Delightful. Logan snorted and crossed his long legs. "In the time I've been here, members of the *ton* would hardly agree with your description."

Fiona sniffed and straightened where she sat—as though the suggestion affronted her. The sunlight filtering into the room lit her hair afire. "Then you shall prove them wrong tonight."

"All in one night? Indeed? What is so special about tonight that so much shall be accomplished?" he asked suspiciously.

A glint flashed in her eyes and she suddenly took on the air of a general entering battle. "Listen well. The box is already occupied by Mr. Hamilton's cousin, Lady Libba, and her grandfather, the Earl Thrumgoodie. And there are two other guests, I believe." She waggled her fingers and shrugged as though those were of no consequence. "Lady Libba is your quarry. She is quite the lauded heiress. "And"—she paused for emphasis—"quite looking for a match."

"Ah." He sighed with understanding. "And yet that does not mean she will take a liking to—"

"Oh, Logan. Posh!" Fiona cut him off, waving a hand in his direction. "Be serious, will you?"

He shook his head, mystified.

She gave him a sobering look, motioning to his person. "You're every girl's dream. Every inch of you is a feast for the female eye. How many village maids did you bed back home? I can't recall a time Mama wasn't on her knees praying for your wretched soul."

"Er, thank you?" he murmured wryly. "Yet I wouldn't take it as a certainty that she'll fall at my feet."

"Oh, she'll happily fall. Trust me. They all would . . . if you would only choose one." Fiona pinned him with her gaze, her amber-hued eyes direct and faintly accusing. " 'Tis the reason you came here, after all. Let's not dally about it further."

He gave her a sharp, two-fingered salute.

She returned her attention to her letter. "I'll send Alexander's valet to help attend you this evening. I'll not have you looking like the barbarian everyone claims."

"Simply because I was the only gentleman

present bearing a knife at the last soiree." He grinned, recalling the scene. "A certain marchioness was much grateful I was present to rescue her when she swooned."

Fiona snorted and shook her head. "By slicing open her gown and stays."

"Anyone could see she was blue from lack of air."

"Laugh all you like, that story now precedes you everywhere you go. It's not a story that requires embellishment, but somehow it manages to sound worse with every retelling."

"If your faith in me has any merit, I'll win over this Lady Libba withstanding all the prattling from the dames of the *ton*."

He did not care for the notion of people—strangers—discussing him as though they knew a single thing about him. Especially a bunch of over-privileged English aristocrats.

Fiona smiled in satisfaction. "Of course. I have utter faith in your prowess."

Instead of humoring such rot with a response, he rose smoothly to his feet, all the more determined to find a wife and return home.

Chapter Three

"Have I said how lovely you look tonight, my dear?"

Staring into the earl's rheumy gaze, Cleo couldn't help wondering whether he could actually see her clearly. "Thank you, my lord."

Lord Thrumgoodie lifted a shaky, beringed hand and unerringly confiscated her gloved hand. Not too blind, she supposed. She watched in dread as he pressed his chalky-dry lips to the back of it.

Cleo smiled thinly. "You are really too kind, my lord."

Beyond the earl's shoulder, his great-nephew glared. It was simple enough to read the contempt in Hamilton's stare. She quickly averted her gaze and turned her attention to Lord Thrumgoodie, vowing to ignore the wretch.

As the earl's heir, Mr. Hamilton often accompanied them. Fortunately, he primarily occupied himself at his estate outside Town. When he did visit, he at least feigned to like her in front of the earl and others. The contemptuous glances were for her eyes only.

The earl patted her hand with his trembling one, still clinging to it. "I speak only the truth, my dear."

Cleo stifled her cringe. If she was going to marry the man, she really needed to learn to better abide his touch. It wasn't often that he made overtures—and she knew on good authority that the old earl's nether parts were not in working order. She wasn't above listening to servants' gossip, and her maid had turned out to be most garrulous. With no prodding, Berthe had become well acquainted with the earl's servants, gleaning all she could about the man Cleo was considering marrying.

That Thrumgoodie had fathered only one child with his first wife nearly fifty years ago was common enough knowledge. Since then there had been four more wives, all unable to produce offspring. Two of those wives even had children from previous marriages. All of which pointed to the earl's inability to sire further children. Less common knowledge was that in recent years the old earl had attempted to ravish a few maids in his employ. All to no success. Berthe had put it crudely: *The ol' man's cannon is cracked.*

As far as Cleo was concerned, he was the perfect candidate for matrimony. The last thing she wanted was some young, virile male to inflict upon her all the misery her mother had endured.

Thanks to Jack Hadley's newfound interest in his daughters, she had a dowry to rival Croesus himself. Yet in exchange she was expected to wed someone titled. Someone to help elevate her father's social standing among the *ton*. That was the trade-off.

After her half sister Grier married the Prince of Maldania, Cleo had thought Jack's ambitions for her might lessen somewhat. One of his daughters had married a prince, after all. But she wasn't off the hook. Her father still wanted an English nobleman for a son-in-law.

"I'm so excited." Lady Libba bounced her generous frame upon the theater seat.

Cleo glanced down at the program in her hand, nodding. "Yes. I've heard several good things about the score."

Libba slapped her with her fan. "Not the opera, you silly hen. McKinney." She quickly glanced around as if uttering the name alone might set the hounds of hell upon them.

Cleo blinked. "Who?"

"Oh, Cleo! Have you been living under a rock?" She inched her chair closer, bouncing even more as she did so. "McKinney will soon be joining us."

Cleo glanced at the two remaining seats, still vacant. Presumably the mysterious McKinney would occupy one. "I thought a Mr. and Mrs. Blackwell were invited to join us." She'd overheard Hamilton mention that he'd invited his old school friend.

Libba bobbed her head in agreement. "They were, but Mr. Hamilton sent a letter around explaining that Mrs. Blackwell was not feeling quite the thing, so his brother-in-law, Lord McKinney, is joining us."

"I see." Cleo stared at Libba, seeing nothing at all. Apparently this McKinney should be known to her—at least in reputation.

Libba fluttered her fan as if suddenly overheated. "I've been fairly panting to meet him. He's all everyone is talking about—ever since he drew a sword and sliced Lady Chesterfeld's gown to ribbons." Libba made a motion across her dress that looked as though she were fending off bees.

"Left her stark naked on the ballroom floor. He's a perfect savage." Her eyes danced with delight, attesting that this was not a mark against him.

A perfect savage. Cleo's lips twisted in a sardonic smile. Seemed rather a contradiction to her but she didn't bother pointing that out. Instead, she said most soberly, "If that were true—"

"Oh it is!" Libba stared crossly at her, evidently resenting that her tale should be doubted.

"I'm sure it didn't happen quite like that. He would have been tossed in gaol, certainly, and not about to join us in an opera box."

Libba readjusted her plump figure on the chair with a sniff. "You shall see."

With an indulgent smile, Cleo lifted her opera glasses and eyed the crowd pouring into their seats below. She was so engrossed in appreciating the ladies in all their finery—and musing how much her mother would love to witness such a sight—that she did not take heed of the newcomers entering their box until Libba slapped her with her fan again.

"Come now, stop your woolgathering," Libba called out in an overly loud voice. "We've company!"

Cleo resisted the urge to rub her bare arm where the fan struck her. Libba really could be an annoying creature. The girl nodded her head meaningfully toward the back of the box where two gentlemen stood, exchanging greetings with Hamilton.

She assessed the new arrivals, her gaze sliding over a nice-looking fellow with sandy-brown hair and smiling eyes. When her attention turned to the man a step behind him, her breath caught in her throat.

There was no mistaking him. Libba's perfect savage had arrived.

Chapter Four

Lord McKinney stood a head taller than the other gentlemen. He was a veritable brick wall with impossibly broad shoulders. He filled out his jacket to perfection—no padding necessary. No wonder the ladies of the *ton* were all atwitter. The image of him cutting away some lady's gown with a sword was rather easy to envision.

His smoky gaze swept over the box, briefly appraising Libba before moving on—to her. Too late, she didn't have time to look away. Their gazes collided. His eyes reminded her of a storm rolling in off the sea.

The air trapped in her lungs. She locked her jaw and tightened her lips, refusing to so much as smile lest he mistake the gesture for interest.

Her resolve only deepened as those gray eyes

turned speculative. He evaluated her where she sat, ramrod straight in her seat, hands folded tightly in her lap. She felt stripped of her gown, exposed and vulnerable as he scanned her features, lingering on her mouth for a long moment before dropping to survey her décolletage, modestly displayed in her heart-shaped bodice.

She resisted the urge to press her hand there like some squeamish schoolgirl. Heat flooded her cheeks, and by the time his gaze lifted back to her face, she was certain her cheeks were the color of the red velvet drapes. His dark hair, in need of a trim, fell forward on his brow, begging for a woman's hands to touch . . . caress. She damned herself for the fanciful notion.

Her gaze snapped away at the sound of Lord Thrumgoodie's jarring tones. "Eh! Who are these two gents?"

Hamilton edged closer to his uncle, explaining, "This is the old school friend I was telling you about, Blackwell, and his brother-in-law, Lord McKinney."

The earl nodded, but Cleo was unconvinced he had heard—or understood. Thrumgoodie possessed far too much pride, however, to beg his nephew to repeat himself.

"Ladies, allow me to present Mr. Blackwell and

Lord McKinney. Gentlemen, my cousin, Lady Libba." There was a weighty pause before he introduced Cleo, as if she were an afterthought. "And Miss Cleopatra Hadley."

Cleo stifled the wince that always followed when she heard that dreadful name her mother had chosen for her spoken aloud. Given the life she had lived up until now, it was a mockery.

The gentlemen took their turns bowing over first Libba's and then Cleo's hands.

"A pleasure," Mr. Blackwell murmured. "Thank you for including us. My wife is abject over missing such a delightful evening. She adores the opera."

"Indeed," Hamilton replied, all graciousness. "We are sorry to miss her lovely company, to be sure, but glad you could join us. We shall rehash our youth with stories of our days at Abernathy Hall." Hamilton clapped Blackwell on the back. He nodded cheerfully at Lord McKinney, as if that pardoned his exclusion.

The "perfect savage" nodded in acknowledgement and Cleo wondered if he would deign to speak. The lights dimmed and everyone lowered into their seats.

Hamilton dropped back to sit beside Blackwell, so Lord McKinney took the vacant seat beside Libba. It could not have been arranged any better.

Libba did not bother to hide her ear-to-ear smile. Unable to contain her excitement, her hands shook upon her lap.

"How are you enjoying London?" Libba inquired amid the opening notes.

Lord McKinney opened his mouth to answer her, but she did not give him a chance, rushing ahead with her next question. "Have you visited Persephone's Emporium yet? Or Haverty's? You must stroll Bond Street. The most splendid shopping in the world. It's simply brilliant. I'm certain you've never seen the like. Certainly not in Scotland. That is where you are from, is it not? I've heard of you, of course . . ."

McKinney nodded, shifting to face her better as she prattled on and on about shopping, of all things. A glazed look fell over his eyes.

Cleo couldn't help herself. A smile twitched her lips. He was probably reconsidering the wisdom of accompanying his brother-in-law.

His gaze caught sight of her as she fought down laughter, that same speculative look on his face as before.

Thankfully, the curtains lifted at that moment and the performance began, snaring everyone's attention and silencing Libba. *A blessing*, Cleo couldn't help but think. Especially for Lord McKinney.

Cleo soon lost herself in the music and drama

unfolding below. She did not even immediately notice when the old earl's hand crept upon her shoulder.

She started at the realization, glancing sideways as though a spider rested there. His thin, cold fingers brushed her flesh before settling upon the curl of hair draped there. He stroked her hair until she was quite certain the curl had unwound itself. Her throat tightened and she struggled to swallow. Her pleasure in the opera quickly vanished. For being defunct in matters of intimacy, he was certainly fond of touching her, but then she supposed touching was the only thing left to him.

Hoping to subtly dislodge his hand, she angled her head as though she needed to stretch her neck—or perhaps better see the corner of the stage. The action turned her body, and she found herself locking eyes with Lord McKinney.

His eyes gleamed darkly in the shadows, but even in the dim lighting she didn't miss the knowing look there. The barest smirk tainted his well-sculpted lips.

She'd seen the look before, scorn the moment someone realized that she and the earl were more than passing acquaintances. The judgment was always evident once they comprehended he was her beau. They deemed her a greedy social climber, after the earl for his title.

She quickly faced forward again, her spine an unyielding rod. Lord McKinney's stare burned into the side of her face. Her hands knotted in her lap. The intermission couldn't come quickly enough. As soon as the curtain lowered, she hastily stood and murmured her excuses. Lifting her skirts, she fled, gaze averted.

The corridor was not yet crowded. Fortunate for her, she reached the sanctuary of the retiring room before it was invaded by too many other ladies and claimed a seat.

As it filled up with chattering women, she pretended to fiddle with her hair in front of one of the gilded mirrors, feigning great concentration and using this time to compose herself.

"Did you see him? McKinney? Sitting bold as you please up in one of the boxes?"

Cleo blinked hard at the mention of the Scotsman. Could she not escape him even here, in the ladies' retiring room?

"I don't care if he is some savage, he's the most delicious-looking specimen to ever set foot in Town," a young woman uttered, readjusting her generous bosom inside her snug-fitting bodice.

"He's on the hunt for an heiress, you know."

A sigh followed this remark. The lady released her breasts and puckered her lips for her reflection, angling her head as though seeking the most flattering pose. "Aren't they all? One of four girls, I'm certain my dowry couldn't tempt him. I must look to my other assets." She and her friend giggled at this. Cleo rolled her eyes. Ninnies.

Lowering her hands from her hair, Cleo rose to her feet more abruptly than she'd intended. The girls paused in their ministrations, sending her curious looks. She pasted a vacant smile on her face and departed the retiring room. In the corridor, she struggled through the mad press of overly perfumed bodies. In these moments, she missed being able to step outside and inhale the salty sea air.

Arriving at the entrance to their box, she hesitated, reluctant to rejoin the group within. She closed her eyes in a slow blink, only to find McKinney's scornful gaze in the dark of her mind. Blast! The fact that such a brief encounter should trouble her was utter absurdity. Who cared what a single stranger thought of her?

Lingering in the threshold, she glanced inside. Thrumgoodie was nowhere in sight. Or Libba. Only the three gentlemen remained. She stared at their backs, on the verge of gathering her nerve and stepping across the threshold when she heard Hamilton mutter, "Blasted female. She's got blunt enough of her own, so we know she's only after his title . . ."

She registered no other words as anger shot through her. How dare he gossip about her? Mortifying heat swept through her. She stared at the long line of McKinney's back, trying to gauge his reaction. Not that it should matter. Not that it did.

From the look he'd sent her earlier, she knew he'd already begun to form an ill opinion of her. This no doubt cemented it.

"Come, move now, Cleo, you're blocking the way."

At the sound of Libba's voice, the three men turned around.

Even if she wanted to flee, she couldn't any longer. Not without looking like a weak-hearted girl ready to collapse beneath the first strong wind. She couldn't let Hamilton know he got beneath her skin. If she was to marry into his family, he'd best learn now that he held no power over her . . . that he failed to affect her.

After all, she was Jack Hadley's bastard. The past year had toughened her skin. She'd endured the ugly whispers of the *ton*. What was he but another ugly voice on the wind?

Lifting her chin, she met Hamilton's stare, hoping to convey how little she thought of him. He met her gaze with no regret, no shame. In fact, he looked quite pleased to have been caught in the process of disparaging her. Mr. Blackwell looked appropriately uncomfortable, tugging at his cravat as if it were suddenly too tight. Her gaze slid to Lord McKinney.

He stared back at her unflinchingly, his gray eyes as cool as fog coming in off the water. With features carved of stone. It was as if he saw nothing when he gazed upon her. Nothing worth seeing, at any rate.

Anger rose up bitterly in her mouth. In her first glimpse of him she had recognized warm interest in his gray eyes. He'd looked at her as though she were a lady of worth—a lady worth . . . well, considering. Now he looked at her like she was beneath his regard.

And it stung. Silly of her to care, she admitted. It's not as though she could consider him. He was handsome, young, and virile—everything she wished to avoid. And yet, her eyes burned with a sudden sting of unwanted emotion.

With her chin still angled high, she strolled into the box and took her seat, staring straight ahead and telling herself she didn't feel the gaze of the man sitting two seats over, coldly judging her.

He'd already made up his mind about her. Which was fine. She knew his sort. He'd probably gambled everything away at faro and needed an heiress to keep some decrepit estate from falling down around his ears. Once he secured his heiress, he'd stow her away there and keep her fat with his seed. Thank you, but no. Libba was welcome to him.

It was just as well he formed an ill opinion of her. She intended to cling to her poor opinion of him.

As Logan sat through the remainder of the performance two seats away from Miss Cleopatra Hadley, only one thought raced through his mind. *What a shameful waste.*

It's not as though she were the most beautiful woman he'd ever clapped eyes upon. Her midnight dark hair was fine enough—with a lovely glossy gleam to it. But it was her eyes. They shone with a sharp intelligence—a directness he had not seen in many a woman. It reached out and grabbed him, captured his attention as no lady had since he'd arrived in Town. There was something there at work behind her gaze.

His first hope had been that this was the Lady Libba he was here to court. He quickly discovered Libba was the garrulous chit wearing a profusion of peach ruffles. The fascinating Miss Hadley was courting the old man with one foot in the grave.

The longer he sat there with Lady Libba scooted close to his side, her nasal voice whispering inane remarks throughout the performance, the longer he mulled over the irony of finally meeting an heiress who intrigued him—and she happened to be intent on marrying an ancient English lord.

At the end of the performance, he wove through the crush with Lady Libba's hand tucked into his elbow. At least he had gained the girl's favor—precisely what he'd set out to do this night. He should be pleased with himself on that score and count the evening a success.

He glanced back to spot Miss Hadley following at a much slower pace on the arm of the earl. Her gaze briefly locked with his before narrowing and looking away. Her nostrils flared as though she'd caught wind of something unpleasant.

Shrugging, he faced forward. Dismissing the chit as beneath his concern, he glanced down at Lady Libba clinging to his arm and made his first tactical move in winning himself an heiress. "Have I mentioned how lovely you are, my lady?"

She blushed and tittered and swatted his arm. "Oh, la! Lord McKinney, you're a terrible flirt!"

Chapter Five

Cleo brushed her hair vigorously until the dark mass crackled all around her like a brewing storm. The evening had left her disconcerted. She wanted to place the blame on Hamilton and his vicious tongue, but she'd only be lying to herself. He was only partly to blame for her consternation. The rest of the blame could be laid at the feet of him. The Scot. McKinney. That moment when those cool, gray eyes had looked at her with scorn was etched inside her mind.

She jumped as a gentle knock sounded at her bedchamber door. Setting down her brush, she bade entrance, assuming it was Berthe returning to see if she required anything else for the night.

Instead of the maid, she watched as the man who had sired her stepped inside her bedchamber. Jack Hadley. She felt none of her initial tension as she gazed upon the barrel-chested man. Over the months, they'd come to almost an accord. Not that she forgot or forgave him anything . . . but she acknowledged that he was a different man from that of twenty years ago. She saw regret in the worn lines of his face and longing in his eyes.

While it might appear that he longed for position and rank—which he ostensibly hoped to gain through marrying her to some titled lord—she sensed he longed for something else. Something more. A connection to others. Belonging. Money hadn't bought him that yet. Even if he didn't realize it, she suspected that was the true reason he had tracked her down. And not just Cleo, but two other illegitimate daughters. Jack Hadley wanted a family.

He nodded at her reflection in the mirror. "How was your evening?"

She turned to face him. "Fine, thank you."

He looked as though he would like to say something more, but then shook his head as though thinking better of it. "Well, I won't keep you. Good night."

In the threshold, he suddenly stopped and turned. "You know . . . this courtship with the earl . . ." His voice faded away.

She nodded. "Yes."

He rubbed a hand against the back of his neck. She'd never seen Jack Hadley discomposed like this. But then, she seemed to be constantly reevaluating him.

"Yes?" she prompted.

"The earl is older than I am."

A smile twitched her lips. "I'm aware of that."

He looked rather pleadingly at her. "You're a young woman, Cleo. You don't have to settle on him. I realize he's titled, but—"

"I'm quite satisfied with the earl's courtship."

Jack looked at her rather doubtfully. "Are you? Truly? Because I don't want you to feel I'm forcing—"

"No one can force me to marry anyone." She smiled at him with an arched brow. "Not even the great Jack Hadley."

He snorted. "Well, your sisters seem to fear that I'm bullying you into this."

"I'll talk to them." Or at least she would talk to Marguerite. She'd have to post a missive to Grier in Maldania.

He looked somewhat relieved at this and she suspected that they must have been badgering him a great deal over the matter. No one could understand her motives for accepting the earl's suit. Which did not affect her one way or another. Her reasons were her own.

Jack stepped inside her chamber. "In fact, it's rather nice having you about. I don't see any point in your rushing into matrimony. The year you've been here has been . . . nice."

"Indeed?" Despite herself, her heart thawed another notch. Her stepfather had never spoken a kind word to her. She really must be starved for a father's care.

She quickly reminded herself that this is the same Jack who, a year ago, had been anxious to herd up his offspring and marry them off. Marguerite and Grier had actually obliged him—and rather quickly. Perhaps he regretted that now? Regretted that he didn't have more time to acquaint himself with his other two daughters.

He looked a little lonely right then. And sad. Suddenly she had a notion of what might be bothering him. "Any luck on locating the Higgins woman?"

Several weeks ago, Jack had confessed he might have fathered another child with his former housekeeper. He sighed and shook his head. "The Pinkerton man I hired believes he may have found a lead on her. In Yorkshire."

"I'm sure he'll find her," she murmured, even though she wasn't certain of any such thing. She couldn't help wondering whether this Higgins woman even wanted to be found. Her father believed he had sired a child with her, and perhaps he had. Perhaps she was happily married and wanted to forget Jack Hadley.

Staring at Jack, she felt a twinge of her old resentment. Jack had certainly been prolific in spreading his seed all about the country and leaving heartache in his wake. Still . . . if she had another sister or brother out there, she would like to know them.

Jack plucked at an invisible piece of lint on his sleeve. "Well, I won't keep you from your bed."

"Good night," she murmured, watching him depart and musing over how she could not despise the man who had rejected her mother—and her. She had assumed the hatred would always be there.

When she first arrived, she had been quite willing to lay the blame for her mother's wretched life at his feet. But Cleo didn't have it in her to hate the man. At least her mother's needs were being tended now. She also recognized that her mother had made her choices with open eyes. She'd known Jack Hadley was not the marrying kind and yet she'd gone to his bed anyway.

Her mother had paid for that mistake. And Cleo had learned from it. She would choose a different path. Even though she didn't hate Jack any longer . . . she wouldn't place her total trust in him. A smart, carefully chosen marriage would give her the lifelong security she sought.

Setting the brush down, Cleo used the small step stool to climb into bed. As she sank beneath the luxurious quilted silk coverlet, she marveled that this should be her bed—*her life*. She would never have to worry about an aching belly again.

And if she chose carefully, wisely, she wouldn't have to contend with a man wreaking destruction over her life and body. To say nothing of her heart.

For two days, she avoided Thrumgoodie, in no mood to see again his wretched nephew, who had taken residence at the earl's Mayfair mansion during his visit. She frequently replayed that moment when she'd stumbled upon him gossiping about her to Mr. Blackwell and Lord McKinney. The wretch.

Then she realized that she was being cowardly. The last thing she wanted Hamilton to think was that he'd succeeded in running her off. Indeed not. With that thought in mind, she accepted the earl's invitation to dinner. Her father, invited as well, accompanied her. He reveled in these affairs, mingling among the peerage over glittering crystal and the finest port. Wearing the rich, garish colors his tailor convinced him were the height of *ton* fashion. He enjoyed nothing more.

It was a small dinner party, no more than a dozen guests. Cleo dressed in her best, feeling fortified in a gown of bronze silk that made the hidden lights gleam in her dark hair. At least that's what the modiste had told her when she selected the fabric. She only hoped she wasn't being led astray as her father was.

Jack helped her from her cloak and handed it to a waiting groom. Offering his arm, he led her into the drawing room where everyone was gathered before dinner. As they approached, she could hear the familiar din of Lady Libba hammering away at the keys. From the sound of it, the pianoforte might very well crumble beneath the onslaught.

"Hope she bloody well quits that racket soon," her father murmured in her ear. "Might turn off my appetite."

Despite herself Cleo chuckled and grinned, all gaiety when she entered the room.

As though a magnet drew her, her eyes landed on him first. The sight of Lord McKinney startled her as it shouldn't. He stood straight as an oak beside the pianoforte, turning the pages when Libba indicated he should.

He spotted her, too. His direct stare flustered her. Her fingers flexed on Jack's arm and he sent her a curious glance. Inwardly, she commanded herself to recall herself—who she was, what she was about.

She greeted first the earl and then the other guests. Unfortunately that meant she had to eventually face Lord McKinney again and exchange pleasantries.

As Libba finished playing, Cleo nodded in greeting. "Good evening, Libba. Lord McKinney."

His gaze skimmed her, from the top of her head to the toes of her golden slippers, and then he looked away, dismissing her. She squared her shoulders and reminded herself that she was not here to gain his favor.

She took her seat on a settee beside the earl.

It shouldn't have surprised her to see McKinney here again. If he was hunting for an heiress, Libba was that. And he was a feast for the eyes. There was no question that Libba was all gushing encouragement. She was his for the taking.

When dinner was announced, Cleo rose quickly, glad for a change of scene.

"Ah, my dear Cleo," the earl said in his croaking voice. He waved his pale, thin hand on the air. "Come. A little assistance, please?"

With an obligatory smile, she offered her hand. He used it to haul himself from the chair. She staggered before catching herself, rooting her slippers into the carpet so she didn't lose her balance.

He gripped her shoulder to right himself, crushing the capped sleeve of her gown. She fought back a grimace as he leaned against her, resisting the temptation to step away, quite convinced that if she did so he would collapse.

His labored breath blew moistly against her cheek. "I need but a moment to catch my breath," he panted.

She nodded and watched as everyone filed out of the room in to dinner.

The hairs at her nape began to tingle and she had a certain sensation that she was being watched. She swiveled her head, surveying the last of the guests as they emptied the room. Nothing. It appeared everyone—

And then she spotted him.

Instead of escorting Libba in to dinner, he lingered in the corner, holding a glass of brandy lightly in his hand and surveying her and the earl.

His stare was penetrating, yet unreadable. Her face heated as he gazed at her. Mortification burned through her. She was acutely conscious of what he saw—the earl clutching her in an undignified manner as though she were a nursemaid and not a lady.

Thrumgoodie coughed hoarsely, regaining her

attention. He struggled to regain his legs. His grip on her hand intensified. The fingers on her shoulder dug in deep and painfully. She bowed a bit beneath the pressure and stopped shy of crying out.

Abruptly, a deep voice rumbled near her ear. "I'll help you there."

She sagged with relief. Even if it was him. She didn't think she could see Thrumgoodie all the way to the dining room without assistance, and no one else had lingered to see if she or the earl needed any help. She didn't let herself consider why McKinney stayed behind. She was simply relieved he had.

The earl's head snapped in his direction. "Eh? Who are you?"

"McKinney, my lord."

"Oh, Libba's beau." He nodded as if remembering.

Libba's beau. The reminder left a foul taste in her mouth and suddenly she didn't want his help.

She tried to reclaim the earl's hand. "We're managing quite well, Lord McKinney. Thank you for your consideration, but it's not necessary."

He looked at her with those unreadable gray eyes. Just when she assumed he would turn and walk away, he made an exasperated sound and shook his head. Stepping close, he brushed her aside as if she were of no account.

Before she could so much as squeak, he took hold of Thrumgoodie's hand that gripped her shoulder fiercely and guided him from the room, taking the old man's weight into himself as if he were nothing more than a feather.

After a stunned moment, she followed, resenting that he should have been the one to stay behind and help her. When they at last settled in at the dining table, she focused her attention on her companions, grateful they were neither Hamilton nor McKinney. Still, she found it quite difficult to focus on the words of the soft-spoken lady beside her. Not with Libba laughing uproariously every few moments.

Cleo found herself sneaking baleful glances down the table. Libba threw back her head and leaned her entire body to the side, swatting the Scotman's arm again and again. She held her ribs as if they ached from laughter.

Lord McKinney talked with ease, his broad hand waving carelessly on the air, a mild smile playing on his well-carved lips. Cleo narrowed her eyes on him and felt a fresh surge of dislike. He couldn't be that genuinely amusing or charming. Nor could he honestly find Libba's braying enjoyable. He doubtlessly played puppet to Libba, hanging on her every word and acting as though she truly had something interesting to say. The man belonged on stage. It would have been comical if it did not annoy her so much. She stabbed at a small roasted potato on her plate with uncharacteristic force.

Suddenly he looked up to catch her watching him. She possessed too much pride to look away as if she were guilty of some crime, so she held his stare, lifting the potato to her lips and chewing as if his scrutiny failed to affect her.

He must have read some of her distaste for him on her face, for the smile he had worn so easily for Libba faded and his eyes turned to hard chips of winter gray. Again, the condemning judgment. As his gleaming gaze watched her watching him, that night at the opera came back in a flood.

Jack, thankfully, paid her little note, too intent on impressing the young widow beside him to notice the stare-down between her and McKinney. Deciding she'd wasted enough of her time on the man, she looked away for good, determined to not give him another thought.

Chapter Six

$\mathcal{A}$t the end of the meal, the ladies retired to the drawing room while the men adjourned to the library for their cigars. And not a moment too soon. Cleo desperately wanted a moment to compose herself and forget the way Lord McKinney had looked at her—that cold-eyed stare rattled her to the core.

Did he disdain her for letting a man old enough to be her grandfather court her? Or did her lack of pedigree offend? That stuck in the craw of enough members of the *ton*. She supposed even a Scottish lord might consider himself her better.

If that was the case, he was worse than Hamilton. Hamilton she at least understood. His nastiness derived from his fear that she'd marry his great-uncle—and he'd have to share Thrumgood-ie's inheritance with her.

Libba's voice pulled her from her thoughts. "I'm the luckiest girl in the whole empire," she gushed beside Cleo.

"Indeed," Cleo murmured, stamping back her nausea at Libba's excessive prattling.

"No man can rival him. Not in looks or charm." She clapped her hands together and shivered in delight. "I can't wait for our wedding night. Can you imagine his expertise in the boudoir?"

Cleo's cheeks burned as she envisioned his virile form . . . stripped free of his evening attire. Unlike most gentlemen of the *ton*, he would prob-ably look better out of his garments. She cleared her throat. "It seems soon to harbor such thoughts, does it not?"

"Oh, I know everything about him. He lives in a castle in the Highlands." Her eyes danced with de-light. "I'm quite sure he strolls about in a kilt. Can you imagine the sight of his delicious bare legs?"

Heat crawled up her neck to her face as she imagined McKinney's bare legs. She swallowed. Not an image she needed in her head. He already spent too much time in her thoughts.

"Libba, really . . . you shouldn't say such things."

"Oh, don't be such a prude, Cleo. You are

female. How can you look at him without thinking such things?"

Cleo didn't bother explaining that she was immune to virile, handsome men. She'd trained herself to resist the flirtations of young men, all too aware that such a path led to misery.

She shrugged. "You really believe you know *everything* about the man?"

Libba nodded. "Indeed. I do. He's the one."

"Let's recount, shall we?" Cleo counted off on her fingers. "He lives in the highlands. In a castle. He's seeking a wife." She shook her head, searching Libba's face for anything else she might wish to add.

Libba nodded, smiling rather blankly.

Cleo sighed with exasperation. "That hardly constitutes *knowing* a man, does it? Would you really go off into the wilds with him? Totally at his mercy?" Just the notion made Cleo's skin shiver.

A dreamy expression came over Libba's features. "Hmm. Yes."

"Never mind." Cleo rolled her eyes. The girl was hopeless.

"Oh, Cleo." Libba nudged her shoulder roughly. "Haven't you any trust? Any faith? Sometimes you have to trust your instincts about a person."

Cleo sniffed. Like her mother had trusted? First

Jack Hadley. And then her stepfather. Not Cleo— not a chance.

Libba continued. "I'm fairly certain he means to offer for me. Perhaps even this week . . ."

Cleo blinked. "So soon?"

"Oh, yes. You've been hiding away with that headache of yours for the last two days so you wouldn't know, but he called on me the day after the opera with a bouquet of hothouse roses.

"Of course he did. He knows a good catch when he sees one," Cleo replied wryly, but Libba missed her sarcasm and continued talking.

" . . . And the day after that he took me for a ride in the park. Tomorrow we shall stroll Bond Street. I do hope he will propose soon," she rushed to say. "Grandfather's health is so precarious. The last thing I want is Hamilton acting as my guardian . . . or having to delay my wedding because Grandfather died." Comprehension suddenly broke across Libba's features. "Oh, how dreadful of me. I did not mean to imply that Grandfather might soon die. I know you're very . . . fond of him."

Cleo smiled weakly and patted Libba's hand. The girl meant well. She just couldn't be accused of keen intelligence. She could never fault Libba for being unkind. Unlike Hamilton, she was tolerant of Cleo's budding relationship with her grandfather. "No worries, Libba."

Libba clutched Cleo's hand in each of her own. "And he is exceedingly fond of you, too. You've brought new life into him."

Cleo's smile grew pained.

Libba's head dipped closer as she whispered conspiratorially, "I believe he intends to offer for you very soon."

At this confidence, Cleo's stomach sank. Foolish, of course. They'd been courting for months. This was what she'd been working toward, after all. An easy, uncomplicated match. Safe.

Above all safe.

"W-wonderful."

"Isn't it?" Libba's head bobbed happily. "He swore he would never wed again after his last wife died. Sorry luck, that." Libba gave her hand another squeeze. "He'll likely outlive us all. Wait and see."

"I dearly hope so," Cleo returned. Not a lie. She truly did not yearn for widowhood . . . as the gossips were fond of declaring. She simply wished to keep her body to herself—and not lose her spirit under the grind of some man's boot heel. The earl's days of grinding his boot heels were long past. He was unthreatening in that regard . . . spending most of his days in a prolonged nap.

She need only envision her mother's haggard face, or recall one of the tiny corpses she'd carried to the churchyard, to know the kind of life she wanted.

Still, the thought that she might soon have to finalize her decision and accept Thrumgoodie's proposal knotted her stomach.

"Pardon me, Libba. I'm in need of some air." She rose to her feet and slipped out the drawing room's balcony doors.

She shivered at the sudden plunge into chilled air. She wished she'd brought her shawl but wasn't about to go back into the house to fetch it. She moved away from the door. The feminine chatter from within faded as she strolled along the verandah that wrapped around the side of the house.

Chafing her arms, she stared up at the night and squinted, wondering where the stars had vanished. She'd always been able to see them at home. She and her mother were fond of picking out the constellations.

"Can't see a thing through all the smog."

Cleo gasped and spun around.

Standing several feet away, the Scot propped a lean hip against the stone railing, his booted feet crossed at the ankles.

"What are you doing out here?" she demanded.

"Could ask you the same."

She crossed her arms, suddenly unsure what to do with them.

It dawned on her that they'd never even spoken at any length. Just a brief two- or three-worded greeting. For as much as he'd filled her awareness . . . occupied her thoughts, this struck her as strange.

She shivered anew. It was too dark to see his eyes but she imagined they still looked at her with that cold disapproval.

"Tired of the chatter?" he asked, his dark head nodding toward the drawing room.

She soaked up the sound of his voice. The faint brogue rolled through her like warm honey. She shook her head for thinking such a way, angry at herself for letting his voice affect her.

"I needed some fresh air," she murmured, her voice a tight squeak.

"Bracing yourself for the earl's cold touch?"

She sucked in a sharp breath, his words as shocking as a dousing of water. "Pardon me?"

"You heard me well enough."

"Surely not. My ears must be mistaken to have heard you say something so unconscionably rude."

He chuckled and the sound grated. Suddenly, his laughter stopped and silence stretched between them until he asked, "How old are you?"

She hesitated, but ultimately answered him. "Three and twenty."

"That young?"

"You thought me older?"

"You must confess there aren't many girls of your tender years who would consider a man in his eightieth year a prime candidate for a husband."

She pulled back her shoulders. "You know no bounds, my lord. I'm not sure why anything about me should interest you."

He shrugged. "You're a curiosity, I confess."

"Perhaps I look beyond the superficial shell of a person."

He chuckled and the sound rippled though her like dribbling honey. "Oh, indeed? Then do tell. Share with me what it is about the old earl that you find so endearing?"

She stared at him in mutinous silence and she was quite certain that he was enjoying himself. At her expense. His eyes gleamed in the gloom and she felt the overwhelming urge to strike him.

He continued in that rolling burr of his, mocking, "Is it his scintillating conversation?"

"Go to hell." The words exploded from her lips before she could stop herself. Immediately, she regretted them. She regretted the hot emotion he'd roused within her . . . the unreasonable urge to lash out. She'd never been like this before . . . so defensive, so hostile. Not even with Roger, and he'd justifiably earned her ire on countless occasions. Daily.

He chuckled, seemingly delighted with her outburst. "You're the first woman I've met in this godforsaken city to utter anything quite so . . . honest. It's a welcome bit of fresh air."

This declaration bordered on a compliment. Decidedly uncomfortable that he might actually admire her in some fashion, she turned to go. "We shouldn't be out here . . . alone together."

He chuckled anew, this sound lower, deeper. It slid seductively along her spine. She stopped, shooting a glance over her shoulder at the dim shape of him. "What's so amusing?" she queried, the annoyance in her voice crisp and sharp.

"You did not strike me as the type to worry about what others might say."

His comment hit its mark—no doubt as he'd intended. Her annoyance flared. She stepped closer. Closer than comfortable, but she couldn't back down after he'd waved a flag like that before her face.

"Because if I did care what others think or say about me I would what?" Another step. "Conduct myself differently?"

Even in the gloom, she detected a bend to his lips. He was smiling. "Your words. Not mine."

She inhaled thinly through her nostrils. "You really shouldn't listen to gossip, Lord McKinney. It's usually untrue."

"Usually," he returned. She could hear the smile in his voice. "But you know what they say."

"And what would that be?"

"There's always a kernel of truth to every rumor . . ."

Meaning he believed Hamilton's scathing words about her—that she was naught but a title chaser.

She squared back her shoulders. "I hear you are quite good with a knife. Is that gossip or truth?"

He chuckled again. "I know my way around a blade."

"You're incorrigible."

"I've been called worse."

"I'm certain of that."

He pushed himself off the railing and advanced. In a few softly thudding steps he was directly in front of her. "You're a familiar story to me, Miss Hadley."

Her skin tightened warily. She dropped her head back to peer up at his shadowed features. She should turn and walk away, but she couldn't resist the bait. "What do you mean by that?"

Shivering, she hugged herself tighter, telling herself it was the chill in the air and not his proximity—or the way his eyes glimmered down at her. "Wasting yourself on someone you can never care about . . . I understand that all too well."

Her breath seized for a moment at his words . . . at what sounded like regret in his voice. She finally breathed again. "I'm wasting nothing."

He lifted one shoulder in a half shrug. "Not yet. But you're on the cusp. Like me."

"You don't know me. We're nothing alike." With that, she spun around and marched away, her slippered feet moving quickly beneath her skirts.

His voice followed her. "Run along, Miss Hadley. I'm sure Lord Thrumgoodie is missing you. He needs someone to guide him about the furniture, after all."

She swallowed down an epithet, but kept walking, refusing to believe that any part of him was like her, that he might know her or see inside her.

Logan watched her flee, aggravated with himself. What was he doing needling her? He all but admitted that he cared nothing for Libba. Not a smart move on his part. What if she persuaded Libba of that fact?

He dragged a hand over his face and stared blindly out at the night. She brought out the worst in him. He couldn't explain it. She wasn't doing anything he wasn't doing—simply looking for the best match possible—but she stirred feelings inside him, made him unaccountably angry . . . made him *feel*.

He shook his head, reaching for the cool calm of indifference. Nothing had changed. She had her agenda. He had his. They'd both marry people they felt nothing for.

Chapter Seven

The following morning Cleo set out on a walk through the park.

Berthe accompanied her. Rather silly considering all the solitary walks Cleo had taken in her life. But that was all in the past—as Jack had reminded her the first time she tried to step outside unaccompanied.

Country bred, Berthe did not mind her brisk pace—or the early hour. A still, windless air draped the park—as if the world had not yet woken, and Cleo could almost pretend she wasn't in the bustling city at all.

Berthe puffed beside her, the cheeks in her narrow, angular face flushed a ruddy red in the chill morning. "A mite fast today, aren't you, miss?"

Cleo nodded to a nearby bench. "Feel free to have a seat."

She shook her head. "Just pondering your need for such haste. No more than that."

Cleo smiled. Berthe had come to read her well. There was an undeniable parallel between Cleo's moods and her urge for brisk walks.

They continued on, the only sound their rasping breaths. An occasional rider streaked along a bridle path, reveling in the freedom of the park in the early-morning hour.

The path wound, cutting into a heavy cluster of trees. A twig snapped behind them and Cleo glanced over her shoulder. Leaves scuttled across the path, but nothing else moved. Shrugging, she faced forward again . . . only to stop and glance behind them again several moments later, an uneasy feeling sweeping over her.

Berthe followed her gaze. "What?"

Cleo shook her head. "Nothing. Just . . ."

"What?"

"Nothing." Turning about, she moved two strides before a shadow fell across their path.

Cleo gasped. Berthe yelped and took a hasty step in front of Cleo.

With a sinking sensation, Cleo gazed at the man in front of them and placed a hand on Berthe's arm. "Don't be alarmed."

The maid glanced back and forth between Cleo and the stranger.

"He's my stepfather," Cleo explained, staring sullenly at Roger. His face appeared more bloated and dissipated than she remembered, and she could guess that he'd been spending some of Jack's money on a healthy portion of gin.

"Your stepfather?" She looked him up and down, clearly unimpressed. "Don't you know how to make a proper call? It doesn't include sneaking up on a lady and giving her a fright—I don't care if she is your stepdaughter!"

His lip curled. "Mind yer affairs and step away while I have a word with my daughter."

Berthe straightened with an indignant huff of breath.

"Stepdaughter," Cleo interjected even as she nodded to Berthe, indicating for her to give them a moment.

Frowning, Berthe moved off the path—out of hearing range but not out of sight. The maid's gaze never left Roger, and Cleo had no doubt that Berthe would attack at the slightest behest.

His gaze crawled over her like a slow-moving serpent. "Aren't you the fine-looking lady? Looks like you've landed yourself in quite the cozy little nest."

Cleo crossed her arms and cut straight to the point. "What do you want?" She knew he wasn't interested in idle chatter. If he was here, it was because he needed something from her . . . and the fact that he hadn't gone directly to the house told her he wanted to stay clear of Jack.

His red-rimmed eyes didn't blink at her bald question. "Money."

She blinked and cocked her head to the side. "Jack's man gave you plenty when he—"

"You didn't expect that to last, did you? That was almost a year ago."

"It's gone? That was enough to last two years."

He shrugged. "What can I say? My standard of living has significantly increased." He tugged on the lapels of his coat. "I'm a gentleman now."

She didn't even acknowledge the absurdity of that comment. "What did you do with the money?"

He stared at her, thin lipped. Crossing his thick arms across his chest, he asked, "Does it matter? It's gone."

She supposed it didn't matter. She sighed. "I'll go to Jack and—"

"I already done that. Months ago."

He'd gone to Jack? He'd run through the money months ago?

Roger continued, "The tight-fisted bastard offered me a paltry sum to come only every fortnight. An *allowance*, he called it. Treats me like a bleeding child."

"It's better than nothing. He owes you nothing," Cleo sharply reminded.

"I married his whore." Roger thrust his face close to snarl. "Raised his brat."

She took a bracing breath.

"I want more." He pounded his chest. "I deserve it."

She shook her head, wondering in what twisted reality he resided if he thought he deserved anything. "I can't make him give you more."

Roger stepped closer, the wool of his coat brushing her. "You forget about your family, Cleo? Your sisters and brothers?" His gaze narrowed. "Bess asks for you still. You remember her?"

Cleo's throat tightened. She nodded. "Of course I remember her."

"Because it's been hard these last months. Little Bess is so frail." He shrugged. "It's been cold . . . and coal isn't cheap."

Her gloved fingers curled and uncurled in anger. He'd had more than enough money for coal . . . and food, and clothes. Cleo cursed herself. She should have known this would happen—that

Roger would hoard the money for his own vices while her mother and siblings suffered.

She suddenly doubted whether her mother and the children saw a penny of it. Of course her mother wouldn't have wanted to complain to Cleo. Her mother never complained. She just endured.

"I'm close to marrying." She held up a hand in supplication. "I can give you money of my own then. You won't have to go through Jack."

He looked her over appraisingly. "Found yourself a ripe pigeon, have you? Are you certain he'll give you free rein of his purse?"

She nodded. "Yes. But I'll require a promise from you in exchange."

A guarded look came over his face. "And what would that be?"

"I get the children. And Mama, too."

He scratched his bristly jaw, obviously considering her words. "And what will I get?"

"Money. Freedom. You won't have a brood of children beneath your feet. You can live the life of a gentleman . . . go off and spend your money however you please—"

"I can do that anyway—and keep my kin."

"No. You can't." She sucked in a breath. "You won't get a penny from me unless you agree to these terms."

His eyes narrowed. "The boys. Adam and Conrad. They're getting older. They can be useful—"

"I want them. All of them."

"That's going to cost you."

Loathing curled in the pit of her belly. "What kind of man negotiates the sale of his children?"

He shrugged. "What can I say? I'm an entrepreneur."

"I'll pay whatever you ask. But I get all of them. Or I walk. That's the arrangement." She held her breath tight inside her chest, hoping he'd believe her bluff—that she'd walk away from her family. No matter the situation, she'd never do that—could never turn her back on them.

He studied her, clearly contemplating her offer, weighing if there was any disadvantage to him.

"Very well," he finally relented. "You can have the children. They're naught but trouble, anyway. But I keep your mother."

A protest surged hotly to her lips. "No!" Her mother would not live much longer if she remained with him. Of this she was certain. "I'll pay you."

"You can't pay me enough for her." He thrust his face close. Spittle flew from his lips. "She's my wife. I keep her."

Gazing into his eyes, she knew he would never

relent on this point. Her shoulders slumped in defeat. "Very well."

He smiled suddenly. "I'm glad we had this talk." Shivering in the morning chill, he flipped up the collar of his coat.

Glaring at him, she marveled that she could ever despise anyone so much.

Squinting out at the tree-shrouded horizon, he murmured mildly, "Best be quick and get yourself to the altar. Don't know how long the little ones can fare without proper care. Life can be so . . . taxing." He glanced back at her, an eyebrow winging high. "As you well know."

With that parting comment ringing ominously in her ears, he drifted off down the path.

The next afternoon Marguerite surprised Cleo with a visit. Even if Cleo hadn't grown fond of her half sister in the last year, she would have been delighted to see her for the distraction alone. She'd suffered a restless night, her encounter with her stepfather replaying through her mind, filling her with a gnawing sense of urgency. She must do something and soon. She might not be able to save her mother, but she could still save the children.

Deciding an outing would do her some good, Cleo suggested they visit her favorite place, a bookshop she had discovered shortly after arriving in Town.

The bell chimed over the door as they entered the shop. Cleo inhaled, loving the musty, leathery aroma. Mr. Schumacher greeted them warmly, coming around his wide oak counter.

"Ladies! So good to see you again. Anything I can help you with today?"

"Just browsing, Mr. Schumacher," she replied, untying her bonnet's ribbons beneath her chin.

Marguerite did the same, smoothing a hand over the top of her raven-dark hair.

"Well, you always manage to find something with no assistance from me. Enjoy! Let me know if you need anything." Beaming, he gestured widely with his hands, welcoming them to peruse the towering shelves stuffed haphazardly with books. Cleo was certain they were organized in some order and fashion that Mr. Schumacher alone understood. Patrons, however, were hopeless to understand what that pattern might be.

Marguerite trailed behind her, evidently content to let Cleo browse the many books. Cleo pulled out one title and then slid it back in its home, strolling along and running her fingers over spines.

"See anything you like?"

"Not yet." She looked over her shoulder with a smile. "But I will."

"Of that I have no doubt. You read more than any soul I've ever known."

"Books were such a rarity growing up. The only thing I ever read with any regularity was Mama's Bible. Or sheet music. When I practiced the pianoforte at the rectory, the vicar would sometimes let me read from his collection of books." She smiled at the memory. "The reverend was a good man, but his reading preferences were different from my own. He didn't own a single novel."

She selected a battered novel by Mrs. Radcliffe and tucked it beneath her arm.

Marguerite arched a dark eyebrow. "I'd hazard to say he would not have approved of that one."

She laughed. "Most assuredly."

Cleo exclaimed with delight as she found a thin volume of poems. Thumbing through it, she saw that it was all melodramatic rubbish. The best kind. Pleased, she hugged the book close.

"I'll be back. I want to see if there are any books of children's rhymes. My friend Fallon enjoys reading to her daughter." Marguerite moved down the aisle.

Cleo continued to browse as Marguerite moved off. Surrounded by so many books, she could forget the world around her . . . especially so close to the chance of escaping into other worlds. Better worlds.

"Good morning, Miss Hadley."

As the familiar Scottish voice ribboned its way through her, she questioned her sanity and whether she had conjured the words from memory. Surely he couldn't be here of all places. Not in the one place in this city she considered hers.

Inhaling a bracing breath, she turned. Her ears had not deceived her. Her skin heated as she recalled their last encounter and his intimation that they were alike.

"Lord McKinney," she murmured, pleased at the flatness of her voice. "What are you doing here?" Blunt to the point of rudeness perhaps, but she didn't really care. After their last exchange, she needed to keep things aloof.

"It's a bookshop. I'm looking for a book." His gray eyes narrowed. "What? You don't think I'm following you, do you?"

She lifted her chin. "Of course not."

He nodded slowly, those gray eyes of his watching her closely as if he really believed she thought that.

She waved at the books. "You don't strike me as much of a reader."

"I don't know whether to be offended or complimented."

She frowned, wondering how he could have read a compliment in that.

He elaborated, "You either think me a dullard uninterested in books . . ."

"Or?" she prompted at his pause.

"Well, that you think of me at all to form any opinion is quite gratifying."

She exhaled. "I assure you I don't think of you." Pulling her books close, she moved to walk past him. He stepped directly in her path, blocking her way. He stood so close she had to tilt her head back to meet his gaze.

"Liar." He breathed the word more than he actually said it. Her heart stuttered inside her chest.

"Now who's laboring under delusions of grandeur?"

The flat line of his mouth curved ever so slightly. "It's fair to say I've thought of you perhaps . . ." he tilted his head as though searching, "once. Oh, very well. Twice."

She snorted. "Well, not me."

He shrugged one broad shoulder. "I suppose I'm not such an enigma." His gaze dropped from her face, eyeing the modest cut of her dress as if it were anything but modest. The flesh of her chest warmed beneath his perusal.

"I couldn't say. Now if you'll let me pass."

Instead of obliging, he plucked the books from

her hands. She protested and tried to reclaim the books, but he held them out of her reach, reading their covers.

"Poetry," he mused, scanning the volume. He looked at her second selection. "Ah. And Mrs. Radcliffe." He made a clucking sound. "I would never have suspected it of you."

Her lips pursed as she fought back the urge to demand what he meant by that.

"Oh, you look like you're sucking lemons. Go ahead, Miss Hadley. Ask before you explode. You know you want to."

She shook her head, loathing that he should read her so clearly. "I have nothing to ask you."

"You're a stubborn chit." He waved the books before her. "Very well. I'll go ahead and enlighten you. This is not the reading material I would have credited as your preference."

"And why is that?" she snapped.

"So . . . emotional. Romantic and fanciful." He scanned her face as though committing her every feature to memory. "These are the books a young girl reads . . . a dreamer." His words fanned her cheek in a warm breath. "Not someone who would commit herself to a doddering old man—"

"Enough," she bit out. "I'll not bear your scorn. Especially as you're no different from me."

His dark eyebrow winged high. "Oh, now we're alike, are we?"

She closed her eyes. She hadn't meant to admit that. Opening her eyes, she confessed, "Very well. We're both great pretenders, fooling poor souls into thinking we care about them when we have our own agendas. Is that not so?"

A muscle feathered across his jaw and she surmised that her words hit a nerve. A surge of satisfaction wound through her.

"You opened my eyes to that," she added.

He didn't answer, simply continued to stare at her as if perhaps he didn't know her quite so well after all.

This time he did not stop her as she swept past him. At the end of the aisle, she spotted her sister watching her avidly, her bright gaze rife with questions as it drifted from her to Lord McKinney.

"Who is that?"

Cleo looked over her shoulder where he stood, still watching her. "No one," she murmured.

"He's not looking at you as no one would," Marguerite remarked.

No, he wasn't. He was looking after her like he wished to strangle her. At least she thought that was what his intense expression meant. She was not entirely sure.

Overcome with the need to hasten away, she took her sister's arm. "Come, let us go."

Satisfied that she had put him in his place, she fell into step beside Marguerite.

"I'm not sure you should look so smug," Marguerite interrupted her thoughts. "He's staring daggers at you right now."

A quick glance over her shoulder confirmed he had moved to the end of the aisle to watch her retreat. "Of course he is." She shrugged. "We loathe each other."

Marguerite arched a slim eyebrow. "Indeed, do you now?" Her lips twitched.

"What's so amusing?" she asked as they descended the short steps that led to the front of the shop.

"Loathing is such strong sentiment."

Cleo frowned. She was right of course. Strong sentiment shouldn't be applied to a man she had characterized as no one only moments before. "Perhaps loathing is too strong a word then. He irks me," she corrected.

She chuckled lightly.

"Marguerite," she growled. "Why are you laughing now?"

"I met a man who irked me once, too. Extremely so. I may have even fancied that I loathed him."

Sighing and expecting a lesson was coming, she asked wearily, "And? What happened to him?"

"Oh, Ash? I married him."

No words could have more effectively stolen her breath. It took her a moment to recover her speech. "Well, I can assure you that that will never happen. The notion is absurd. It's too disturbing to even contemplate. I'm quite satisified with Thrumgoodie. I'm hoping for a proposal soon."

"If you say so," Marguerite agreed in an aggravatingly amiable tone. She sent another glance over her shoulder. "Only if one compared him and Thrumgoodie side by side . . ."

"If one were superficial enough to do that," Cleo inserted pertly.

Marguerite giggled. "Have you seen my husband?" She smiled in rapt memory. "Never underestimate the appeal of virility in a man."

Oh, Cleo never had. Which is why she was determined to choose Thrumgoodie over gentlemen like McKinney.

By the time Logan reached the front of the store with books in hand for Fiona's little ones, Miss Hadley was nowhere to be seen. For the best, he resolved.

She had done a brilliant job getting beneath his

skin. With their every encounter, she only buried herself deeper and deeper. Claiming they were both great pretenders was vexingly true. Courting Libba, fawning over her and plying her with empty compliments . . . it was a torment. But he had to.

He couldn't fathom what drove Miss Hadley into the arms of a relic like Thrumgoodie. The allure of a title? Was it that simple? From all accounts, she didn't require Thrumgoodie's money. Shaking his head, he told himself he would probably never know what drove her. And why should he bother trying to find out? They weren't even friends. Once he was married to Libba, he might see her at the occasional function—if she married Thrumgoodie, of course—but no more than that.

He nodded at the shopkeeper behind the counter and murmured an appropriate farewell as he took his parcel of books and left the shop, more determined than ever to put Cleopatra Hadley from his mind.

Chapter Eight

Cleo knew the moment she accepted the invitation to Lady Doddingham's garden party that she would come face to face with Lord McKinney again. Hopefully, preparing herself for the encounter would make it less . . . *less*. A dull conversation with the Scotsman would not be remiss. Or even no conversation at all. As she stared out at the sea of manicured lawn, she caught no glimpse of him. For the time being, she breathed easier.

Lady Doddingham was Libba's godmother. Those close ties to Lord Thrumgoodie explained why Cleo had earned an invitation to what was customarily the first event of the season and a most coveted affair. As Libba explained, anyone who was anyone attended.

She had Thrumgoodie to thank for most of her

invitations about Town. Jack's wealth only carried so much pull, she'd learned. Her sister marrying a prince didn't benefit him as greatly as he would have hoped. Not when the first thing Grier did was pack up and move to Maldania.

If her father chose to relocate to the country of Maldania, he wouldn't have to grease any palms to see that he was invited to the best soirees. Here, however, was another story . . . and why he still craved a highborn English son-in-law.

She sipped from her crystal flute and continued to scan the garden, searching for a dark-haired man who would stand a head taller than other gentlemen present. Just as Cleo was invited, she knew Libba would have insisted upon McKinney's inclusion. Indeed, Libba would have seen that his name was on the top of Lady Doddingham's list.

"What a perfectly lovely day," Hamilton remarked as he came up alongside of her.

She forced a bright smile and blinked, blinded by his garishly bright purple cravat. Apparently the *ton* dressed more colorfully for garden parties. He wasn't the only one present wearing colors to rival a peacock's plumes.

"Indeed," she agreed with stiff politeness.

"Even if you are here," he returned.

She congratulated herself when her smile didn't

falter at his jab. "The day is remarkably warm. I so feared it would rain."

He smiled tightly, no doubt annoyed she hadn't risen to his bait. "Would rain have kept you away then? Perhaps I should issue forth a quick prayer for a downpour so that I may be delivered from you."

She snorted, doubting the good Lord even heard this devil's prayers. Even as she thought this, she held her tongue and glanced around, hoping for rescue. There wasn't a friendly face anywhere amid the elaborate flower arrangements and yellow-striped linens.

"Looking for my uncle? I believe he had an accident." His voice dropped on the last word and he motioned near the front of his trousers so that she had no confusion to what he was referring. Mortifying heat crept over her face. "He has those problems, you know," Hamilton continued with a *tsk* of his tongue. "A man his age . . . he has a great many . . . ailments. Incontinence. Impotence."

If possible, the heat in her face only intensified. "How dare you speak of such matters to me? You go too far. Your uncle would not appreciate it."

In the distance she spotted Thrumgoodie walking in his wobbly gait along the buffet table and her anger only burned hotter. "I see you were making sport. Your uncle is over there."

"Oh, so he is." Hamilton shrugged. "Doesn't alter anything I told you. Marry him and you'll only be getting half a man."

"I realize you're only speaking out of concern." Her voice dripped sarcasm. "You're such an altruist."

At her tone, his mocking smile vanished to be replaced with a very nasty sneer. "Oh, make no mistake. I'm not a nice man. Heed me well. Stay away from my uncle. Go sniff after some other title. If you think we don't rub on well now, just wait and see what happens if you actually marry my uncle."

Cleo sipped from her flute before saying, "Hmm, let me consider this scenario. Me . . . marrying the earl. What would happen? Oh, I remember," she exclaimed with false brightness. "I get half of your inheritance." Smiling sweetly, she whirled away. But not before a muttered *bitch* stung her ears.

She fought to keep the smile on her face until she was certain he could no longer see her. Lifting her skirts, she descended the stone steps into the garden, past the milling guests. She walked until the chatter, clink of crystal and harp strings were but a distant song.

She bypassed a maze of hedges and veered off the pebbled path into a press of trees that crowded one side of a pond. Doddingham's estate was only just outside the city, but it felt as though she were lost amid the country. Far away from the city. The *ton* and all its watching eyes. She inhaled a deep breath, smelling the leaves and loamy earth. Some of the tension ebbed from her shoulders. Until that moment, she hadn't realized her eyes stung. She rubbed at them until the sensation faded.

Heedless of the snags it might give her gown of buttercream silk, she expelled a great breath and leaned against a thick oak tree. Staring out at the pond's glassy surface, she wondered if she should not heed Hamilton's warning and focus her attentions elsewhere. Although finding another man to meet her criteria might prove a challenge.

The words she'd uttered to her mother—the vow she'd made to herself—weighed on her. She'd dallied long enough. She needed to see her mother and all her siblings properly cared for. Roger had made it clear she was short on time. No more gnawing hunger. No wretched sickness. No miserable squalor. Marrying Thrumgoodie would see to that. It would grant her the freedom and independence to live her life and use her money as she wished without sacrificing her body and heart to a man who would use and abuse both.

Thrumgoodie was the one. She might never find a gentleman so perfectly suited to her needs. He was safe and unthreatening.

The sting was back in her eyes again. She blinked several times as the doubts pressed in on her. Blast it. Moisture built in her eyes and she wiped at them furiously, marveling at her sudden emotion. Because of Hamilton? She snorted. He hadn't aggravated her to such a degree before. Maybe the tenor of his threats had altered today and frightened her?

She shook her head, quickly dismissing that. No. She wasn't afraid of him. Living beneath her stepfather's roof, she'd tasted the bitterness of fear before. When she was a girl, Roger's alcohol-laced voice had spit angry words that shadowed every moment. Those days had been a haze of unrelenting dread.

Fear didn't make her doubt herself now. But something else—someone else—did.

A certain gentleman's taunting voice and derisive remarks suddenly had her questioning herself. Absurd. Leaning her head back against the tree, she listened to the thoughts warring inside her head. She wasn't hurting anyone. Lord Thrumgoodie would be thrilled for her companionship . . . thrilled to call her wife. Why did a certain cad have to give her second thoughts?

Steps sounded on the path and she jerked her gaze up, spotting Hamilton advancing down the path. Had he followed her? He hadn't noticed her yet. With a small gasp, she dove into the press of shrubbery edging the pond. Drastic perhaps, but the last thing she wanted was to be cornered alone by the vile man.

Holding her breath as though that would somehow make her quieter, she lifted her skirts and moved deeper into the undergrowth, hoping her gown wasn't detectable from the path.

She glanced over her shoulder, making sure she wasn't being followed. A branch snagged her hair and she winced, attempting to free herself without ruining her coiffure.

"Allow me."

She froze at the sound of the deep voice. Her stomach dipped as strong fingers delicately freed the strands of her hair.

She quickly stepped back several paces, surveying who else hid in the shrubbery alongside her. "Lord McKinney," she greeted.

"Miss Hadley." He motioned to the tight press of trees and undergrowth surrounding them. "Seeking a moment alone?"

"You could say that. And you?"

He smiled, but there was no humor in it. "Likewise." His cool gray gaze flitted over her.

She evaluated him in turn. He wore a deep blue jacket with tan trousers. Apparently he'd eschewed the vivid colors that seemed requisite at a garden party.

They said nothing more, simply considered each other thoughtfully. After a moment, he moved. She watched warily as he closed the space between them, his booted feet crackling over twigs and fallen leaves.

"I've been giving some thought to what you said," he finally announced.

"Have you?" She tried to reveal none of her surprise that he should be thinking about anything she said. "And what was it I said requiring such reflection?"

"That we are both great pretenders, fooling poor souls into thinking we care about them for our own agenda."

"Ah, yes. That."

"And you're right. We're both playing at this game of securing a spouse."

She angled her head. "Game?"

A rueful smile curved his lips. "Hunting for a wife, or in your case a husband, is nothing more than a game."

He continued, "That being the case, we shouldn't be sniping at one another. It serves no purpose."

She crossed her arms awkwardly. "No. I suppose not." What was he suggesting? That they actually be friends? Warning bells rang in her ears.

"Splendid."

She nodded, feeling like an awkward schoolgirl. It was easier before this truce. Silence descended and her heart beat a loud rhythm in her ears.

"Well. I suppose I should get back."

That muscle feathered his jaw again, and she knew she'd displeased him. "Want me to check and see if Hamilton is gone?" he asked idly.

"Why? I'm not hiding," she lied.

His lips curved in a slow, seductive smile that she was certain got him most anything he ever wanted. "Indeed?" He leaned back against a tree, the picture of a relaxed gentleman, totally at ease, without a care in the world. "I am."

From Libba? Of course he was. Not about to commiserate with him regarding the need to hide from one's beau, she nodded and strode past him, heedless of her step. Her foot caught on a root, and she went flying, narrowly escaping a hard fall as he caught her.

Strong hands flexed around her arms. "Are you all right?"

"Fine," she replied breathlessly.

Something flared hotly in his eyes as they gazed at each other. "You're always running from me."

"Apparently not very gracefully."

"This time, no. But I sense that worked for the best."

A shudder traveled through her. "Why is that?"

He angled his head. "I have my hands on you."

Her hand fisted in his jacket, alerting her to the fact that she even touched him. Everything else faded—who she was, where she was. It all happened in a blur, too fast to process. A haze clouded her mind. She was out of control, past considering propriety and how vastly dangerous the situation had become.

And yet when he tugged her closer and trapped her arms between them, lifting her off her feet and against him, sanity returned.

She caught a flash of gray eyes before his head dove toward hers. Determined to resist, the press of his lips on hers galvanized her, made her struggle.

She bit down on his lip.

He pulled back with a cutting curse.

Locked in his embrace, chests squashed close, she glared at him. He glared back. For several moments their panting breaths mingled as they stared incomprehensibly at each other.

She noted a change in his eyes then. They no longer looked so cold. The condemnation wasn't there. None of the calculating judgment of before. It was as if he saw her. Now. For the first time.

And there was fire in his eyes.

His head descended and this time she didn't

move. Not the barest flinch. Her breathing ceased altogether as his lips claimed hers with a swiftness, a surety, and skill that she felt ripple through the whole of her body.

His hands splayed against her back, each finger burning an imprint through her gown. Her body came alive as his lips moved over hers, caressing, possessing, melting her from the inside out. Her knees weakened and trembled. She clutched fistfuls of his jacket in her hands—to keep from falling, to pull him close. Both.

Heat sprang in patches all over her. Suddenly her dress felt constrictive, too tight. She moaned against his mouth and he deepened the kiss, parting the seam of her lips—or perhaps she opened to him. Either way his tongue slipped inside her mouth. Warm and deft, smooth and skillful, he tasted her, sliding his tongue against hers.

Her belly clenched and a twisting ache started between her legs. Just like that. One kiss and she was shattered and aching for this man. She never wanted it to end, and yet a voice worked its way through her, fighting its way to the surface as though from a deep, hidden place. A forgotten place where logic and her true purpose dwelled.

Stop this! Stop this madness!

She broke away with a shocked gasp. Unbelievably, she'd let passion seize her. A circumstance she would never have believed possible. She was nothing like her mother . . . like other girls who craved a man's kisses.

He held her, but not tightly anymore. Not as a prisoner. Standing in the circle of his arms, she blinked up at him, unable to leave just yet. She had to understand. Had to process for herself what it was that had just happened . . . and if he was as shocked as she was.

His heavy-lidded gaze drilled into her with a relentless intensity, peeling away her layers bit by bit. At least it seemed that way. For a panicked moment, she felt certain those gray eyes saw her. Saw everything. That he read her fear, that he understood what motivated her. Likely because of her runaway tongue. She'd shared too much . . .

Horrified, she stumbled free.

She took several steps back, still gazing at him and confronting the knowledge that she wasn't immune.

He'd aroused her as she'd never thought possible.

She lifted her hand and touched her lips. His gaze followed the movement. His eyes darkened, reminding her of a stormy night. The hunger there was unmistakable. She recognized it. Felt its echo inside herself.

It seemed neither one of them could manage speech. He looked as astonished as she felt. She only hoped that his shock would soon translate into regret. Eventually. That his low opinion of her would return in full force and this moment would soon be a dim memory.

Turning, she fled.

She'd forget this ever happened. She'd forget him. Even if forced into proximity again, she'd treat him as she would a stranger. Because that's all he could ever be.

Chapter Nine

$\mathcal{L}$ogan watched her go, his body throbbing and alive as it hadn't felt in years. Certainly not since he'd traveled across the country and began courting vapid young misses who thrilled him about as much as a glass of day-old milk.

"Cleopatra," he murmured, his lips still tender and warm from the taste of her. For the first time he not only said her name, he allowed himself to think it. To feel it in his blood.

In that moment, something turned, something shifted inside him as definite as a key turning in its lock. She moved from the category where she'd been residing in his mind.

She wasn't the cold, uninteresting female he'd first thought her to be. Far from it. He could still feel the delicious shape of her in his hands, against his body. And perhaps he'd known this all along. Why else had she consumed so much of his thoughts?

He followed in her wake, moving slowly across the pebbled path bisecting the lush lawn, coming to terms with this new realization. And grappling with what it signified.

Later that night in her bed, Cleo stared into the dark, her hand pressed to lips that still felt overly warm and tender. He had kissed her.

She had kissed him back.

She caught herself just short of smiling. Rolling onto her side, she struck her pillow several times.

Was this how it had been for her mother? She could almost empathize. Which was a frightening consideration when she had judged her mother weak and without sense all these years. With a sigh, she sat up and struck her pillow anew, using more vigor.

Feeling slightly better, she dropped back down and glared up at the dark canopy overhead.

Her mind raced ahead, contemplating when she would likely next see him. The Fordham ball was the day after tomorrow. She'd clarify matters with him then. He would not mistake her meaning. She'd be steadfast and resolved.

Tempting or not, she wouldn't succumb. His

lips would not come near her again. And she'd make sure he knew that.

Cleo's feet tapped to the music, longing to dance, but knowing that would be unlikely. Lord Thrumgoodie was hardly a candidate. Understandably. He had no wish to break a hip. Rather than take to the dancing floor, he occupied himself at one of the card tables. A far safer pursuit. She assumed that all the other gentlemen considered her off the market because they never asked her.

Cleo currently stood along the edge of the ballroom beside a pouting Libba. She tried to focus on the swirl of colorful gowns, but it was difficult standing next to Libba. The girl had no shortage of gentlemen willing to partner her on the dance floor. With her pedigree and dowry, all manner of men pursued her. And yet she chose to spend her evening whining beside Cleo, rejecting dance partner after dance partner.

She stared straight ahead as Libba dismissed yet another gentleman with a feeble lie. "Forgive me, Reginald, but my head is aching most miserably."

Cleo inhaled. Viable men sought her, and yet Libba had set her cap for only one.

An uncomfortable knot formed in her gut as she recalled the kiss she and McKinney had shared. As much as she regretted it and knew it could never happen again, oddly enough, in these moments with Libba, it gave her a secret delight. Until it occurred to her that he may have kissed Libba, too. Then she felt only jealous and panicky.

As the callow Reginald retreated, freshly rejected, Libba spun to face her. "Oh, where is he?" She stamped her foot in a fit of pique. "I know he received an invitation. I made certain of it."

"Then I'm sure he'll be here," Cleo replied.

"He's changed his mind about me." Her eyes stared abjectly ahead.

Cleo's pulse stuttered at her neck with treacherous hope. "W-why do you say that?"

"He hasn't called upon me in two days."

Since the day of our kiss.

"Perhaps he's ill," she offered lamely, her mind spinning.

Libba gazed at her desperately. "Nor has he sent word. This is so unlike his previous behavior. What if he's met someone else?"

Cleo coughed, her face suddenly hot. "I find that unlikely."

"Perhaps someone with a larger dowry—"

"Whose dowry could compare to yours?"

Libba waved a hand. "It's not impossible. Yours surpasses mine from all accounts I've heard."

At this comment, Cleo strangled on a breath. "I haven't your grace or charm or social standing . . . no one could compete with you on those points."

Libba shrugged. "Ah, well. That's true. I do have a great deal to offer."

Cleo nodded.

"Perhaps he is ill and just didn't want me to worry." Libba cocked her head as though considering this doubtful explanation.

"Yes, I'm sure that's it," Cleo lied.

Cleo spied another of Libba's young swains weaving his way toward her, his face flushed with eagerness. "You really should dance. The last thing Lord McKinney would wish is for you to wallow away during his absence," she suggested.

"Perhaps." Her lips pulled into a little moue. "And it would do me good if word got back to him how popular I am."

"Oh. Naturally." Cleo nodded. And perhaps another gentleman might catch her fancy and turn her off from Lord McKinney. Not a bad thing, however small the chance. Especially as Cleo was beginning to fear that he had in fact experienced a change of heart regarding his pursuit of Libba. A fact for which she felt heartily to blame.

Could their one kiss have persuaded him to forget Libba?

Of course not. She scoffed at the absurd notion.

It was one kiss. She wasn't so egotistical to think her lips possessed the power to change one man's matrimonial plans.

She watched in satisfaction as Libba finally accepted a partner and was swept away on the dance floor. Cleo inhaled, at peace for the moment with a respite from Libba. Her gaze scanned the room, looking for her father even as she assumed that he was still in the card room with Lord Thrumgoodie. When it came to whist, the two were a pair. They could play for hours.

Her gaze suddenly halted amid its survey of the room. There, in the threshold, stood her McKinney.

She blinked and silently cursed the mental slip. Not *her* anything!

His gray eyes scanned the room and she spun around before he could see her. So much for her determination to face him. She fled, hoping he hadn't spotted her—or that he couldn't recognize the back of her.

She wove her way through bodies. Holding up her skirts, she disappeared down a corridor, telling herself she needed but a moment alone to gather her nerve . . . to regain her composure before she issued her warning that he keep his hands—and lips—to himself.

She passed the buzzing card room. A glance

inside revealed the crowd of gentlemen—even a few ladies. Not a very good hiding place.

She pushed ahead. Feeling very much like a panicked hare, she hurried forward without direction, no destination in mind. She couldn't imagine McKinney staying too long. He always seemed to possess an air of ennui in large gatherings—like he'd rather be somewhere, anywhere, else. Or perhaps that was simply wishful thinking. He'd arrived late. Perhaps he intended to stay a good while.

Perhaps if he can't locate you, he'll leave.

She shook her head at the arrogant thought. If she believed that, then she believed his reason for coming here tonight was because of her. For all she knew that kiss meant nothing to him and he was here to continue his courtship of Libba. That seemed the most logical conclusion.

She soon found herself in the portrait gallery. She strolled down the long length, gazing at several stern faces staring down at her—a long line of proper-looking aristocrats. She snorted, thinking of her own ancestors. Peasants, all. None could have imagined any descendant of theirs ever strolling the floors of such a grand house. A year ago she would not have thought such a thing possible.

Steps sounded in the distance, echoing off the marbled floor. She started, looking swiftly to the left and right. Her first thought was that he was coming after her.

Even as she recognized this as foolish and unlikely, she dove behind a potted fern. It was a rather large specimen. Even so, she doubted she was totally hidden to the discerning eye. Her peacock blue skirts peeped out from around the fern. And yet, she held herself utterly still.

It only sounded like one pair of feet. A man's tread. Her heart thudded in her chest. She bit her lip and turned her face away from the offending branch poking near her eye. Probably just someone wandering through to view the gallery.

Even as she reasoned this, she held her breath, listening. The steps rang out with an echo as they entered the gallery.

And then they stopped altogether.

Too many leaves obscured her view, and she didn't wish to rustle them with her fingers. She imagined some innocuous soul standing there, studying one of the portraits. Just as she was counting herself ten kinds of fool for concealing herself behind a fern, a voice rumbled across the air.

"Are you going to hide there forever?

She jerked, the wretchedly familiar voice with its velvet burr like a slap.

He spoke again, "I can see your dress. Come now. Show yourself."

"Hiding?" She stepped out from behind the fern and smoothed both hands over her skirts. Lifting her chin, she adopted an even tone and blinked innocently. "How absurd. Why would I hide?"

"Because you're avoiding me."

"I'm not avoiding you. Why would I even bother to do such a thing?" She snorted lightly, applauding herself for how calm and unaffected she sounded.

He angled his head and swept her a hot look that brought everything back. His mouth on hers. His hands moving over her back. That impossibly broad chest pressed against her.

Heat crawled up her face. With a look like that, he clearly wanted her to remember.

"Oh. Because of that?" She waved a hand dismissively. "A mistake to be sure, but it won't happen again." It was the closest she could bring herself to discussing what had happened.

He stepped closer, his boot heels clicking on the floor. His gray eyes were as stormy as a night sea and she felt a stab of alarm that only intensified at his next words. "I would very much like to kiss you again."

Her eyes widened. She hadn't expected such bluntness—nor the way those very direct words made her belly flutter.

Her breath fell faster. "That's quite impossible."

"Why?"

She shook her head, baffled that he should even have to ask. That she should need to explain. "You know why."

He shook his head slowly. "I've considered it, and no. I don't know why we cannot. We're both marriage-bound and obviously suited."

"Because of a mere kiss you think we are suited?"

"Mere?" His dark eyebrows winged high. He was close enough now. Too close. He reached for her and she knew instantly he meant to prove her wrong, to take her in his arms again and show her there was nothing *mere* about their kiss.

She danced out of his range and held up a hand to ward him off. "Very well!" she quickly admitted, hoping to avert the disaster of his lips landing on hers again. "It was . . . nice."

That stopped him. "Nice?" he demanded.

Her heart flipped as she gazed at his face—so handsome in his indignation that the sight made her chest ache.

"More than nice," she amended, taking a sliding step backward.

His gray eyes darkened and she knew she'd annoyed him. "Liar."

She flinched.

"I want you," he declared, stepping nearer again. "And you want me, too."

She shook her head. "You're making too much of this." She took another step back and bumped into a bust of some long-dead ancestor. It wobbled dangerously and she quickly turned, grabbing it and steadying it with her shaking hands.

She exhaled with relief and turned to find him there, practically on top of her. She gasped. Unable to back up a step again without sending the bust careening to the floor, she held her ground. Her hands wobbled uncertainly between them before surrendering and coming to rest on his splendidly broad chest.

His heart thudded strong and deep against her palms, and she was achingly reminded of his words—could hear them in her head. *I want you.*

There was no mistaking his intent even if he hadn't said such an outrageous thing. She could see it in his eyes . . . smell it on the musky, intoxicating aroma of him. In the way he held his body against her, all tense muscles ready to spring.

She moistened her lips and asked, grasping at straws, "What about Libba?"

"Come now." His stare searched her face, missing nothing. "I've promised her nothing."

"Formally, yes, no proposal has been issued, but the expectation is there all the same."

"Everyone has expectations. Disappointments are a way of life. She'll forget me in time and favor someone else."

Cleo shook her head, her heart thundering in her chest. She doubted that. He was quite unforgettable. She glanced at his too handsome face and then looked away. But too late. The strong lines, the dark slashing eyebrows and steel gray eyes were there, permanently etched in her mind.

God, she was her mother's daughter, to lose her head over the first handsome man to pay her such attentions, to pursue her as a hungry predator might.

He reached down to caress the fat sausage curl draped over her bare shoulder. "Like satin," he murmured. "Molten chocolate."

"I don't understand." The words rasped slowly from her lips, her thoughts churning sluggishly through her head. His nearness, his touch did that to her—addled her head. "You're saying you no longer wish to court Libba because . . ." She stopped, unable to put it into words.

His lips curled in a half smile, crooked and enticing. "I'm a pragmatic man." His hand turned so that his fingertips stroked the bend of her throat, where her neck and shoulder connected.

"Uh-huh." She struggled to focus, something exceedingly difficult with his velvet touch on her.

Was this seduction then? This sensation of sinking deeply, inexorably into a pool of sensation.

"There's only one lady I've met that fires my mind and blood. How can I turn from her?"

She gazed up at him, feeling utterly bemused. "Who's that?"

He smiled that devilish grin again. "You. It only makes sense that you and I should court."

Court? He wanted a legitimate relationship with her? She blinked, some of the fog dissipating as reality fought its way to the surface.

"You're mad," she whispered, and then reminded him. "And I'm no lady. Just a bastard. You can't mean to entertain . . ."

He frowned, looking rather disappointed with her. "I don't care about the circumstances of your birth. We're both seeking the same thing. Why not choose each other?"

No words could have struck terror to her heart with more speed. She wiggled free of him, heedless of the delicious friction it created between their bodies.

With a growl, he grabbed hold of her wrist and forced her back around to face him. If possible, they now stood even closer than before. His arms came up to wrap around her, his hands warm and all-encompassing against her spine. The temptation to soak up his touch, lean into him like a purring cat was cruelly beguiling.

She struggled against this—against him. He was a brick wall. Immovable. Overwhelming. She was again reminded why virile, muscular men were so repellent to her. She loathed this sensation of being somehow fragile and easily broken. Prey for a man who could use her and crush her if she left herself vulnerable. Her mother's face flashed before her eyes, older and more weary than her actual years, broken and defeated.

Not me. Never me.

"Hold still," he bit out.

She ceased her struggles and glared up at him. A lock of hair fell into her face, waving like a flag in the wind before her eyes. She blew at it and shook her head, trying to force it back.

His gaze scanned her, devouring her face, missing nothing. "What are you so afraid of?"

The question landed like a perfectly targeted arrow, quivering throughout her body.

"N-nothing," she quickly denied.

"You're lying. I see the fear in your eyes."

"Perhaps your unwanted attentions alarm me."

"I alarm you, but not because you don't want me."

"Your arrogance knows no bounds."

"Are you afraid of getting hurt? Is that it?"

Was she that transparent then? Blast! She clamped her lips shut, determined to say nothing else that confirmed his suspicions.

His eyes narrowed on her face. A muscle feathered tensely across his tight jaw. He looked dangerous and she was reminded how little she knew of this man.

Mentally, she recounted what little she knew of him that she could call fact. He hailed from the Highlands. He possessed a crumbling castle. He used a knife to cut through the stays of ladies' gowns.

And she trembled with desire in his arms. Fact.

"Has someone hurt you before?" he pressed, his eyes darkening.

Her eyes widened. He thought someone had ravished her?

"No," she quickly assured, mortification sweeping over her. She hadn't lived the perfect childhood, but no one had hurt her in that manner. "Nothing like that."

"But there is something that puts fear in your eyes."

She silently cursed her slip and the implication that she was frightened. "What you call fear is modesty and good sense." She moistened her lips. "I've set my cap for the earl and ask that you respect that."

"Why? Is it his title? I know a Scottish title isn't the same as an English one, but a life as my wife would—"

"Wife?" she echoed. He'd only spoken of courtship. This was the first time he had dared utter the word *wife*. And blast her defiant heart if she didn't experience a small thrill . . . if her blood didn't rush just a little bit faster in her veins.

"I've a mind to wed you." His deep voice shot through her like a bolt of lightning. His eyes studied her intently, watching her reaction.

Masculinity rippled off him in waves. Altogether he presented no minor temptation. The same trap her mother and countless other women had fallen into yawned before her. Would she be strong enough to resist?

He stared at her for a long moment, his hands flexing over her arms. "I came to London to find a wife."

"An heiress," she quickly corrected.

Something shuttered over his eyes. He didn't like the reminder, which was why she'd made it, determined to wedge a wall between them. He didn't want her. Not fully, at any rate. If she weren't in possession of a dowry, he wouldn't be discussing marriage with her.

"Very well. I came to Town looking for an heiress. You're the first one I've met who so much as piques my interest." He swallowed, the cords of his throat working. "I'll have you, Miss Hadley."

I'll have you.

Her skin prickled. As though she were a possession to be claimed. A female to be conquered and crushed beneath his will. Not just once but every day of her life. The words were just what she needed to hear to regain her senses and shake free of her mother's curse.

"You can't have me." No man ever would. Even as she worked to fulfill her arrangement with her stepfather, she would still see to that.

"Why?" he asked, his voice maddeningly calm. "Give me one reason."

Her mind searched, grasping for anything but the truth. She wouldn't confide that to him and risk him empathizing with her plight. His wanting her was bad enough. She didn't need for him to like her. Then he might pursue her with more fervor than he already was. "I can't do that to Lord Thrumgoodie."

His look turned skeptical. "Oh, you care about him that much?"

"Of course. I wouldn't want to crush him." She bit her lip at the lie. "He means a great deal to me."

He snorted. "You can come up with a better excuse than that." His lips quirked in a half smile.

"Come now. A blood oath, is that it? He's holding your kitten hostage?"

She started to smile and then caught herself. "Just take my words to heart. You and I can never be." Wrenching free, she hastened away, experiencing the strongest sense of déjà vu. She was fleeing him again, the weight of his stare heavy on her back. She hardened her heart and didn't stop. Didn't look back.

If she must, she would keep repeating this moment. However many times necessary, she would run. She'd never stop running from him.

Eventually he'd give up. He had too much pride to chase her forever. And she wouldn't be free that long anyway. If all went her way she'd soon be married to Thrumgoodie. A bitter taste rose in her throat that she fought to swallow. McKinney needed money. He needed an heiress. He'd have to find that in another female.

Logan watched her flee with a curse hot on his lips. That hadn't gone as he'd hoped. He dragged a hand through his hair. A boy of ten and five could have handled that with more finesse.

He'd never fumbled with the fairer sex before. Cleopatra Hadley was the first. He clasped his fingers behind his neck and looked up at the ceiling.

Like Antony, he intended to win her heart, too. Hopefully, it wouldn't take him as long though—nor would it end as tragically.

His every instinct told him the best way to go about winning her was to seduce her. Or perhaps his mounting desire for her pushed him in that direction. Either way, it was a strategy he would very much enjoy employing.

Feeling refreshed with purpose, he strolled from the gallery, hands locked behind his back, whistling an old ballad from home under his breath.

He wouldn't be nearly so confident if he weren't positive she wanted him, too. Only fear held her back. A fear he was going to have to defeat . . . once he figured out what provoked it.

So intent on his next move with the complicated and fascinating Miss Hadley, he never noticed the shadowy figure watching him from the corner of the gallery, or that those eyes glowed with an unholy light, the calculating purpose there unwavering and determined enough to rival his own.

Chapter Ten

Over Cleo's protests, Jack insisted on entertaining Lord Thrumgoodie and his family. It wasn't an evening spent with Thrumgoodie that bothered her so much—she'd already determined to increase her efforts with him and garner that proposal she so desperately needed—but rather the prospect of an evening with the others on her father's list of guests. She supposed she couldn't get around Hamilton—he was Lord Thrumgoodie's houseguest after all. But Lord McKinney?

"He is a nobleman," her father had explained when she'd asked why they must invite him. "And he's courting Lady Libba. Why should you care one way or another if he attends, Cleo?"

She held her tongue in the face of her father's inquisitive stare. How could she explain that the man provoked her? That, incredible as it seemed, he wanted to marry her?

She couldn't. And that's how she found herself in her father's drawing room, suffering through a musicale. Normally, she would have enjoyed such a diversion, but not sandwiched between Thrumgoodie and Hamilton. Nor with McKinney's warm gaze heating her back.

The conversation with her stepfather replayed itself over and over in her head, and she knew she must extend every effort at encouraging Thrumgoodie. Not an easy task with Hamiltion there, interrupting and insinuating himself between them at every turn.

Cleo looked up as Berthe slipped inside the room and motioned for her to step outside. She eagerly rose and murmured her excuses, skirting around Thrumgoodie and Hamilton.

The soprano her father had engaged for the afternoon sang beautifully, but Cleo was not sorry to leave. It was altogether draining, pretending to ignore Hamilton's scathing looks . . . pretending the sound of Libba fawning over McKinney didn't nauseate her.

"Berthe?" Her slippers fell silently over the marbled floor as she approached the maid. "What is it?"

Berthe smiled anxiously. "This missive came for you, miss." She extended the letter toward Cleo. "It's from your mother. I knew you would want to read it at once."

Cleo grinned. "You know me well, Berthe." Clasping the missive to her chest, she hurried into the neighboring library for a private moment, the smell of books and leather comforting.

As often as she wrote home, her mother had only managed a few letters. Cleo hadn't let it dismay her, well understanding how busy her mother must be—especially without Cleo's help.

Excitement pumped through her as she settled onto the settee before the fire and tore open the missive. Her mother's familiar scrawl leapt off the page. As she scanned the parchment, the smile slipped from her face. Her excitement vanished. Cold washed over her, prickling her flesh.

She pressed a hand against her chest, over the sudden painful pounding of her heart.

"No." She shook her head and read the words again, hoping, praying she'd read them wrong . . . that she misunderstood somehow.

Pain blossomed in her chest and spread throughout her body as the letter fluttered to the ground. She pressed her chest harder, pushing against the tightness at its center. Her breath came fast and hard and she still couldn't breathe, couldn't take enough air inside her constricting lungs.

She slid on her side onto the settee, gazing blindly into the crackling flames until they blurred in front of her.

This couldn't have happened. *It didn't happen*. Bess wasn't gone. She wasn't dead.

Logan watched the doors, waiting for Cleo's return. As the minutes ticked by, he began to suspect that she wasn't coming back.

The soprano finished yet another song. As everyone erupted into applause, Logan excused himself, lifting Libba's clinging hand from his arm and freeing himself. Libba was a taxing creature, and he could only feel sympathy for the man that married her. Thankfully that would not be him. As soon as he persuaded Cleo to marry him, he could dispense with this farce of a courtship.

Free of the drawing room, he expelled a deep breath. He leaned back against the wall and rubbed his forehead. Hopefully, he'd win over Cleo soon.

A small sniffling sound caught his attention. He looked to the right. The double doors leading to the library were cracked. Firelight spilled out into the corridor. He turned and stepped into the path of light, pushing the doors open wider with the flat of his hand.

Cleo lay curled on the settee, her face buried into a cushion. He approached silently, the sound of his steps deadened on the carpet. Her shoulders shook, heaving with silent sobs. Her hair had fallen partially undone, the rich dark waves falling down her back.

He blinked and looked around him, as though he might find the answer to her present condition somewhere within the room. She always came across so composed, prickly and invulnerable. The sight of her weeping left an uncomfortable feeling in the pit of his stomach. He'd been around females before. All his life. His sister, even his mother, the strongest woman he'd ever known . . . all had cried on his shoulder at one time or another.

He cleared his throat. That didn't seem to have any effect on her.

"Cleo?" He lowered a hand to her shoulder and gave a gentle squeeze. "What happened?"

She muttered something unintelligible. He sank down on the settee beside her. Something crinkled beneath his shoe. Bending down, he grasped a wrinkled sheet of parchment. He looked from her to the letter, guessing it had something to do with her present mood.

Scanning the letter, his heart sank. Lifting his gaze back to Cleo, he asked, "Bess? Your sister?"

A long moment passed before she rolled to face him. Her face was wet from crying, her eyes red-rimmed and . . . haunted. "Yes."

He shook his head. "I'm so sorry."

"I should have been there." She wiped at her face with both hands.

"How old was she?"

"Three."

He cursed low beneath his breath.

She shook her head, sending loose tendrils flying around her face. "I should have been there."

He waved the letter. "Your mother said it was consumption."

"Doesn't matter," she said quickly. "It shouldn't have happened. She was healthy when I left." She beat a fisted hand to her lap.

"You can't blame yourself."

"Can't I?" She wet her lips and looked at him rather desperately, her eyes alive with a wild light. "I should have wed by now. Then I could have saved her."

"How does your marrying have anything to do with Bess getting sick?"

"You don't understand."

His hand tightened on her. "Then explain it to me."

She released a deep, shuddering breath. "My stepfather did this. Roger barely kept us in clothes. Or warm. Or fed. He certainly would never see that we received the care of a physician." Her lip curled in disgust. "He agreed that I could take the children once I married. As long as I paid him, I could have them." Her face crumpled then. "Not my mother though. He won't let her go." Tears swam down her cheeks.

He pulled back in horror at what she described. "He's holding them hostage?"

"In essence, yes." She sucked in a deep breath and shook her head as though trying to stave off the tears. "I've dragged my feet . . . left them in his care for too long." Her fist beat in her lap with renewed vigor. "Stupid, stupid. He's never cared if any of us lived or died before. It's my fault."

He cupped her face, letting the warm wet of her tears soak into his palms. "She died because she was sick. That wasn't your fault. Nor is it your fault that you're at the mercy of an animal."

Tears shimmered in her eyes as she gazed up at him. The sight clawed through him. "I wasn't there to carry her."

"Carry her?" He frowned, angling his head, his thumbs gently stroking her cheeks. "Where?"

"To the churchyard. It's my responsibility. I

always carry them to the church. I *always* carry them."

"What do you mean, you . . ." His voice tapered off, suspicion sinking its teeth into him, making him dread her next words.

"Rose, James, Lottie, and Helen. I carried them all. I should have carried her, too. I wasn't there for her."

He could only stare at her, speechless for a long moment, struggling to comprehend what she was saying. "Wait. You mean you . . . take the bodies away?"

She nodded once and his gut clenched thinking about her walking to the churchyard holding the dead bodies of her siblings. His throat tightened up on him, but he still managed to say, "That should never have been your burden."

"Should it have been my stepfather's? He wouldn't waste his time with such a task. Nor would I wish him to." Her eyes glittered passionately. "They deserved someone who cares to walk them to their final rest. I'm the one who's supposed to carry them." Her head bowed and she choked out, "Oh, Bess. I'm so sorry."

He hauled her into his arms, unable to stop himself, unable to stand her suffering for something that was out of her control. He knew her pain was inescapable. He'd lost both his brother and father. He understood grief. She'd just lost her sister. Nothing would ever take away that ache. But he'd be damned if he'd let her think any of it was her fault. "Don't blame yourself. You loved her. She had that love . . . she always will."

Her body trembled against him and he held her tighter as if he could somehow take her anguish inside himself. She pulled back enough to look up at him. He scraped the loose tendrils of hair back from where they clung to her damp cheeks.

"Thank you," she whispered. "It means a lot to hear that . . . to be reminded of that."

Noses practically touching, he nodded, his gut suddenly clenching tightly in a way that he'd never felt before. Staring down into her tear-filled gaze, he felt like he was drowning. One thing for certain, he'd never met a woman like Cleopatra Hadley. She was stronger than he could have ever known . . . and he wanted her for his wife with a fierceness that stole his breath.

"Miss!" A maid rushed into the room. "Are you all right?" She eyed Logan suspiciously—as if he were the cause for her distress.

Cleo pulled away, sniffing loudly and wiping indelicately at her nose. He hated to leave her, but knew his presence here, with her, was vastly inappropriate. He read as much in the gaze of her maid. Cleo wasn't his to comfort, as much as he might like her to be. At least not yet.

And yet a new purpose consumed him. Whether she ever belonged to him or not, there was something he could do for her.

Cleo watched Logan depart, staring hungrily at the broad expanse of his back. The gnawing ache at the center of her chest only intensified as he moved away from her. Somehow when he'd held her, talked to her . . . her pain had felt . . . less.

"Miss?" Berthe brushed a tendril back from her face. "Did he hurt you?"

"No, Berthe," she whispered. "He didn't hurt me."

Quite the opposite. Shaking her head, she told herself that she shouldn't let herself feel this way. Because she was now more determined than ever to marry Thrumgoodie. She lost Bess. She would not lose anyone else.

Chapter Eleven

Logan stared grimly at the man sniveling in the carriage across from him. Cleo's stepfather clutched both hands over his nose, trying to staunch the flow of blood.

"What do you want from me?" he asked in a nasal whine. "I have money in my vest pocket. And I can get more . . ."

From Cleo, no doubt, after he sold her his children. Logan's hands clenched and unclenched at his sides.

"Easy," Alexander advised from beside him, well aware of the hostility pumping through him . . . and his overwhelming urge to do more than land the two punches that it took to haul Roger out of the brothel and inside their carriage.

With Alexander's help, it hadn't taken long to

track him down. Apparently Roger spent most of his time at a seedy brothel in St. Giles. What better way to spend the money Jack had given him than on women of ill repute?

"Who are you? What do you want?" Roger demanded as they rolled to a stop in front of one of Alexander's ships.

Logan grabbed him by the front of his jacket and dragged him from the carriage. The briney dock air immediately washed over him, mingling with the stench of rotted trash.

"We have a mutual acquaintance," he growled, cutting through the fog and following Alexander up the rickety ramp, his hand clamped around the cuff of Roger's coat.

"Who?"

Logan shook his head, unwilling to even mention Cleo's name to this bastard—as if that would somehow sully her.

Reaching the ship's deck, he spun Roger around so that they stood face to face. "You like to sell children."

His eyes widened, and the understanding was there . . . mingled with fear. "What? No! What are you talking about. I never—"

"Your family. You haven't done a very good job taking care of them, Roger."

"What business is it of yours?" he railed. "They're mine!"

"Too many have died on your watch. They're not yours anymore. Do you understand?"

"Go to hell!"

Logan hauled back and struck him in the face, punctuating his words with the pound of his fist. "Not your children. Not your wife. Understand?"

Roger moaned and nodded, his head lolling before he managed to straighten his neck and focus on Logan. "What are you going to do with me?"

Logan released him. Roger staggered and fell. "You'll take this ship to South Africa. Stay there. Go somewhere else." He fished a pouch of gold from his pocket and tossed it on the deck beside the man. Roger dove for it. "I don't care as long as you never return here. Never set foot in England again."

Roger nodded jerkily, clutching the pouch close.

Logan bent down and hauled him up by his mussed cravat. Roger fixed unblinking eyes on Logan's face. "If you ever show your face here again, I'll see you never draw another breath. Nothing will stop me from making that happen. Is that clear?"

If possible, Roger's eyes widened further. Understanding glimmered there . . . and defeat. "Yes."

Logan released him and wiped his hands on his breeches as if he could rid himself of the feel of the man that brought such misery on Cleo and her family.

He looked up at Alexander, who stood beside the ship's captain. The pair watched grimly. He nodded to them both. "I'm done here."

"We'll see him belowdecks and make sure he doesn't sneak off." The captain motioned to his men to fetch Roger.

"Thank you," he murmured, although he doubted it was necessary. Roger wouldn't attempt to leave the ship. He was nothing more than a bully. Spineless and desperate to feel in control, he wouldn't dare return where Logan's threat could become a reality. He'd stay on the ship and sail wherever she took him. He'd never return. Cleo and her family were free.

He turned and departed the ship, his boots thudding heavily on the ramp, his mind already moving ahead to when he might next see Cleo.

"This is rich!" Fiona crowed. "My brother, the darling of every lass within a league's ride from McKinney, the very one likely to be found beneath a milkmaid's skirts rather than about his chores, needs advice on wooing a lady?"

"Are you finished, Fiona?" Logan asked, already regretting asking Fiona for her input in winning over Cleo.

She waved a hand at him amid her riotous giggles.

"Fiona, dear, be kind," Alexander chided. "Can't you see he's fond of this one?"

She gasped for breath. "Of course, of course. Forgive me, Logan." She wiped tears of merriment from her eyes. "I'll be serious. Especially as this one seems to have captured your fancy."

He recalled the efforts he had taken to see that Cleo was happy . . . that her family was safe from her stepfather. Yes. She had more than captured his fancy. "I'd appreciate that."

She nodded, adopting a more somber expression. "Yes, well . . . let me ask you, have you kissed her yet? Back home, every lass claimed your lips to be nectar of the gods."

Tossing his napkin upon the table, he stood to leave the room.

"No, no, stop! Sit yourself back down." She waved an imperious finger at his chair, again reminding him of their departed mother. "It's a legitimate question."

At her arched eyebrow, he admitted, "Aye, I've

kissed her and she appeared to like it well enough, but she's still determined to marry the old man."

"Hmm." Fiona tapped her lips. "If you can't seduce her body, you'd best turn to her mind."

He blinked. "Her mind?"

Fiona threw her toast in his direction. She always was a horrible aim. "Yes, you oaf. It's that thing between your ears. Most women happen to possess one, too."

"Oh, then just yours was left out at birth?" he returned.

Fiona continued blithely as if she hadn't heard the barb. "Discover her interests, her hobbies, her favorite books . . . engage her on a different level." Fiona's gaze locked with his, all seriousness. "Persuade her. Convince her that she can't have anyone else but you. Make the notion of any other man intolerable because no one but you will do. Make her believe no other man will care about her as you do."

Leaning back in his chair, he brought his cup of steaming coffee to his lips, inhaling the chicory aroma and considering his sister's words. He arched a brow at Alexander, silently inviting him to chime in.

"She's right." He smiled fondly at Fiona, plucking her hand off the table and kissing the back of it. "That's the way it is between us."

"Spare me," Logan muttered, although the sight did twist something inside his gut. He was happy that his sister had found such contentment in her marriage, and he possibly wondered if he could find a measure of the same for himself.

And yet he was certain that Cleopatra Hadley was not a woman easily persuaded into anything. Especially now that he understood that fear for her family drove her. She'd settled on Thrumgoodie . . . believed him to be her salvation. It would not be easy to sway her from that notion . . . and he was not inclined to inform that he'd put her stepfather on a ship for South Africa. He didn't want her coming to him out of gratitude. He wanted her to want him.

A groom arrived with a tray bearing several envelopes upon it. He set the tray down beside Fiona. With a smile, she took the envelopes and began perusing them, as she was accustomed to do during breakfast. In the years since she'd married, his sister seemed to have grown into herself. She actually appeared to enjoy her life here. Living in Town with all its diversions suited her.

"Ah, appears to be an invitation for you, Logan." She tossed a letter in his direction. "You're not a total pariah after all."

Alexander chuckled and Fiona flashed him an approving smile.

With a grunt, Logan tore open the letter and scanned the elegantly worded missive.

"Well?" Fiona prompted.

"I've been invited to a house party."

"My, my, you have made friends. I've underestimated you, Logan."

"Mr. Hamilton requests the honor of my company . . ."

"And will you be going?"

"I think if a certain lady is in attendance . . . and I fully expect she will be . . . then I most certainly will be there." Immediately he envisioned himself slipping into Cleo's bedchamber in the dead of night and waking her with a heated kiss.

"Heaven help her," Alexander murmured, shaking his head side to side. "If you're anything like your sister, the chit doesn't stand a chance."

"Anything like me?" Fiona blinked. "Who do you think I learned it from?"

Logan gazed at the invitation in his hand, their voices fading to the background.

He didn't care for Hamilton. Even if he hadn't been so quick to malign Cleo that first evening at the opera, there was simply something in his eyes that Logan distrusted. And yet if she was there, he'd tolerate the fellow. It was a small thing for him to bear in order to win her. And what better venue than a house party to convince her she should choose him over old Thrumgoodie? Certainly he'd be able to steal her away for a private word. On multiple occasions. A slow smile curved his lips. Perhaps more than words would be exchanged.

What on earth am I doing here?

It was a question Cleo had asked herself again and again, too many times to recall at this point.

She'd been shocked initially to even garner an invitation to Hamilton's estate . . . until she reminded herself that Hamilton strove to secure his grand-uncle's blessing. And having her in attendance went far in pleasing Lord Thrumgoodie.

She might have felt more comfortable if Jack had accompanied her, but business kept him in Town. So she'd come alone, traveling with Libba and the earl. After Roger's visit, she knew every day that she dallied her brothers and sisters suffered.

The carriage ride had been nothing short of a trial. She'd endured Libba waxing on and on about McKinney. Although he still hadn't called upon her—apparently she hadn't seen him at Lady Fordham's ball—he had accepted the invitation to Hamilton's house party. A fact that had filled Cleo with delight and dread. Confusing to be sure.

She had no desire to marry the man . . . as he'd outrageously offered. He was the complete antithesis of what she desired in a husband. His virility was overwhelming to her senses. If she married him she'd end up as broken as her mother. Not a year would pass before her belly swelled with child. An image of the babies she'd carried so solemnly to that lonely churchyard flashed through her mind. A shudder racked her. She couldn't endure that. And the babies would be hers, so the misery would only be amplified. She couldn't even fathom it.

One thing for certain, she refused to live it. No matter that for those few minutes in the garden and the library, she'd found herself at ease with him. Even comfortable and relaxed. Such peace could never last.

She glanced out at the horizon. Dusk approached, tingeing the sky a faint purple orange, and she began to hope that McKinney had changed his mind and decided not to attend.

"Can I get you anything, my lord?" she inquired from where she sat beside Thrumgoodie in a reclining chair.

His hands shook lightly where they were folded in his lap over his blanketed legs. He seemed very different from the man she'd met almost a year ago. His energy was waning, and she suspected

Libba had spoken the truth when she said her grandfather's health was on the decline.

The wind blew softly, lifting the ends of her shawl. She pulled the soft pashmina closer around her and stared out at the figures dotting the lawn. The loud *thwack* of Libba's mallet carried across the air. She crowed with delight, waving her arms in the air like she'd won some grand prize.

Thrumgoodie clapped his gnarled hands. His rheumy gaze swung to Cleo. "Looks to be a rousing game, indeed! Certain you don't want to play, my dear? I won't mind if you leave me for a bit. Not so long as you return soon." He winked one rheumy eye.

She shook her head. "I'm quite content to sit here with you." Safe from Hamilton's probing gaze. There was a cunning behind his gaze that she didn't trust. Her unease around him was only pronounced by being here beneath his very roof. She'd entered the enemy camp.

He reached for her hand. "You're such a darling to keep an old man company as you do."

She patted the back of his hand. "No hardship, my lord."

"Sometimes I feel selfish keeping a young dove such as you to myself." He looked wistful for a moment. "I'm no young buck anymore." He motioned to the lawn. "You should be frolicking out there instead, with others your age."

"But I want to be here." She inhaled through her nose, adding on a gust of breath: "With you."

Did he hear the hesitation in her voice?

He stared at her for a long moment and she felt as though he were deciding something, assessing her and then weighing something inside of himself.

She held her breath, sensing this moment was important . . . that her future and whether it rested with him was being decided. At least on his part.

His hold on her hand tightened, surprisingly strong for one so aged. "Cleopatra," he began, stopping to cough and work his throat clear.

She nodded, a tightness closing around her throat. This was it.

He would ask for her hand now.

Her flesh grew tight and itchy. She blinked suddenly aching eyes. "Yes?"

Abruptly his gaze shifted, lifting to settle on something over her shoulder. "Ah, McKinney, my good man!" he exclaimed. "Was beginning to think you wouldn't make it!"

Blast the man! Must he ruin everything? Without even a word he managed to thwart her. His mere presence did the trick.

She shot a fulminating glare over her shoulder

at him. His eyes locked on her, the gray glittering with amusement, and she knew he knew. Not that his presence displeased her, although she was certain he knew that to be true. No. He knew that he had interrupted something important. He winked at her.

Infernal man! She fumed, not even aware of the words passing between the two men, entirely too irate that he had chosen this moment to arrive. And beneath her annoyance, was another emotion that equally disturbed her. *Relief.*

What was wrong with her? She was finally close to getting what she wanted.

She rose abruptly. "Pardon me. I'll fetch us something to read from the library."

"Ah, my dear, you're such a solicitous creature." He looked up at her. "Always thinking of others. Always concerned with my comfort."

"A paragon," McKinney murmured.

Her fists curled deeper into the fabric of her skirts. Those eyes continued to glitter at her. Emotion surged within her and she inhaled a calming breath, reminding herself that there was no reason McKinney should affect her whatsoever. He meant nothing to her. Truly.

She inched another step away. "A book sounds lovely, does it not?"

"Brilliant, my dear." Thrumgoodie looked at

McKinney again. "She has a lovely reading voice. You shall see. Sit. Stay."

Like he was a lapdog to be commanded.

"I'm sure Lord McKinney would be far more interested in joining the game than listening to me read." She motioned to the lawn where the others played.

McKinney looked out at the others then back to her. "I think I'd enjoy relaxing here with the both of you."

"Lord McKinney!" Libba's loud squeal carried over the air. Cleo sighed inwardly as she watched Libba lope across the lawn like a great anxious puppy, holding her skirts up in two hands to keep from tripping. "You made it!"

McKinney executed a sharp bow. "I couldn't miss what promised to be a titillating event— especially with your lovely self in attendance."

Empty flattery. How well he delivered it. Cleo looked away so no one would notice her rolling eyes. Silken-tongued devil. Just days ago he'd kissed her. Proposed to her. This moment only served to remind her to believe in nothing he said.

Apparently he'd arrived to press his suit on Libba. Her rejection must have woken him to the fact that he stood a better chance on landing Libba. He'd get nowhere with Cleo and well he knew it. If he needed an heiress—and quickly—Libba was the one to win.

It stung a little, she had to admit. That he could so quickly give up on her after vowing to want her, after those moments they shared in the library when he held and comforted her. He'd almost convinced her he cared for her. Further evidence that he wasn't to be trusted.

"You must join us for croquet," Libba gushed, clapping her hands merrily.

McKinney splayed a hand to his chest. "I confess to weariness from my journey. Perhaps tomorrow."

"Do let the man sit down and partake of some refreshment before you sink your clutches into him, Libba." Her grandfather shooed her away with a waving motion of his hand.

She pouted. "Very well. I shall let you relax, but later you shall be mine." She wagged a finger playfully at him.

Cleo felt like retching.

McKinney inclined his head in seeming agreement. It was really too much. She couldn't stomach it. Would she have to endure such tripe all week long? Oh, the misery.

Intent on escape now more than ever, she took a step toward the house. "I'll be but a moment, my lord."

"Of course, my dear. Take your time. Choose something you like, as well."

Nodding, she could not stop her gaze from sliding to McKinney. His eyes were inscrutable as he watched her move away. She prayed he would not be here when she returned. She found it unlikely he wanted to listen to her read to the earl. Perhaps if she took her time, he'd be gone when she returned.

As she slipped inside and made her way into the library that was precisely her hope.

Chapter Twelve

Watching her leave, Logan was quite certain she would take Thrumgoodie's advice to heart and dawdle in choosing a book . . . if for no other reason than to avoid him.

"She's a fine one." Thrumgoodie's voice almost startled him from his musings. He glanced swiftly to the old man to see his gaze trained on where Miss Hadley had disappeared.

"Nothing silly about her. Not like so many of these women." He waved his bent and crooked fingers toward the lawn where Libba and two other ladies played their game with the gentleman. "She's lived a different sort of life before this. You can see it in her eyes. It makes all the difference."

Logan would agree with that. She wasn't vacuous or spoiled or vain. She loved others more than herself. She was willing to sacrifice herself for her family. Need for her tightened inside him.

Life in the Highlands wasn't like life in Town. There weren't the teas and vast entertainments. No operas and balls and shopping jaunts to Bond Street. But he did not suspect she would miss any of that. Heat unfurled in his gut. They could find other ways to divert themselves. He could see her at his side, helping him rebuild his castle, helping him tend to the crofter's needs and assisting him in the care of his siblings.

He could especially see her in his bed in the long, cold nights of winter—the fire from his fireplace gilding her skin as he sank himself between her thighs.

He blinked, swallowed, disturbed to find himself uncomfortably hard. Damn the lass. She did this to him and she wasn't even within sight. At any rate, it was all a fantasy until he persuaded her to marry him.

"Too bad I happened upon her so late in life. If I were a younger man, I could be a real husband to her . . . instead of this . . . shell." He punched a gnarled fist upon his blanket-covered thigh.

Logan blinked, startled at the old man's bluntness, and not a little dismayed. It sounded as though Thrumgoodie had made up his mind and intended to marry Miss Hadley. He sounded so certain, in fact, that Logan wondered if they weren't already betrothed. When he'd arrived, he'd felt as though he were interrupting an intimate moment between the two of them and felt only satisfaction in shattering their closeness. It never occurred to him that Thrumgoodie could have already proposed.

"I suppose I'll get about the matter of proposing," he continued. "Haven't got too much time left. Not that I can get down on a knee these days, but I'll manage. She accepts me as I am. A rare trait in a female, to be so accepting. And she's exceedingly solicitous of my needs. More than anyone else . . . even the servants."

Logan heaved a sigh of relief. He wasn't too late then. But he best not dally. Thrumgoodie spoke as though a proposal was imminent.

Followed on the heels of this relief, he felt a surge of anger. Did she really wish to marry a man who regarded her as little more than a servant?

Thrumgoodie broke into his musings: "Have you ever been married?"

"No."

"Well, think hard before you settle on someone . . . it's not a decision to enter into lightly. Choose the female best capable of serving your needs."

Logan grimaced. He made a wife sound like a slave to her husband. His mother had been a true partner to his father. She'd ruled their family like a general before and after his death. When his father left for the Crimea, his mother had been the one to put food on the table and oversee the crofter's grievances. She was so much more than his father's servant.

Thrumgoodie's voice droned on. "Most gentlemen spend more time picking out a cravat than a wife. I could never understand that. A potential wife should be weighed with the same consideration a man employs while selecting his steed."

Logan blinked at the oddness of this conversation. Strange consul indeed, considering he was presumably here to court Thrumgoodie's granddaughter. The strangeness was even greater if one knew Logan's true motives—that he was intent on wooing Miss Hadley. As he sat beside her decrepit beau, listening to him dole out advice on matrimony, he focused on how he might steal Miss Hadley out from under him. The irony wasn't lost on him.

He wasn't above taking advantage of the situation. Not just for himself but for Miss Hadley, too. She deserved more than an old man who, by his own admission, could never be a real husband to her.

The silence stretched and he stared at the double

doors in the distance where she'd departed, longing to give pursuit. "You've known Miss Hadley long?" he asked.

Thrumgoodie broke into laughter that ended in a horrible hacking cough. Regaining his breath, he gasped, "Do you ever really know a woman?"

Logan cocked an eyebrow and stared again in the direction where Miss Hadley had disappeared. He supposed there was some truth to that. Except he felt like he knew her. Comforting her as she wept over her baby sister, her grief over not being there to carry her to the churchyard . . . he had learned everything he needed to know about her in that moment.

Logan rose to his feet. He didn't have time to squander—not with Thrumgoodie so very close to proposing.

Cleo finally narrowed her selection to a volume of romantic poetry. Thrumgoodie had, after all, suggested she choose something she would enjoy, too. She perused further, in no hurry to return to the lawn where she'd left him with Lord McKinney. She need wait only a little while. As determined as she was, Libba would doubtlessly override his protests and claim him.

"Have you found a book that meets your satisfaction?"

She whipped her head around, struggling to keep her expression cool and composed. "What are you doing here? I thought you needed to relax."

"I feel quite invigorated actually." He leaned against the wall just inside the library, arms crossed over his chest. He looked very masculine and formidable—definitely not like a man in need of rest.

She feigned boredom, sliding the book she'd been perusing back on the shelf. "Interesting. You should play croquet with the others then."

He pushed off from the wall and began walking toward her, his long legs quickly covering the distance between them.

Something about his gait—his very appearance—struck her as predatory. Not the first time. The gray of his eyes seemed dark, almost charcoal . . . and intense in a way that made the tiny hairs at the back of her neck prickle.

"Games are fun," he agreed, inclining his head in a partial nod. His dark stare held her for a long, tense moment. He took a final step, stopping himself directly before her. Only a scant inch separated his chest from hers. Her neckline was modest, but the exposed flesh above her breasts tingled. His gaze scanned her face before dropping to her throat, her chest. "But I'm not playing at anything when it comes to you."

She held her breath, riveted by his eyes, his face, the movement of his lips as he spoke.

She swallowed and recovered her voice. "No? What do you call proclaiming your intent to court me one day, and then showing up here the next day to woo Libba? Sounds like a man with a penchant for games to me."

A slow smile curved his mouth. "You sound jealous." He splayed one hand against the bookshelf above her shoulder. She glanced at the strong length of that arm before looking back at his face.

He arched a dark brow at her in that infuriating way of his.

She snorted. "I'm not jealous. I'm merely pointing out your duplicitous nature."

"Have no fear, sweetheart—"

"Don't call me that."

He continued as though he hadn't heard her speak. Leaning in closer, his arm brushed her cheek. "I've not changed my mind."

She ignored the small thrill his words created in her. "I really couldn't care one way or another, Lord McKinney."

He drew in a deep breath. The motion lifted his broad chest, grazing the front of her dress. Her breasts tightened, the tips hardening in the most treacherous manner.

"You're a horrible liar. You care." He brushed

her cheek with the back of his fingers. Her heart seized at the touch. "And I really think you should start calling me Logan."

"That wouldn't be appropriate."

"After all we've shared . . . the least we can do is address each other by our Christian names."

Her face burned at the reminder of her past transgressions.

"I'm a breath away from gaining a proposal from Thrumgoodie. I don't think you should be touching me like this . . . or continuing engaging me in these private discussions."

His hand stilled on her face. "You'll not do it. You'll not marry that old man."

"You think not?" She lifted her chin, cursing that her voice shook.

He nodded. "You won't go through with it."

"I wouldn't wager on that. For months now I've been working toward that very goal."

"Why?" he demanded, his voice hard. "You don't care for him."

"Cast no stones here," she charged. "You were pursuing Libba, a girl you don't care for—"

"And I've come to my senses. I want you."

"Merely because I'm the more tolerable choice," she sneered. "You wouldn't be standing here if not for my bridal settlement."

"What do you want me to say?" he asked, his words a growling rush. "That I'm not in need of funds? I am. Yes, you have the money my family desperately needs. But you also have my undivided interest. You fill my thoughts. I ache for you. More than any female I've met since leaving home. Hell, even before then. What more can I say?"

Their gazes locked, clung. She searched his face, both reveling in and frightened from his stark declaration. In his expression she thought she read a small measure of discomfort . . . as if the declaration had surprised him, too.

She ignored the slight softening of her heart and pushed the echo of his words from her mind.

"I don't want you to say anything," she whispered. "Again." Please, no more words like that. "I-I don't care," she stammered.

"Do you want me to profess my love?"

She choked and jerked as though slapped. "N-no! I would not believe you if you did."

At his decidedly relieved look, she rolled her eyes. Apparently he believed in the sentiment of love as much as she did.

Desperate to end this, she shoved past him, but he grabbed her arm and turned her back around. "You feel something for me. I know it." His hand flexed and she felt the imprint of each of his fingers like a brand.

She exhaled thinly through her nostrils. "Again, your high opinion of yourself staggers me." She jabbed a finger dead center in his chest. "You and your smoldering looks and your impressive—" She motioned wildly to his person, biting back the word *body*, refusing to reveal how much she had made a study of him. "It may work on every other lady within sight—"

"You find me impressive?" He smiled again and she yearned to wipe the smirk from his handsome face.

"I'm not some wee lass from the local village ready to swoon at the mere sight of you."

He scowled at her mocking imitation of his slight burr, but she didn't allow herself the smallest stab of guilt. She couldn't relent when it came to him. He was too tempting by far, and she could never let him suspect that she found him appealing.

He shook his head as if her words finally penetrated.

She didn't want what other girls wanted. She didn't want some young swain, virile and strapping and handsome of face. He had to understand that. Those were merely superficial trappings. Attraction never lasted. It only plunged a woman into degradation and pain. In the complete loss of one's self.

"Are you beginning to understand? Your energies are best served elsewhere." She hadn't the time for this. For him. Roger's wretched face and words flashed across her mind.

His gaze narrowed. "I think perhaps I know you better than yourself."

She opened her mouth to let him know precisely what she thought of that outrageous claim when his head suddenly dipped toward her, smothering her words.

His mouth took hers completely, roughly. He crushed her against him, trapping her hands between them. His lips devoured hers. His tongue slid inside her mouth, tasting, possessing. She was helpless against the onslaught. She sagged against him, incapable of standing without the support of his solid length holding her up.

His hands cupped her cheeks, positioning her for him. The rasping sensation of his broad palms on her face made her knees tremble.

She moaned, sagging against him, sinking into his kiss, drowning in the deliciousness of the moment.

He broke away with a shuddering breath. His hands slid from her face as he stepped back.

She swayed, on the verge of collapsing. He

quickly reached out a hand to grasp her elbow and steady her. She hissed at the touch. He dropped his hand as if he felt the sting of contact, too.

"There. You see," he murmured. "You didn't expect that of yourself, did you?" He paused a beat. "I did. You've passion in you." A corner of his mouth lifted. "A passion for me, it would seem."

Shaming fury swept over her. Blast him!

"You have no bounds," she growled. Yanking her arm free, she hugged the book she still clutched in her hands to her chest. "Don't look so smug. A kiss proves nothing. It's an animal urge. Nothing more. Fortunately I'm more than a base beast. I possess the power of logic and reasoning." She tapped the side of her head to illustrate her point. "And there is no reason beneath the heavens that I should entertain the notion of marrying you." Not with Roger's threat hanging over her head. She'd already lost Bess. She couldn't risk anyone else.

With a swirl of her skirts, she stalked away. As her heart hammered like a drum, she brushed her fingers over her lips and wondered why her hand should tremble so much. She knew what she was about—she had since she first accepted her father's bargain. Especially since Roger's visit. And what she was about did not involve the likes of him. Losing Bess only drove that home.

Once outside, she crossed the lawn toward Thrumgoodie, pasting a smile on her face. The sooner the earl proposed, the sooner she said yes. And the sooner Lord McKinney ceased to torment her.

Chapter Thirteen

Following dinner that evening, Cleo tucked herself away in the back of the drawing room as Libba banged away on the pianoforte. Abiding one of her stepfather's drunken rampages would prove more enjoyable than such a racket. From the painful fidgeting of the others, she knew she wasn't the only one suffering.

Logan maintained a perfectly neutral expression, staring at Libba with polite interest. The man belonged on stage.

"Let's take a walk," Thrumgoodie suggested, struggling up from his chair. "Can only abide so much of that claptrap for one evening."

She blinked at the unusual request. The man wasn't one for casual strolls. For obvious reasons. They tired him greatly. Still, she quickly rose and accepted his arm, although she was more or less the one to guide him toward the balcony doors.

A glance over her shoulder revealed Logan still gazing faithfully upon Libba. Perhaps he'd finally listened to her and accepted that she would never return his interest. A heaviness settled deep in her chest and she hastily looked away from him— only to clash gazes with Hamilton standing near the fireplace.

He glared at her from across the room, his stare flickering from her to his uncle and back again. It didn't take a grand intellect to understand that her presence here upset him. She resisted the childish urge to stick her tongue out at him.

She turned her attention away, quite happy to forget both Hamilton and Logan. She needn't let them cast a pall over her evening.

The French doors were partially cracked to allow some air to flow inside the stuffy room.

"A moment alone, at last," Thrumgoodie sighed into the night as they cleared the threshold. "Libba was given all the best instructors, but I'm afraid some people are simply not born musicians."

She slowed her steps to match his dragging pace.

"It's a lovely night," she agreed. "Even with a nip to the air, it's far finer than the city. You can see the stars here."

Thrumgoodie patted her hand as they neared

the stone balustrade. "This fine evening is only matched by you, my pet. Such a delightful companion to an old goat like myself."

"You mustn't call yourself such things," she protested with a smile, feeling strangely nervous. Odd that. They'd been alone before. And it's not that she feared he would behave inappropriately. The man could barely walk unassisted. He wasn't likely to pounce on her.

Several moments passed. Neither said anything as they absorbed the night humming all around them. A faint hint of rain rode the air and she wished it away, not looking forward to the prospect of staying indoors all day tomorrow with everyone. She'd go mad trapped in close confines with Libba, Hamilton, and Thrumgoodie. To say nothing of Logan and his effect on her.

She glanced toward the open doors behind them. Dull light glowed through the sheer curtains. Voices carried on the air over the discordant notes of Libba's playing, and she thought she detected Logan's deep voice among the others. Shaking her head, she chastised herself for such straying thoughts. She couldn't afford to care about him.

She forced her attention back to Thrumgoodie, realizing he was speaking.

" . . . it shouldn't come as any surprise that I've

grown fond of your company over the last few months. You've been a bright light into my fading days."

She tensed and straightened, pulling back her shoulders. This was it.

The moment she'd been waiting for.

She focused on his face, but a movement over his shoulder attracted her notice. She peered, squinting, but could only make out a shadowed figure there.

"You're far finer than I deserve. I realize you could have any of the young bucks about Town. And yet, I cannot resist stealing you for myself. I would be honored to call you my own, Miss Hadley."

The shadow just beyond his shoulder took shape then, moving slightly closer to the light spilling out from the drawing room.

Cast in shadow, Logan's face was even more inscrutable than usual. Only his eyes gleamed like twin torches of light.

"Cleo, my pet. Did you hear me? I'm asking you to be my wife." He released a chuckle that sounded like a coughing duck. "Have I overwhelmed you, my dear?"

She shook her head before recovering her voice. "You've knocked me speechless, my lord."

Again, that dying, hacking laugh.

And still Logan's shadow watched, unmoving from a distance. Did he think she would not? She had told him. She had warned him.

Still, she had not imagined it would be this hard. Especially with her stepfather's words hanging over her head. Nor had she imagined she would have a witness—especially not in the form of McKinney.

She moistened her lips. "I'm flattered and humbled by your offer."

Blast him. She could feel the censure radiating off him. She'd done nothing—was about to do nothing for which she should feel any shame. Remember Bess. Think of the others.

She released a gust of air, unaware she'd been holding it inside. "I'd be delighted to marry you."

Even though the shadow did not move, she felt as though he had. Something passed over him—through him. A reaction of some kind. A ripple of emotion that reached out to wrap around her. Or perhaps she just imagined it.

Perhaps the reaction was simply hers alone.

Thrumgoodie grasped her hand and pressed cold, dry lips to the back of it. Her flesh puckered with goose bumps at the contact. "You've made me the very happiest of men. I cannot wait to proclaim from the rooftops that you've agreed to be mine."

A lump clogged her throat. She looked down

at the earl's genuinely delighted face. He gazed at her expectantly and she realized she needed to say something. "Nor can I," she murmured, disconcerted at the total emptiness she felt at finally reaching this moment.

Shouldn't she feel something? Triumph at the very least? Possibly relief? She'd have marriage, security, limitless funds to rescue her siblings from Roger. They'd never have to know wretched poverty again.

Nothing. She reached inside herself and poked around, prodded carefully in all the places that should feel.

And still nothing. She felt only a yawning void inside.

Lifting her gaze from Thrumgoodie, she searched for Logan's shadowy figure. Only he was gone.

His shadow no longer watched her, assessing in silence. He was gone. Her gaze scanned the parted French doors, searching for a glimpse of him. Her emptiness only seemed to stretch wider, yawn all the deeper until breathing suddenly became difficult, impossible with her too-tight chest.

And that wasn't right. This sensation wasn't part of the plan. Not part of the plan at all.

"Come, my pet. Let's share the news with everyone."

Thrumgoodie clutched her hand and leaned against her side as they made their way back into the drawing room.

Libba was rising from her seat before the piano-forte, her face flushed from her energetic play.

The earl waved an arm unsteadily in the air. "Attention, everyone!"

All heads swung in their direction. Cleo searched the half dozen faces present, seeking only one. Even Hamilton's intent stare meant nothing. The anger glittering in his gaze did not even rattle her. She sought only for a glimpse of Logan, wondering where he had gone.

"The lovely Miss Hadley has obliged to make me the happiest of men by becoming my wife."

A smattering of applause broke out through the room. Several mocking glances were exchanged between guests, no doubt forming their own snide opinions on the matter of her marriage to Thrumgoodie. Libba clapped fiercely, the only one who seemed genuinely pleased. Hamilton glowered at her, and a shiver skated down her spine. She looked away, unable to bear the hostility of his gaze.

Again, she scanned the room, needing, irrationally, to see his face. Even as logic insinuated itself, reminding her that she'd brought this about, that she'd chosen Thrumgoodie . . . it failed to matter.

She needed to see Logan with the same compulsion of one who couldn't look away from a terrible accident. She had to see . . . had to know . . .

She shook her head and turned her attention to the well-wishers surrounding her. Libba was at the forefront of the group, chattering on about the church and dress patterns and the wedding breakfast. The words were dizzying, the velocity carrying all the speed of gunfire.

Hamilton seized her hand and leaned close. Pressing his cheek to hers, he spoke into her ear, his voice low and furious, "Congratulations . . . cousin."

This latter word was uttered with such venom that she suddenly couldn't stomach his touch. She wrenched her hand free and took a step back. He stared at her with such open enmity that she glanced around, certain everyone else could see it, too.

Only no one looked at him. Everyone focused either on her or the earl, exclaiming their well wishes.

Hamilton drifted away, fading to the back of the group, but his stare remained fixated on her, a scalding imprint that she couldn't ignore no matter how hard she tried.

She'd actually done it.

He hadn't thought she would. When it came

right down to it, he'd assumed she wouldn't be able to actually agree. Not when she kissed him the way she had. Not when her eyes looked at him with his own hunger echoed in their depths.

Cleopatra Hadley and old Thrumgoodie did not make sense on any level. She and Logan made sense. At least that was what he had fooled himself into believing.

He paced his bedchamber, telling himself he might as well fetch his mount and leave. He nodded once, hard and decisive. In his present mood, that was precisely what he intended to do. He had no intention of marrying Libba, so remaining here was only a waste of time for both of them. He owed no one an explanation. They could wonder all they liked about what happened to him come morning.

She would know, of course.

Striding to his wardrobe, he grabbed his satchel and began tossing his garments inside. Damn if he was going to stay another moment and witness the farce of Cleo and Thrumgoodie celebrating their betrothal.

A soft knock sounded at the door.

He whipped around, spotting the slip of paper the moment it slid beneath his door.

He tossed down the shirt he held and strode toward the door. Grasping the latch, he yanked the door open and peered out into the shadowed corridor. No one. Nothing save flickering shadows.

Bending down, he snatched up the small slip of paper in one motion. The neatly worded scrawl stared up at him, the message brief, but to the point.

Meet me in my room.

C.

Bitter fury coursed through him. She wanted to see him? Now? He growled low in his throat. What remained to be said? She'd made her choice. He'd watched as she said yes to another man. A veritable slap in the face after he'd bared his soul to her—confessing to want her as he'd never wanted another woman.

He crumpled the parchment into his fist and strode across the room. Flinging open the grate, he was on the verge of tossing it to the coals. With a grunt, he slammed the grate shut again, and walked a short, hard line back and forth across his chamber, stuffing the note into his pocket.

There was nothing left to say, and yet he couldn't leave without seeing her one last time . . . without satisfying his curiosity and hearing what she had to say to him.

He'd see her. And then he'd go. He'd wasted enough time here already. He'd not waste another moment on a female that wanted nothing to do with him . . . who preferred a cold, empty future to the one they could have had together—one that would at least have been vital and alive. They would have had their share of fights, he was certain. But there would have been passion.

He returned to his satchel and finished packing absently, his thoughts elsewhere. When he left Scotland, he'd thought this matter of finding a wife would be a relatively easy feat. True, she needed to possess a dowry of means, but he'd been certain there were females enough to fit that requirement. He couldn't have known that he'd fixate his desires on the one female who didn't want him—who would prefer a man with one foot in the grave over him.

But after tonight that wouldn't matter. She wouldn't matter. Because he was moving on.

He'd never see her again.

Chapter Fourteen

Cleo brushed her hair until her scalp tingled. Glaring at her reflection, she set her brush down with a sharp click.

Angling her head, she studied herself. "What's wrong with you?" The fact that she was talking to herself didn't daunt her in the least.

Shaking her head, she rose to her feet. Untying the sash of her night rail, she dropped it at the foot of her bed, an enormous beast that could have slept her and several of her half-siblings. The thought of her siblings fortified her, reminding her that she was on the right path. Even if her chest felt heavy and tight, this was what she needed to do.

A maid had already pulled back the coverlet. She climbed within and pulled the soft bedding up to her chin. Staring up at the canopy, her thoughts invariably drifted to Logan. She told herself she was only concerned. She had no wish to hurt his feelings. She told herself that was the only reason she worried. Not because she cared about him . . .

She'd been unable to escape for at least another hour after Thrumgoodie announced their engagement. She'd suffered a toast of champagne. Libba had insisted Hamilton's servants fetch his finest champagne for the occasion. He'd looked none too happy about that, of course, but no one seemed to notice. Just as no one seemed aware that Logan was absent from the festivities. Even Libba was too caught up in the revelry to notice. And yet Cleo noticed.

It was just the beginning, she realized with a bitter swallow. There would be dinners and parties, and more toasts to endure. She hadn't anticipated all of that. Hopefully, the earl could arrange a short engagement so as not to drag it out.

With a sigh, she turned onto her side, lifting up on an elbow to punch her pillow with decided vigor. Falling onto her back, she allowed doubt and regret to creep in.

What am I doing? I cannot do this. Bitter emotion soured her stomach, and for a moment she feared she would be sick, the evening's champagne acid in her stomach.

A soft knock at her door had her lurching upright. Frowning, she imagined Libba stood on the other side, too agitated from an evening of carousing to sleep yet. She was an easily excited creature even without adding spirits.

Flinging back her covers, Cleo marched toward the door and pulled it open with an admonition for Libba to march herself back to bed ready on her lips.

Only Libba did not stand there.

She gaped. Her head fell back to take him in. He wore only trousers and a shirt. No vest. No jacket. A pair of Hessians hugged his muscular legs up to the knees. The white lawn of his shirt contrasted sharply to the darker exposed flesh of his neck. Her throat felt suddenly dry, and she fought to swallow.

She wanted to demand an explanation for his presence outside her bedroom, but speech failed her. She'd thought so much of him tonight, wondering where he'd disappeared to during the impromptu celebration of her forthcoming marriage, wondering if she'd hurt him—hoping she hadn't. She was unable to erase the memory of his shadow, standing witness as she accepted Thrumgoodie's offer.

Without a word, he strode past her, his shoulder brushing her arm. She swallowed a hiss at the contact.

For a moment, she couldn't move. Her head spun. Reeling and bewildered, she took a quick glance up and down the empty corridor. Satisfied no one had seen him enter her room, she closed the door, sealing them in as effectively as if they were in a tomb.

She knew she could demand he leave. She should. Nothing about this was proper or seemly. If he was discovered, she'd be ruined, all her hopes for her family lost.

She wasn't sure why she was letting any of this happen. Only that she felt compelled—like some other force was guiding her to behave against her will. Against all reasoning. She was willingly betrothed to another man—the precise man she wanted for a husband. The man she'd set out to land for herself.

And yet the precise man she did not want, she had just permitted inside her bedchamber. There had to be a cell in Bedlam for people like her.

He prowled a small circle before stopping in the center of the room. Facing her, his arms hung at his sides, hands clenched in tight fists.

Tension swam on the air, so tangible she could touch it.

She'd never seen him look like this before. The flesh surrounding his eyes seemed tighter. A tiny tic worked madly at the corner of the right eye. His chest rose and fell, lifting against his white shirt.

She couldn't stand to look at the accusation in his face. She looked away, and her gaze fastened on the exposed stretch of his throat, on the skin there that looked so warm and inviting.

"You did it," he murmured.

He might as well have yelled the words. She jumped at the whisper. She breathed in and out before answering, "I said I would."

"Yes." He nodded, moving slowly, advancing on her. "You did."

No censure. Not even anger. Just that tension about him. A coil ready to spring. A lion about to pounce.

Ironic considering she moved first, coming at him in a gliding step.

And that's all he needed to act.

He met her, enveloping her in his arms and lifting her off her feet. His mouth swooped over hers. Her hands slid up to cup his face, holding, reveling in the rasp of his bristly cheeks. His tongue was in her mouth, mating fiercely with her own. His hands clutched her back, the strong dig of his fingers rough and thrilling.

They clung to each other with equal fervor, their lips locked in a devouring kiss that went on and on. His hands slid down, cupped her bottom through the thin fabric of her nightgown. She gasped as he lifted her easily, guiding her legs around him.

Everything about this should have horrified her, but she could only feel. Only taste. She had thought she'd never see him again. That he was lost to her. Nothing could make her break away right now.

Her world jarred slightly with his every step. Soon she was descending back onto the bed, all his splendid weight falling atop her, directly between her splayed thighs. Her nightgown slipped and cool air drifted over her exposed legs.

He released her lips and dragged his hot mouth down her throat just as his hand slid along her rib cage. He nipped her throat and then kissed the bruised flesh, laving with his tongue. She moaned, arching under him, sensation flooding her.

She didn't know it could be like this. His hand closed over her breast and she gasped, seized with a want so deep that she forgot everything. Who she was . . . what she'd always wanted for herself. For her family. For once the visage of her stepfather didn't intrude. The only thing she wanted right now was this. Him.

His hand kneaded her breast until she was

panting and writhing beneath him. When his lips closed over the hard tip, sucking through the thin fabric of her gown, she arched her back with a sharp cry as hot sensation rippled through her.

His mouth pulled at her, taking her deep. The wet fabric of her gown only served to chafe her overly sensitized nipple. She weaved her fingers through his hair, holding him to her with hungry desperation, determined that he give more. She wanted her nightgown gone—his clothes to melt away. She yearned to feel his skin, to experience the hardness of his body against hers . . . his flesh to her flesh . . .

She was lost. Oblivious to reason. To the world around her.

To the click of the opening door . . .

She was heat imploding in his arms. Logan was overwhelmed with the taste and feel of her. He hadn't come here for this. At least not consciously. She'd agreed to marry another man. As far as he was concerned, she was beyond his reach. She'd seen to that. It infuriated him, but there was nothing to do about it now short of abducting her.

And yet here he was. Here they were. Lost together. With each other.

He heard the gasp. It registered dully, sinking into his awareness slowly. He lifted his head from her delectable breast and blinked as if waking from a dream.

Instantly, the trio standing in the threshold took shape. His gut clenched at the sight of Libba, her expression one of horror and disbelief. Thrumgoodie stood there, too, looking more ashen than usual, clutching his nephew's arm as though it were the only thing keeping him from collapsing.

Logan sat up quickly and stood back from the bed, reaching down to cover Cleo's legs with her nightgown. A hasty assessment told him there was little he could do to help her appearance. She looked like a woman thoroughly ravished.

Her dark hair floated like a nimbus around the wanton curve of her body. Her clouded gaze seemed unable to focus. She propped herself on her elbows and stared up at him beneath heavy lids.

"Cleo," he whispered harshly, gazing intently at her flushed face. She looked appealing as hell, and he cursed the crowd of intruders.

Of course, better that they arrived when they did. He winced at the idea of them arriving five minutes later. Given more time, he had a fairly good idea of the scene they would have witnessed. Now that would have been a scandal to live down.

He glanced swiftly at their audience and then back at Cleo again. She murmured his name, extending her arms in invitation. Her fingers touched his neck. He grabbed her wrists to stop her from going any further. "Cleo," he said more sharply. "We're not alone."

That did the trick.

Her eyes widened, and he knew in that precise moment full comprehension had hit. She stiffened and scrambled off the bed, dropping to her feet a good distance from him. She clutched the modest neckline of her nightgown to her throat, which only managed to pull the fabric tighter against her breasts.

Her lucid gaze scanned the room, stopping on the crowd gathered near the door. Since he'd last looked, the trio had grown in number. Where three had stood, now seven hovered. Four of Hamilton's guests—more witnesses.

Hellfire. He couldn't care less about himself or his reputation. But Cleo . . . she'd never survive this. It quickly became apparent to him that her betrothal to Thrumgoodie had come to a swift end. Normally, this would have pleased him, but not at this cost. People could be cruel, and he'd not have her suffer the viperous tongues of the *ton* once this night became public knowledge. Which would take no less than twenty-four hours. From the gleam in the eyes of Hamilton's guests, they'd likely be on their way to Town tomorrow to share this juiciest tidbit.

Libba gained her voice. She couldn't stop squawking and sputtering, hurling words he would never have suspected she even knew, and her venom wasn't reserved all for him.

"You devious little witch! How dare you? After everything I've done for you? I should never have taken you under my wing! To think I protected you from all the wolves of the *ton* that wanted to gobble a little nobody—a bastard—like you up!" Libba motioned to Thrumgoodie. "I even pushed you at my grandfather, although it's obvious you only want his title!"

Cleo's face only burned brighter.

"See, uncle. I warned you," Hamilton patted Thrumgoodie's arm as though to console him.

Logan snorted, stifling the urge to plant his fist in the man's face. The fact that the three of them had strolled into Cleo's chamber seemed a little too convenient. It would never have occurred to Thrumgoodie or Libba to burst unannounced into Cleo's room in the middle of the night. Logan knew who was behind this.

Hamilton shook his head as though aggrieved, but Logan read the triumph in his gaze. "What can you expect from someone of such low birth? Better you learn now before you married the harlot."

Cleo flinched. Logan couldn't stand it another moment. Not the slurs, not the wounded look in her eyes. He strode forward and knocked Hamilton off his feet with one punch.

Hamilton howled and clutched his nose. "Out! Out!" he screeched. "Leave my house and take your whore with you!"

Logan saw red. Bending down, he hauled the worthless excuse for a man to his feet.

Libba grabbed his arm. "Stop! You beast! Unhand him, you savage!"

Logan shook her off him with great restraint.

Then he felt Cleo's touch on his arm. He looked down at her. "Enough," she murmured. He stilled.

Libba looked between the two of them, the hate in her gaze only intensifying. "Yes, listen to your little harlot."

A flicker of emotion passed over Cleo's face but she didn't acknowledge the insult.

"Oh, a very affecting display," Libba continued. "You're such a marvelous hero!" He winced at the sudden shrillness to her voice.

He released Hamilton and glared at the girl whom he had, for so brief a moment, considered marrying. What a nightmare that would have been.

"What's wrong?" she demanded, thrusting her chin out in a pugnacious angle. "Are you going to strike me, too?"

Suddenly, Cleo spoke, addressing everyone. "I'm sorry you all had to witness such a spectacle."

Logan gazed at her. He wasn't sorry. None of them had any business storming her room in the middle of the night.

She continued, "It wasn't my intention . . ." Her voice cracked, and she shot him a glance. Some of the spark returned to her eyes, and he surmised that she had just reached the same conclusion he had. "What are you all doing in my bedchamber?" Her indignant gaze swept over everyone.

"Good question," he murmured, swinging his gaze toward Hamilton.

The triumph in Hamilton's eyes only glowed brighter. "That's right," he announced with a haughty shake of his head. "I've seen you staring after each other like two hungry dogs. I knew you were lovers and sought to prove it."

"We're not lovers," Cleo hissed with a stamp of her foot. "This was a mistake."

"Oh, it was a mistake indeed," Libba declared. "One that you shall never live down. I don't care if your sister's a princess or your father's as rich as Croesus. Nothing will see you out of this mess. All will shun you. I shall see to it!"

Something indecipherable passed over Cleo's face, and then, in a blink, it was gone. She was all coolness, immune to Libba and anything or anyone else. Inhaling, she turned to the group, her words calm and even. "I'll leave in the morning."

"You'll leave now," Libba ordered, her voice cutting.

Cleo angled her head, holding up a hand in supplication. "I've no means to reach Town. We traveled here together, remember?"

"You think I care?" Libba glanced to her cousin as though seeking support.

Hamilton nodded. "You've abused my hospitality. You've crushed the hearts of my cousin and dear uncle." He motioned to Thrumgoodie, who continued to gaze at Cleo in the manner of a wounded puppy. "How you make it home is of no concern to me." He flicked a scornful glance at Logan. "I'm sure your champion here shall see to your needs."

Cleo looked at him in horror and he knew exactly what she was thinking—the same thought running through his mind.

They were a full day from Town.

She shook her head. "You cannot be serious."

Hamilton answered her by turning his back on them. "Come, uncle, let's see you back to bed. You don't look well."

Thrumgoodie did indeed look unwell. As Hamilton began to guide him around, the old man suddenly grabbed his chest and collapsed into a pitiable heap. Soft little mewls fell from his colorless lips.

Cries filled the air as everyone surrounded him. Logan looked heavenward with a sigh. Things were already bad enough, but if the old man died there would be no way Cleo could survive the ruin of this night.

He glanced at her.

Hands pressed to her cheeks, she watched the unfolding debacle in horror.

"Look what you've done!" Libba shrieked amid the din. "You've killed him! You killed him!"

Almost idly, he wondered if Cleo would finally accept his suit. After all, no one else would have either one of them now.

Chapter Fifteen

Thankfully it was a full moon.

She could see several feet in front of her—enough at least to avoid the ruts and dips in the well-traversed road. The dark air shimmered with a pearlescent glow. It was almost like someone had draped a veil of silver netting over the night. She was glad she wasn't alone . . . and then mad at herself for feeling glad that *he* was here with her. The wretch. He was responsible for this entire mess. If he hadn't shown up in her chamber . . .

She stifled a snort at the thought. Disgust for her behavior filled her. What? She couldn't have exhibited a little self-control? She couldn't have resisted his kisses and caresses? She couldn't have protested as he lowered her to the bed? Her eyes stung as the faces of her siblings filled her mind.

Her stepfather wouldn't wait much longer. Certainly not long enough for her to start over and find a new beau. Blinking, she fought back the wash of tears. It wasn't over. She'd still find a way to save them all. What choice did she have?

She increased her pace and ignored the steady clomp of hoofs behind her. Or at least she pretended to ignore them. She heard every thumping step. Every vibration over the hard ground. She even imagined she felt the hot fan of the horse's breath at her neck. That might have been her fanciful imaginings, but she didn't imagine the sensation of Logan's stare drilling into her back.

He could have ridden ahead—as she urged him to do—but he walked his horse behind her. Infuriating man.

She switched her valise from one sweaty-palmed hand to the other. She'd left her small trunk behind and simply packed the essentials for her trek to the neighboring village. The essentials were more than enough. More than she'd owned when she'd been living at home with her mother a year ago. They'd make do until she reached her father's house.

"Tired?" his voice rang out in the night.

She whirled around. "It's the middle of the night and I'm walking down a country road—no thanks to you. Tired doesn't even touch upon my sentiments."

In the pale glow of the moon, his expression held blank. He merely stared down at her from where he sat atop his mount, his reins loose in his hand. The impatient beast pawed at the ground.

"So you're not tired?" he inquired in a maddeningly even voice.

With a growl of frustration, she whirled back around and continued tromping down the road.

"You're welcome to ride my mount."

She ignored the offer. Again. She was too furious to accept any help from him. He'd ruined everything. She could hardly even manage conversing with him without losing her temper. Best she held her tongue.

They continued for a few more moments before he spoke again. "At the very least, I could attach your valise to the side."

She swung around again, dropping her valise beside her on the ground. "Why are you following me?" She motioned to the road stretching into the darkness ahead of them. "You've a means of transport. Please. Go on your merry way. Don't let some misguided sense of honor keep you traipsing after me."

Moonglow washed over the hard lines of his

face. "I'm not leaving you alone on this road in the middle of the night."

She snorted and crossed her arms over her chest. "Oh, now you're full of chivalry?"

He angled his head at her. The pose sent a small frisson of alarm through her. He looked decidedly dangerous in that moment—certainly the most dangerous creature out in these woods.

"I didn't hear any complaints from you earlier tonight. You didn't even try to send me from your room. In fact, I recall very little was said once you pounced upon me. I must not be so objectionable."

She flinched at the truth of his words. "Trust me . . . you are beyond objectionable." She splayed her hands widely in front of her. "There is no word to describe just how objectionable I find you."

He didn't look amused. "Go ahead and have your little temper tantrum, Cleo. I'm not leaving. You might as well hop up on my horse and save your feet the ache. We'll reach the village faster."

"What is this 'we'? Understand me when I say there is no 'we.' "

"Damn but you're stubborn. When are you going to see there's but one choice for us now?"

She gazed at him uncomprehendingly. Then she looked around her as if the answer lurked somewhere in the dark night. "What choice?"

"You're thoroughly compromised. The shock of

which nearly killed your fiancé. Your only hope is to legitimize us. There will still be talk. No way to quell that. But perhaps you can show your face on the streets of London without being cut direct from every acquaintance to cross your path." He lifted one shoulder in a shrug. "Not that we'll be here very often. Your family can visit—"

"Have you gone mad?" she interrupted his narrative of their imaginary future, fighting against the sudden prickly tightness in her chest. There had to be another choice.

"I'm quite sane."

"Was this your scheme?" Gall rose up hot and swift inside her. "Why did you come to my room tonight? Did you arrange all this?" She swept an arm wide.

"Arrange what? The two of us stuck on a road in the middle of the night?"

"My ruin?" she bit out. "Did you plan all this . . . very convenient that everyone should know to walk into my room—"

"I received your note!" He fished a crumpled piece of parchment from his pocket.

"I didn't send you any note." She took several steps forward and snatched it from his hands. She squinted through the gloom to read the scant words. "I did not write this!"

"I surmised as much. After the fact, of course."

She shook her head. "Who?"

"Hamilton, of course. How else did he know to show up in your room with Thrumgoodie and Libba in tow?"

Of course. It should have occurred to her sooner. "Hamilton must have been thrilled to see his plan work so brilliantly." She laughed brokenly.

"What do you find so amusing?"

"We gave them quite the display, did we not?"

Logan was silent for a long moment. The night hummed around them. "It's obvious we're drawn to each other . . . the attraction is there." Her pulse skipped faster. "You. Me." His voice stroked over her, as deep and endless as the star-studded sky. "It would not seem a horrible alternative."

She nodded, but the motion made her head ache. It would be both horrible and wonderful. She swallowed thickly. If only the wonderful part did not ultimately lead into the horrible. She'd revel in his bed, in his arms. She felt that in her bones. But then the loss would come. The pain. The sorrow. And yet if she could save her family in the process, stop another brother or sister from dying, it could be worth it . . .

Still unconvinced, she backed away from him in a slow step.

He stared at her with grim understanding. "Yet you still refuse."

She moistened her lips. "Attraction isn't everything. It's scarcely anything. I've seen sensible women lose their head over attraction. The price they paid was too high."

"I'm offering honorable marriage."

"She was married, too. Still is," she returned quickly, unable to keep thoughts of her mother at bay. "That only ended up trapping her, keeping her chained and bound forever."

"She?" His eyes glittered. "You're speaking of someone specific? Your mother?"

Cleo tightened her lips. She'd said too much. She was not inclined to unburden her personal history upon him. Upon anyone, for that matter.

"Well," he finally said. "Whoever she was, she certainly made a lasting impression."

With a sigh, Cleo picked her valise back up and handed it to him.

He hesitated only a moment before taking it from her and attaching it to his saddle.

No sense torturing herself. As he said—the sooner they reached the village, the sooner they could acquire accommodations. And the sooner tomorrow would arrive . . . and she'd be on her way to Town.

She could tuck herself away in her father's house and figure out what she was supposed to do now that her plan had been obliterated. She came up with a new plan to save her family—a plan that did not include him.

Once she was settled atop his mount, he led the horse down the rutted road.

"How much longer?" she asked after a few minutes.

He sent her a sideways glance. His lips curled ever faintly but he held silent.

"Now you won't speak to me?" she demanded, looking down at him. "Very adult of you."

"Be quiet," he snapped, his head suddenly cocking to the side.

She pulled back her shoulders, her hackles quivering. "Don't you dare speak to me—"

He reached up and covered her mouth with his hand. She felt her eyes go round in her face.

His eyes glittered up at her. Shaking his head, he motioned with his free hand for her to dismount. She nodded. After a heavy pause, he slipped his hand from her face. Hunkering down, she slid from the horse.

Once she faced him, he pressed his face close to hers and whispered in her ear. "I don't think we're alone."

At these words, her eyes strained, looking left and right into the crowded press of trees. She could see nothing beyond their dark trunks and moon-soaked branches. No movement. No sign of life. Just an utter stillness that went beyond what was normal. And suddenly she realized it was too still, too quiet. The air tightened in her lungs.

He thrust the reins into her suddenly shaking hand and fumbled for a moment with the satchel attached to the saddle. She saw the glint of a knife's blade before he tucked it out of sight.

"Wait here," he instructed in a voice so low she barely heard it.

She grabbed his wrist as he began to move away, practically lurching at him. "You're leaving me," she whispered.

"Wait beside the horse." He peeled her fingers from around his wrist.

She stared uncomprehendingly after him as he crept away, the large shadow of him disappearing into the trees. Was he really leaving her alone when there might be brigands lurking in these woods?

Her fingers clenched around the reins. She looked nervously to the left and right. Feeling inconspicuous—and foolish—standing in the middle of the road, she began walking, one foot falling after the other, crackling upon twigs and leaves covering the road.

Her eyes scanned the yawning stretch of road ahead, and the bowing trees that pressed in on either side of her. And yet the world was still oddly quiet, motionless.

Snap.

She stopped. The sound was close. She glanced at the horse, wondering if the noise had come from him. Her fingers nervously patted his velvety nose as she glanced around again.

She bit back the urge to call out for Logan and lifted her foot to continue—only to stop. She swallowed. Her eyes straining into the murky gloom.

The sensation of someone close, just behind her, raised the tiny hairs on the back of her neck.

She spun around to find two leering men upon her. Gasping, she stumbled back. One of the men grabbed the reins. The horse whinnied and sidestepped at the fierce tug.

It was as if they'd materialized from air. One was as skinny as he was tall, while the other was squatter, solid as a boulder, his eyes sunken and mean-looking.

"Ah, looky," said the skinny one, sweeping her with his gaze and flashing a rot-toothed smile. "A fine bit of lady, aren't you?"

"I'm not alone," she blurted.

"Aye, that's right. Where'd your man go?" He peered into the trees before calling out in jarring tones, "Come out wherever you are! We've got your little dove here."

Nothing. She strained to listen for Logan, but not a sound greeted this.

"Maybe he heard us and decided to look out for his own neck and leave her," the squat one volunteered.

Rot-tooth sneered at his comrade. "Well, it's true you make too much noise, Dixon. Like a herd of elephants you are." Satisfied with his insult, he sniffed and turned his attention back to Cleo, assessing her with a calculating look. "I don't think he'd forget her. Not a fine lady like her."

Cleo took a step back, hoping that was true. Where was Logan? Rot-tooth waved a pistol, motioning her to come closer to him.

Instead, she moved back another step. And another, contemplating how quickly she could mount Logan's horse without getting herself shot.

She didn't get very far before Rot-tooth yanked her against him. She was instantly assailed with the aroma of unwashed body. She struggled, only falling still when she felt the cold tip of the pistol press against her temple.

She closed her eyes in a slow, agonizing blink. Unbelievable as it seemed, she felt only regret faced with this moment that could be her last. Who would help her family now?

She suddenly wished she had allowed Logan more liberties. If she was about to die, the reasons for not tasting the passion he offered her seemed suddenly insignificant.

Before she could contemplate that further, Rottooth's voice ripped through the night. "We have your woman. Unless you want to see her in pieces all over this road, you'll step out now."

She bit her lip until she tasted blood. Was Logan even out there? Her stepfather wouldn't have stuck around for her mother . . . she didn't even know if Jack would have remained in such a situation. Would any man? She didn't have much experience with noble or honorable men—especially when self-preservation was involved.

"He's gone," she declared, turning her head to look back at the villain, and then stopping when he dug the pistol deeper into her head.

"I don't think so," he replied.

"Maybe he did leave her, Ansel."

"And leave his woman? His horse?" Ansel shook his head and turned to face Dixon, lifting the pistol from her head as he did so. She exhaled a breath of relief to feel the weapon removed from her face, even if only temporarily.

"I don't think so," Ansel continued.

The air whistled, and she felt the sudden rush of something launch past her, just inches from her shoulder.

Ansel's grip on her arm vanished and she was free. His body dropped to the ground with a thud. She looked down and choked on a gasp at the sight of the knife imbedded deeply in his shoulder. He choked and made incoherent sounds, twisting his head to look in astonishment at the butt of the knife jutting from his shoulder.

Dixon cursed and fell down beside his friend. "Ansel! Gor, Ansel! You've been stabbed!"

"I know that!" Ansel cried, his face a contortion of pain and panic.

Shaking her head, Cleo jumped to action and scrambled for the forgotten pistol. She located it on the ground several feet away. Snatching up the weapon, she grasped it in her hands and pointed it at the unsavory pair.

She'd barely had time to acclimate to the heavy feel of it before it was plucked from her hand. Strong fingers stole it away as if she weren't gripping it at all.

Her gaze shot to Logan. He stood beside her, his expression revealing none of her anxiety, just stony resolve.

"Now," he announced, his deep voice maddeningly calm. "Listen to me . . . Dixon, is it?"

Without a word, Logan moved, positioning his body between Cleo and the men on the ground. She peered around him to see Dixon's face as he looked up at Logan, his sunken eyes wide and unblinking.

Logan's voice continued, deep and authoritative, "You're going to collect your friend there and disappear back into the trees . . . after you return my knife to me, of course. I'm rather fond of it."

Nodding, Dixon turned to Ansel, grimacing as he pulled the knife free of his shoulder. Ansel cried out and pressed a hand over the gushing wound. Cleo almost felt sorry for him in that moment—until she recalled that he'd threatened to blow her to bits all over the road moments before.

Dixon wiped the blade clean and then offered the dagger back to Logan.

"Very good." Logan secured the knife. "Now, toss down the rest of your weapons. Including Ansel's blade tucked away inside his boot."

"Bastard," Ansel growled as Dixon removed his blade and tossed it to the ground, followed by his own knife.

Logan ignored him and stepped forward to kick the weapons farther away from the men. "Cleo, gather those up."

She quickly obliged, collecting the two knives in her hands. Rising again, she watched the drama unfolding in front of her, marveling that Logan had thrown a knife into her attacker across goodness knows how far a distance. She tried to imagine Thrumgoodie defending her in such a manner and nearly snorted at the implausible image. She quickly chased the thought away. She didn't have

Thrumgoodie in her life anymore, so there was no point comparing him to Logan. Or pondering his inability to protect her. That's not why she'd wanted to marry him in the first place.

And yet a man capable of protecting her wouldn't be remiss. She had never considered that benefit to having a strong, virile man in her life. Perhaps he could give her stepfather the thrashing he deserved. Of course he had to care enough about her to do that, and nothing indicated Logan's feelings for her ran that deeply.

Her gaze devoured the sight of Logan standing with his legs braced, looking so powerful, so strong, in the middle of the road. She filled her lungs with an exhilarated breath. It was a heady sight.

"We'll be keeping these," Logan announced, waving the confiscated pistol and motioning to Cleo with his other hand, indicating the knives she held.

"What are you going to do to us?" Ansel gasped.

"What should I do?" Logan straightened his arm, aiming directly for the man's face. "What would you do?" Tension radiated from every inch of him.

Cleo reached out and rested a hand on Logan's arm, squeezing the tightly corded muscle there gently, hoping to ease him. She whispered his name, drawing his attention. Logan's gaze slid to her and the barely leashed anger there shook something deep inside her. "Don't."

Saving the life of the man who'd been ready and willing to end her life didn't matter. Logan, however, mattered. She didn't want him to dirty his hands this night. Not for her.

With the barest nod, Logan looked back at the unsavory pair on the ground. "Count yourself lucky I don't leave you in pieces all over this road as you threatened to do to her."

A shuddery breath spilled from her.

At those final words, his voice trembled slightly. From rage or emotion, she wasn't certain, but he made his point.

With his face twisted in pain, Ansel muttered some bitter-sounding words of gratitude.

Dixon nodded anxiously, his stocky frame lifting Ansel with ease. "We'll be going. Won't bother you again, sir."

Cleo watched as the pair disappeared into the trees.

Then Logan was there, sliding his hand along her cheek, pulling her to him. "Are you all right?"

She nodded, a lump forming in her throat. For some absurd reason, she felt the urge to weep. A hint of a sob broke free from her lips before she managed to swallow it back. With a deep breath, she reclaimed her composure and pulled away. "Forgive me. I'm rather emotional."

She made out his crooked smile. "You're entitled to that. A man just held a pistol to your head and threatened to kill you. Most females would weep under such circumstances."

"I'm not most females," she countered before she could consider her words. "I'm supposed to be stronger."

"Who says so?"

She held his gaze for a moment, resisting the rejoinder: *Me.*

She'd always expected more from herself. The eldest of her mother's children, she was responsible for keeping everything and everyone together—from shattering within the walls of her stepfather's house.

She was still that. The responsible one who would save them all. She could show no weakness . . . allow no vulnerability in. Not then. Not now.

"It's okay to feel fear." Something flickered in his gaze—a shadow of some emotion she'd never seen from him. "God knows I did when I saw him put that pistol to your head. It took everything for me to stay my hand and wait for the moment when I could get a clean hit on him."

He'd been afraid? For her?

Suddenly his hand on her face became everything, her entire world, where all sensation ended and began. He bowed his head until their foreheads touched. His breath mingled with hers until it felt as though they were one. She closed her eyes against the fanciful thought . . . tried to push it back to that place where she had long buried her dreams.

"We'd better get moving," she suggested, stepping away from him.

His sigh floated on the air. "Very well." He helped her remount, and she heaved her own sigh of relief to escape his touch—to be on their way. One step closer to putting this night behind.

Chapter Sixteen

The village was as still and silent as a tomb. They passed a vicarage at the far end of the lane. Not a single light flowed from its windows. A dog woke and barked as they approached the small inn. If it could be called that. It appeared little more than a house with a crooked shingle hanging outside. A candle glowed from an upstairs window and Cleo took comfort in that. Someone would answer their knock and treat them to a modicum of hospitality. Hopefully, at this late hour they would face few questions.

The door was flung open and a bedraggled woman stood there, a lacy old-fashioned cap askew on her head. A gray-streaked plait hung loose and unraveling over her well-padded shoulder.

She lifted her lantern high to better inspect them. "What can I do for you?"

"We need a room for the night, if you please."

"Late, isn't it?"

"Quite. And we're very tired. We'd prefer a warm bed to the hard earth." Logan flashed her a handsome grin. Cleo rolled her eyes, feeling certain that smile could get him most anything.

The woman looked them over anew, missing nothing. No doubt she was running the odds of them being murderers through her mind. Apparently satisfied with whatever she saw in them—or didn't see—she flicked a hand toward her stable. "The lad is gone for the night. You'll have to tend to your own mount. Our lodgings are small. I've only four bedchambers and all are taken save one. Fortunate for you. Your lady can follow me and I'll see her settled whilst you tend to your mount."

Cleo opened her mouth to object, but Logan sent her a swift shake of his head. "That would be much appreciated," he said smoothly.

The inn mistress's already ruddy cheeks deepened in color. "Yes, well, if you're hungry I suppose I can light the stove and—"

"Please, don't trouble yourself," Cleo assured her.

Right now she merely wanted to fall into a bed and lose herself in sleep . . . where she didn't have to contemplate what was becoming the longest night of her life.

And she especially wouldn't have to ponder the wondrous and confusing feelings the man beside her stirred inside her heart.

As Logan headed off for the stable, the proprietress led her inside, past a small parlor with a dying fire and up the creaking stairs. A man with wild, sleep-mussed hair peeped out from a room as they walked down the narrow corridor.

"Back to bed with you, sir. Just another guest arriving."

With a grunted mutter, the man disappeared inside his room.

"My name is Mrs. Cantrell," she declared as she opened the door to a small gabled room—obviously located at the corner of the house—that smelled of lye.

Entering the room, Cleo rotated in a small circle, surveying where she and Logan would spend the night together. Her gaze drifted to the bed and away. It didn't look big enough for one person. It couldn't possibly fit two. At least not comfortably. Heat swamped her face. Not that she was concerned with it holding two bodies. She certainly wouldn't be sharing the bed with him. Logan might insist they share this room, but she would not share a bed with him.

Her chest tightened almost painfully and she quickly distracted herself by facing Mrs. Cantrell. "Thank you, Mrs. Cantrell. We won't be needing anything else."

Mrs. Cantrell looked unimpressed with this assurance. At this late hour, Cleo supposed that could be understood. "Good night to you then."

Setting the lamp on top of the bureau, she left the room, closing the door behind her with a click.

Cleo studied the room anew, her gaze scanning the way the yellow gold lamplight flickered over the walls. A screen stood along one side of the room. She thought about stepping behind it and changing clothes before Logan returned, but then she recalled she'd left her valise with the horse.

She ducked her head beneath the sloping ceiling as she approached the window and peered out.

The moonlit night stared back, silent and still to her wandering gaze. Not even a breeze disturbed the leaves in the trees. She saw no sign of Logan. The stable was a hulking shadow.

The sound of the door opening behind her brought her whirling around. Logan ducked his head as he entered. Standing inside the small room with its low ceiling only reinforced just how very large he was.

He extended the valise for her to take.

When she didn't move to take it, he gave the barest shrug and set it near the bed.

She was being foolish, she knew. Too afraid to approach him . . . as if he might accost her. In reality, the person she most feared was herself—and the totally unprecedented way she reacted to him. Around him, she no longer knew herself.

She stared from the valise to him. Suddenly the idea of changing into the same nightgown she'd worn earlier—when he had very nearly seduced her—struck her as a very bad plan.

He sat in a chair and began removing his boots. "Aren't you going to change?" He motioned to her valise.

With a reluctant nod, she took her valise and moved behind the screen. She undressed, draping her clothes over the screen with slow, measured movements.

Inhaling a deep breath, she acknowledged that she still couldn't bring herself to strip down to nothing and put that nightgown back on again. Wearing her petticoat and chemise, she stepped around the screen.

Her throat constricted. He was waiting.

He sat upon the bed, his legs stretched out before him with his ankles crossed. And his chest was bare. She gulped. She knew he was no small man, but the muscles there . . . it was just too much. She closed her eyes in a slow, anguished blink. He was the epitome of everything she denied herself. Youth, beauty, virility. If heaven had sent him here to test her, she was on a direct path to failure.

"What are you doing?"

He glanced at the bed. "Hoping to get some sleep."

Sleep? She eyed him suspiciously. "There?" She motioned toward him upon the bed.

"It is a bed."

"And you mean to occupy it? With me?"

"Was there another alternative? It's the only room left. And the hard floor is hardly appealing. Did you wish me to sleep in the stable?"

Cleo stared at him in silence.

He studied her for a moment and then nodded precisely two times. "Apparently you do." His mouth twisted wryly.

She gestured to him, the bed, herself. "This is hardly appropriate."

"You're still concerned with what's seemly?" His look turned incredulous. "After everything that's happened? We've been alone together for hours now. We were caught in a compromising situation by several witnesses."

She shook her head, resisting the childish urge to cover her ears. "You don't understand," she muttered.

"Then explain it to me."

She looked at him starkly, wishing she could. She wasn't about to fall into bed with him simply because her reputation was in tatters and it didn't matter anymore. That didn't make it acceptable.

She crossed her arms over her chest and forced her gaze away from him—all that bronze flesh that looked smooth yet she knew was hard and firm beneath her fingers.

She heard his sigh before he asked, "Are you going to sleep in that?"

She nodded, unable to explain her reason for not putting that nightgown on again—that she was afraid it would carry her back to that moment when she was on the verge of giving herself uninhibitedly to him.

"Get into bed, Cleo."

Her skin prickled at this command. "Don't tell me what to do."

"Do you intend to sleep on the floor then? Because I'm not. Don't think I'll play the gallant gentleman and take the floor so you can have the bed."

"I would never mistake you for gallant," she

retorted even as she wondered why she continued to flay him with her barbed tongue. But she knew why.

His eyes narrowed. "I'm too tired for this."

She was tired, too. And yet she couldn't drop her guard with him. If that meant constantly haranguing him with prickly words, then so be it. Perhaps she'd earn his enmity and then he'd leave her be.

"What are you so afraid of?" he demanded.

The question made her chest ache. How did he know she was afraid?

"Nothing."

You can resist him. Pulling back her shoulders, she strode to the other side of the bed, suppressing her alarm at the sight of how little space remained in the bed beside him.

She pulled back the coverlet on her side of the bed and slid beneath. She lay there for a moment, lacing her hands together atop her chest. She forced her gaze straight ahead, watching the shadows dance over the lighted walls.

"The lamp," she murmured.

"I'll take care of it." He rose and strode across the room. She stared after him, her mouth drying as she appreciated his broad back with its lightly flexing skin.

In moments, they were submerged in darkness.

She heard his footsteps and then a slight rustling beside the bed. She waited for the bed to dip with his weight, but nothing—simply more of that rustling noise.

She moistened her lips before speaking into the dark. "What are you doing?"

"Undressing for bed."

A vision of him discarding his breeches flashed in her mind. "What? You cannot—"

"Unlike you, I prefer to be comfortable at night. I don't typically sleep in my trousers."

"Perhaps you could be atypical for just tonight?" she suggested, her heart beating a panicky rhythm. "For me?"

His side of the bed sank with his weight and she resisted rolling in that direction.

He chuckled low, and the sound was like velvet stroking her goose-puckered flesh. "You're like a nun clutching the bedsheets in fear of a marauding Viking."

She winced at the description, which struck her as strangely appropriate.

He continued. "How did you ever expect to handle your wedding night?"

"I didn't," she muttered so low her voice was barely audible.

And yet he heard.

The bed creaked and she guessed he had

propped himself up on his elbow. She felt him above her, imagined him looking down.

"What did you say?"

She made a low, noncommittal sound.

"Did you say, 'I didn't'?" He made a sound—part laugh, part groan. She winced. His fingers snapped on the air as though he'd made a grand discovery. "You chose Thrumgoodie because he wouldn't be able to perform. That's it, isn't it? You don't want intimacy."

"Yes!" She bolted upright in the bed. "That's it precisely. Is that so unbelievable? Unlike the other females of your undoubtedly vast experience, I don't want to submit my body to a man! I may have to marry, but I don't intend to torture myself through child labor again and again and again with no promise for a healthy child, with no promise that I myself shall even survive." *With no love to make any of it worthwhile.*

Silence fell and stretched between them like a wire pulled taut. She held her breath until her chest ached. The air she was holding escaped, sawing raggedly from her lips.

"Well," he said, his voice devoid of emotion. "That does paint a rather grim picture."

"It's reality," she retorted, blinking eyes that suddenly burned with tears, hating that she should feel so overwrought when he seemed so calm.

"For some women, I suppose, yes. That is a reality they must bear."

"For some women," she agreed fiercely. Like Mama. "But not this one. Not me."

Suddenly she felt the brush of his fingers against her face. She flinched and pulled back from the tantalizing sensation.

"It doesn't have to be that way."

"Oh, no? A man can make such a promise?"

"Well, no—"

"Then I'll take no such risk."

"Life is risk. Would you rather not live life?"

The question had been there, on the fringe of her mind ever since Jack's man arrived on her doorstep. Ever since she met Logan and felt the dangerous feelings he stirred inside her. She'd effectively avoided it until now. "I'll live. But it will be a life of my own choosing." A life that shall improve the lives of her siblings.

"So no to passion . . . no to love?"

She stiffened. *Love?* If it were to be believed, if it were real . . .

He went silent after uttering the word and she wondered if he regretted it. Whether he was as shocked as she was at expressing such a sentiment.

"No children?" he asked, his voice suddenly casual, detached. "Sounds infinitely dull, and you've never struck me as dull."

"It sounds wise," she returned. "Safe."

"Safety." He snorted, his voice suddenly hard and unaccountably angry. "My brother and father died on their way home from the Crimea. After surviving three years of war, their carriage lost a wheel and sent them tumbling down a mountain a two-day ride from home. There's no accounting for when it's your time . . . or what God has planned for you, and you're a fool if you think you can plan your life to avoid risk."

His words deflated her, sapping her of her indignation. She thought of Bess right then—felt the echo of his grief so very keenly. Her fingers itched to reach out and touch him at this confession, but that was just an invitation for disaster. She curled her fingers and sank back down on the bed, struggling to regain her poise.

His voice continued, "I know that you've suffered. That you've known terrible loss. Maybe more than even I can understand. But I know that you can't stop life from happening."

You can't stop life from happening.

With a gulping breath, she marveled that she had ever judged him shallow. There was more to him than she first thought. He continued to reveal himself to her in ways that made him hard to resist.

He sighed and settled back down beside her,

close but still not touching any part of her. "For someone so brave—"

"You think I'm brave?" she asked, her face growing warm at the praise.

"You alone carry your little brothers and sisters to the churchyard following their deaths. Yes, I think you're brave.

"And for someone so brave," he finished, "I don't understand how you can be so afraid."

"What am I afraid of?" she demanded.

A beat of silence hummed between them before he answered. "Everything, it appears."

Everything.

Her eyes burned as the word penetrated—as she absorbed that he was right. As he eased into sleep beside her, she held herself still, reeling with the realization of what she had become—a person she didn't want to be. Yet with her stepfather's threats hanging over her head, she didn't know how she could be anything else.

Chapter Seventeen

The pale light of dawn greeted her as she slowly opened her eyes. For a moment, she stared uncomprehendingly at the single window, absorbing the bluish light creeping between the curtains. Her thoughts were fuzzy and it took her a moment to register where she was . . . and even longer to process who shared the bed alongside her.

In that instant it all flooded over her, and her eyes flew wide.

Every sensation struck her full force. The long press of his body against hers. The weight of his arm draped over her. The span of each of his fingers against her belly. His chest was warm and broad—endless at her back. Her heart thudded violently against her rib cage.

Cleo's thoughts raced, recalling the events of last night.

She was ruined. No mistake about that. Strangely, she couldn't summon much regret about the loss of Thrumgoodie, and she suspected the reason had something to do with the man pressed alongside of her.

"How long are you going to pretend to be asleep?"

In one smooth move, he rolled her onto her back and came over her. His face was inches from hers, their noses almost touching. His thumb grazed her temple, feathering the tiny hairs there.

Even in the dim light, his eyes shone clear and bright, scanning her face as though he were memorizing it. In all her life, another person had not looked at her with such complete intensity.

Her heart stuttered against her chest so violently she was sure he felt it, too. She waited, her flesh tight and prickly with anticipation. Still, he did not move—didn't lower his mouth that remaining half inch.

With a faint groan, she surrendered and lifted her mouth, touching his. It was all he needed, and she realized in some distant corner of her thoughts, that he'd been waiting for her to do this very thing.

Their mouths fused together hotly, devouring, consuming with hungry lips and feverish tongues. She held his face with both hands, clinging to him, desperate and needy.

His hands touched her everywhere, sure and firm, molding to her curves, caressing her in places that made her cry out against his mouth. He made short work of shedding her clothes, tossing them to the floor.

He stared down at her for a long moment. Ideally, this should have been the moment where reason returned in a flood, but he looked so beautiful gazing down at her, his eyes glittering and intense, his dark hair falling across his brow. And then there was his body.

Never had she seen such a sight. Lean and hard, his muscles played along his torso and rippled over his ribs. His sinewy arms were braced on either side of her and she wanted to turn her face and kiss every inch of the sculpted flesh.

He lowered down until his chest mashed into her breasts. The lean line of him aligned with her own naked body and the sensation fired her every nerve. She gasped as his narrow hips settled between her thighs.

His roughened palms glided over the outside of her thighs and her breath caught as those big hands slid beneath her garments, cupping her buttocks. He positioned himself deeply against her, and there was no mistaking the prodding bulge. She moaned at the sensation. And then he began to move. The hard length of him rubbed against her, sliding between her moist, intimate heat without penetrating.

An ache grew low in her belly, shooting a direct line to where he pressed against her. The friction became unbearable. She became slippery and wet against him.

She thrashed her head against the pillow. "Please, please, Logan."

He rubbed deeper, moving in a manner that mimicked the act of lovemaking. She shook, trembled from desire, the need so great in her that she at last convulsed in his arms. Her nails dug into the smooth expanse of his back as fiery sensations rushed through her.

It went on and on. Ripples of pleasure crashed over her like a pounding tide.

She cried out his name and he drowned the sound with a blistering kiss. Suddenly he stilled against her, the throbbing length of him no longer moving and creating that delicious friction . . . and she was left with a vague sense of dissatisfaction. A hunger for more.

His arms, braced on either side of her, shook with restraint. She couldn't help herself. She moved against him, used some wanton part of herself that she didn't know existed inside her—that she had prayed, for years, didn't exist within her.

"What are you doing?" he grit through clenched teeth.

The answer materialized in her mind. "Enjoying life," she returned. "Isn't that what you said I should do?"

"Stop," he commanded, his jaw tense as though in pain.

It was wicked of her, she knew, but she didn't stop.

With an epithet, he slid away from her. She thought he was gone, that she'd pushed him too far, but then his hands were on her thighs again, and she felt him there, his muscled shoulders between her legs.

"What are you doing?" she shrieked.

He splayed a hand on her belly, pinning her to the bed as his head delved between her thighs.

"Showing you," he rasped, the moment before she felt his mouth there, his tongue tasting, licking, sampling her like she was some treat.

She bit her lip to stop from crying out at the sheer sinful shock of it. Then his mouth found the tiny nub buried in her folds. She couldn't describe the wonder of it. She arched off the bed with a strangled shout as his lips sucked.

The waves were back, crashing over her. Hot sensation rolled through her again and again. Still, he didn't stop, continued working his mouth over her like a man on a mission. She writhed like she was on fire beneath him, and she was. She'd never imagined anything like this was even possible—pleasure so acute, so swift and sharp. A pleasure so intense it bordered on pain.

Finally, she drifted back down and he slowed, easing himself away, collapsing at her side.

After some moments, she found her voice in her parched throat. "Why?"

Why didn't you take me, satisfy your own lusts on my body? Why did you only give?

He didn't say anything at first and she thought she was going to be left wondering.

Then he rose from the bed, speaking as he moved to don his clothes. "I just wanted you to know."

Even in the shadowy room, she could identify his state of arousal. It would be hard to miss. The sight of it alone brought the ache back between her legs. Her body, it seemed, knew there was still more he had to show her.

She pulled the sheet around her naked body. "Know what?"

"That not every man is a ravening beast intent on taking his pleasure. That I can control myself." He stopped and came over her suddenly, his flexing arms braced on either side of her. "You can trust me. Some things—like the number of children you have—can be controlled."

He was so close. She found herself straining for his mouth again. And then he was gone from her, shoving off the bed. He pulled on his boots and left the room.

She sat there for a long moment, the sheet hugged to her chest as she wondered how in the span of one day she had come to this point—a woman seriously considering marrying the exact type of man she'd sworn off. A man that could be her total undoing.

She fell back on the bed and inhaled deeply, which only brought the warm, musky scent of him washing over her anew. A rush of longing swept over that she quickly stamped down. This wasn't supposed to be about her. About her wants and desires. She was supposed to be looking out for her family.

She was her mother's daughter, after all, it seemed—quick to lose her head for a handsome man. It should panic her, but oddly she only felt a small frisson of unease. The need to make a decision weighed on her. She kept hearing his words:

You can trust me. Some things—like the number of children you have—can be controlled.

Was that true? She was of a mind to trust him and yet it was so difficult to release her demons and let herself go.

Let herself fall.

Chapter Eighteen

$\mathcal{L}$ogan walked Cleo to the front door of her father's Mayfair mansion, her scent filling his nose. He felt conspicuous as he carried her valise. Even in the dark of night, eyes followed them. Servants peering from windows, people passing in carriages. Anyone who looked at them could see they'd been traveling together. Alone. He wondered if this occurred to her, too. Whether it concerned her in the least. Somehow he didn't think so. Nothing that happened between them last night or this morning appeared to alter her determination not to wed him.

He'd left his horse in the drive alongside the nag he'd acquired for her to ride the rest of the way to Town. A groom rushed to attend to the beasts. She didn't bother knocking at Hadley's front door, simply strode inside.

He stepped behind her, fully intending to follow her, but once over the threshold she turned around and stopped, preventing him from going any further. Apparently, she didn't wish him to join her inside.

He glared down at her, undeniably annoyed. He felt like a lad of thirteen again when Marlena, the young widow from the village, a very worldly nineteen-year-old, had brushed him off after introducing him to the wonders of the female body. He was too old, had seen too much to feel like this.

"I'd like to speak to your father."

"I know you would," she said evenly, giving a brisk nod. "I'll talk to him myself. Explain everything."

Suspicion knotted his stomach. Specifically regarding whether she would actually explain *everything*. Such as how ruined she was . . . and that he wanted to set it to rights and wed her. He glanced beyond her as if he might spot her father. "You can't stop me from talking to him."

She nodded again, the motion swift. "He won't like hearing what happened. It's best if it comes from me. He sets a lot of store in such things."

"Things like your reputation?" he bit out. "Fathers tend to do that."

She winced. "Let me break it to him first. Then you can pay us a call tomorrow."

He angled his head, studying her closely. "What are you saying, Cleo?"

Her chest lifted on a deep breath. "I'll marry you."

His chest eased and loosened. He had to stop himself from grinning like a fool. Especially considering she looked as grim as an undertaker.

She leaned in closer, clutching the edge of the door. "You said I could trust you."

He nodded at her whisper. "You can."

Her eyes locked on his, soulful and deep . . . almost pleading. "I'm counting on that. Don't expect me to be a real wife."

The tightness came back again, seizing his chest. "What can I expect then?"

"I'll try . . . but—" She licked her lips and looked over her shoulder. "Intimacy will be . . . infrequent." Her eyes searched his face, and he read the fear there, the uncertainty. Accepting him was at great cost to her. "And you said there were ways to avoid—" Her voice dipped so low he could scarcely hear her. "Children . . ."

He nodded slowly. She was telling him she might never want children. It wounded more than he expected. And yet not enough to turn away from her. He wanted her. At any cost.

He wasn't one of those men determined to populate the earth with his progeny. He had brothers. His family line would doubtlessly stay within his immediate family. He reminded himself that his goal coming here was to secure an heiress. It wasn't to find himself a broodmare.

He covered her hand where it clutched the edge of the door, her slight fingers smooth beneath his own. "I won't demand it of you. I'll honor your wish."

She released a rattling breath, her expression relieved. With a shaky smile, she slid her hand out from his and closed the door. "I'll see you tomorrow."

The door clicked shut. He stared at it for some moments before turning and walking down the steps.

He'd won his heiress, but he felt no triumph. He hadn't won Cleo.

Not yet.

"Cleo!" Her father's voice boomed across the foyer before she had managed two steps from the door. "You've returned!"

She jumped and turned to face Jack guiltily. Partly because she'd just shoved Logan from the house like some dirty little secret. And partly because she'd hoped to escape upstairs and compose herself before confronting him.

He advanced on her with an anxious expression on his face. "I didn't think Dobson would fetch you this quickly, but all the better. Come. She's in the drawing room."

Her father was expecting her? He'd sent Dobson to fetch her home? "Who's in the drawing room?"

Jack stopped and stared down at her. "Didn't Dobson tell you?"

It appeared she would have to explain everything right now whether she liked it or not. "Dobson didn't fetch me home. I returned on my own."

Jack shook his head. "Thrumgoodie decided to return early?"

"Um, not precisely."

He looked from her to the door, as though he might find the explanation of how she'd gotten here written upon it.

"Lord McKinney brought me back."

"McKinney? You traveled alone with him?" Jack's ruddy complexion darkened, no doubt grasping the implications of this scenario. "Whatever for?"

"I didn't have a choice."

His head cocked to the side. "How's that?"

"You see . . . we were caught." She bit her lip. Releasing the bruised flesh, she added, "In a rather comprising situation. In my bedchamber."

Jack gaped.

"Thrumgoodie was quite upset, as you can imagine." She saw no point in explaining that she'd been engaged to the earl up until that disastrous moment. It would only make Jack's disappointment more acute. "Hamilton saw fit to kick me and Lord McKinney from his house."

"I'll kill him."

"Now, Jack." She rested her hand on his arm. "I'm a grown woman and responsible for my actions. You can't blame Logan any more than you can blame me."

Jack's eyes snapped fire. "I'm not talking about McKinney—although he'll have some explaining to do as well. I'm talking about Hamilton. And Thrumgoodie for that matter. How dare they boot you from the house as if you were some common trash? Thrumgoodie escorted you. I don't care what you did! The man should have seen you safely home."

She squeezed his arm, trying to calm him. "No harm done. And I couldn't really bear to stay in that house a moment longer . . . not after being caught with Logan like that."

Her father huffed and looked down at her. "Logan, is it?"

Her cheeks heated. She managed a nod.

"You care about him?"

She blinked. Partly because the question was so unexpected from Jack. She never expected him to care one way or another. And partly because she didn't wish to consider the notion. She couldn't care for Logan. That would be . . . bad. Bad for her control when it came to keeping him at arm's length.

"I-I suppose. Yes. I do," she answered, guessing that was the answer that would most appease Jack. She couldn't explain her complicated relationship with Logan to him.

He nodded as though satisfied. "I'm assuming he intends to salvage your reputation and—"

"Yes, he's offered."

He waved an arm widely. "Then where is he?"

"I insisted he call on you tomorrow. After you and I had spoken."

He grunted and tugged his jacket down his barrel frame. "Very well. A Scottish lord isn't what I'd hoped for you, but it's something at least."

Her lips twisted. Of course, she couldn't forget her father's mission was to see his daughters well wed. She and Marguerite might not have scored the best matches in his estimation, but at least Grier had not disappointed him.

He clapped his hands. "Come now. I've a surprise for you."

He took her elbow and guided her to the drawing room. She followed, curious to meet the mysterious "she" he'd referred to.

He pushed open one of the double doors with

a flourish. Immediately, Cleo's gaze landed on the female knitting quietly on the sofa, her expression soft and serene, but with a lingering sadness.

She wore a drab dress of wool. It did nothing to compliment her rather pudgy shape—or the bland brown hair pulled back into an equally bland bun.

"Cleo, allow me to present Annalise."

The young woman hastily dropped her needlework and rose to her feet, her expression hopeful and anxious as she gazed at Cleo. A faint awareness tingled at the back of her neck, tightening her skin as she stared at the girl. She almost felt as though she knew her . . . that perhaps they'd met before.

Annalise took a few steps in Cleo's direction. As she did so, Cleo saw she moved with a slight limp. Annalise trained her large brown eyes on Cleo. Brown like the rest of her except that they were large and lovely, framed with remarkably long lashes. They were quite her best feature—extraordinary really.

"Hello," Cleo greeted, looking to her father, uncertain who this stranger was and why he seemed so excited to have her here.

"Hello," Annalise returned. "I've heard a great deal about you from Jack." She wrung her small hands together in front of her.

Jack's smile broadened. "I told Annalise all

about you . . . how quickly you acclimated to Town life and had beaus courting you left and right." He waved a hand like he was swatting flies.

Cleo stifled a snort. It hadn't exactly happened like that. "Er, yes. And will you be in Town long?" She looked helplessly at Jack, unsure what to say to this strange girl and beginning to become annoyed that he wasn't enlightening her as to her identity.

"I should think so," Jack declared, smiling. "She has the bedchamber next to yours."

Cleo looked from Jack to the girl, a sinking suspicion beginning to take hold. If possible, the girl's hopeful expression only intensified, leaving Cleo with no doubt.

She was staring at her sister.

Chapter Nineteen

$\mathscr{A}$nother half sister.

Brushing her hair in long vigorous strokes, Cleo marveled at her father's ability to produce offspring—and solely female offspring at that. Jack had certainly sown his oats across the country.

She set her brush down and stared at herself. "Four?" she asked her reflection, unperturbed that she was talking to herself.

That brought the total count to four. Jack had fathered four daughters, to date, with women he had not bothered to wed. Initially, this only angered her and fed her belief that men were takers, slaking their lusts with no thought to those it affected.

But then her anger dissipated with the knowledge that she had another sister. Her heart softened as she thought about Annalise. Just a few years younger than herself, she didn't have any other family. No siblings. Her mother was gone. She'd thought herself alone and worked long hours as a seamstress apprentice when Jack's man had located her. Now Annalise had Jack and Cleo. And although they were occupied with their new lives, she had Grier and Marguerite, too.

The callow girl was going to need all the help she could get navigating the *ton*. She looked so innocent with those brown eyes so full of hope and faith in all the promises Jack made. Wealth. The sparkling world of the *ton*. A gentleman husband. A titled man—the sort that would never have glanced at her before—was now hers to have.

Cleo shook her head, hoping Annalise wasn't expecting all of that. Disillusionment only awaited her. The *ton* might let her in the door because of Jack's money, but they'd never see her truly as one of them. In their eyes, she'd always be a bastard, one step from the gutters.

She wouldn't be embraced. The wolves would circle, ready to use her, ready to tear her apart and take all that innocence she possessed and squash it underfoot.

Cleo contemplated this as she gazed at her reflection, wondering if she shouldn't warn her . . . shouldn't ask Jack to let her off the hook. Set her up in a nice cottage in some village where she might make genuine friends . . . perhaps one day meet a nice man who cared for her.

But something told her that Annalise wouldn't agree to that. From their brief exchange, she could see that the girl bought into the fairy tale. She wanted everything Jack promised. She wanted her prince and her happily ever after. Jack had convinced her it could be hers.

Sighing, Cleo rose from her vanity table, hoping that her new sister didn't end up hurt too badly.

Hopefully, Marguerite would help her find her way since she wouldn't be here to do so.

Cleo didn't imagine Logan wanted to remain long in London. He had family and duties awaiting him in Scotland. And honestly, she didn't want to remain here either. There'd be a scandal, and she'd rather not be here to serve as fodder for it—even if it meant living with him on some faraway mountaintop.

Not that the prospect didn't alarm her. She was placing herself totally in his hands, away from all that was familiar—Jack, Marguerite. Even Town had become something known.

She would be isolated from everything she knew. It was bad enough when she left her mother and siblings . . . but now she'd have no one. No one but Logan. At least until her siblings joined her. Then they'd have each other. That would have to be enough. She'd make it so.

When Logan arrived the following day, he was immediately led to the garden, where Jack Hadley sat at a small table taking his breakfast beneath a large maple tree.

He'd rather expected Cleo to be absent, but until that moment he hadn't realized how much he longed for the sight of her. He'd only been away from her for a day, but he'd thought of little else.

Jack motioned to the vacant seat across from him. "Have you eaten?"

"Yes, thank you." He lowered himself across from the man who went by the moniker "King of the London Underworld." Logan had no misconception that much of his wealth had been earned through criminal and unsavory practices. It occurred to him that a little fear might be in order when dealing with the man. Only he wasn't afraid. In his mind, fear had to do with regret. And he regretted nothing he'd done with Cleo. He'd change nothing that had happened.

Jack took a healthy bite of kipper and leveled his keen-eyed gaze on Logan, assessing for some moments before announcing, "So. You've compromised my daughter."

Logan didn't so much as blink an eye. This interview was important if he was to gain Hadley's blessing. He did not intend to show weakness.

With his gaze trained on Hadley, he answered, "It appears so."

Hadley chewed some more.

Logan continued. "I seek her hand."

"She mentioned that. And why is it I should sanction such a union?"

For a moment, he considered reminding the man that her reputation was unsalvageable, but he stopped himself. That wasn't why she should marry him. That wasn't why he wanted to marry her.

Settling for the truth, he declared, "I want her. I wanted her before I ruined her at Hamilton's. And the reason she's ruined is because I can't seem to stay away from her."

"And not because of her fat dowry."

He winced. "Initially, it drew me. I have responsibilities . . . a crumbling estate, siblings to provide for." He leaned forward. "But I see your daughter. I—" he paused. "I like her. I appreciate her. More than any fop about Town ever will."

Hadley held his stare for a long moment before slowly nodding. "You have my blessing." He waved his fork in a small circle. "She's in the salon with her sister. I'm sure she'll want to see you so that you may begin making plans. I recommend a hasty wedding . . . it should help stop the worst of the gossip. Perhaps we should journey north to your home and perform the ceremony there? Once we cross the border, there will be no need for a license or posting of banns. And you're a Scotsman, after all. No one shall think it too unseemly."

He wouldn't argue leaving London and returning home with Cleo sooner rather than later. "Very well," he agreed, standing and feeling an inordinate amount of relief. He didn't realize until that moment how anxious he'd been for Hadley's blessing. Now nothing stood in his way from making Cleo his own. Well, nothing except the female herself.

Logan wasn't so dense as to not realize that he still had his work ahead of him. It was going to take time to put Cleo's long-held fears to rest. It wouldn't happen overnight.

But once they married, they would have all the time in the world. Eventually, she'd trust him—and herself.

Then she'd be his.

Cleo was browsing through fashion plates with Annalise when Logan found them in the salon. She stood anxiously at the sight of him, struck anew with the astonishment that she had agreed to marry this man.

He stood tall and handsome, his body strong and lean. He was beyond beautiful. Beyond anything she had let herself dream for herself. Somehow she thought she could control this situation . . . control him. She admitted this to herself with not a small dose of shame.

Annalise cleared her throat softly, and Cleo remembered her presence. She moved back and guided Annalise forward by the elbow. "Lord McKinney, allow me to introduce my sister, Miss Annalise Hadley."

Annalise blinked those large brown eyes, clearly unaccustomed to the surname in reference to herself. She'd get used to it.

"Miss Hadley." He bowed slightly, ever courteous even with surprise reflected in his gray eyes. He'd met Marguerite, and he knew about Grier, but, of course, he'd never heard of a third sister.

Annalise performed a clumsy curtsy, her plump frame wobbling. "Please call me Annalise." She looked quickly at Cleo, verifying if this was acceptable.

The inquiry in her sister's gaze brought back the question of how Logan's conversation had fared with Jack. Whether Annalise and he adopted the use of each other's Christian names largely depended on whether he was about to become her brother-in-law.

Logan leveled his gaze on her. "Jack recommended that we wed in Scotland."

A breath of relief escaped her, followed fast with panic. _I'm really going to marry this man._

He continued, "I suggest we leave tomorrow."

She stared. It was really happening. So soon. And not a grand church wedding, it would seem. But then she didn't really want that. A bunch of people who didn't really like her crammed inside a church, hungry to watch the spectacle of her marriage, hoping for a bit of gossip to carry with them to the next soiree.

Her mother wouldn't have likely attended. Even if her ham-fisted, controlling stepfather allowed her to, she wouldn't have felt comfortable in such elevated company. So why not travel to Scotland and marry in his domain?

"Very well." She glanced at her sister. "Shall we begin packing?"

Annalise nodded, her brown eyes dancing with excitement at the prospect.

An uncomfortable silence stretched. Logan looked as though he wanted to say something more, but a fleeting look at Annalise prevented that.

Annalise must have read the look. She cleared her throat. "If you'll excuse me." She likely thought they wanted the moment alone to kiss and hold each other and whisper sweet words. Cleo grimaced at such a wildly romantic notion . . . but a notion she suspected her half sister harbored.

She slipped from the room and left them alone. They stood with the tea cart between them.

What did one say to the man you were to marry with an understanding in place that there likely would never be intimacy between them? Cleo motioned to the pot. "Would you like some tea?"

"No." He circled the cart, an intent light in his gray eyes.

"Could I ring for something stronger? Coffee?" She resisted the impulse to back up. She had vowed to trust him and that meant not retreating at his approach.

He stopped in front of her and cupped her cheek, his rasping palm holding her face.

"What are you doing?" she whispered, the re-minder burning on her tongue that their marriage wasn't about intimacy. No touching. No sponta-neous caressing.

"Sealing our bargain," he whispered the mo-ment before his lips claimed hers.

She tried to protest but he smothered the sound. It wasn't the type of kiss she thought one might give for sealing a bargain. It was hot and consum-ing, rough and thorough. His tongue sought en-trance to her mouth, sweeping inside and lighting her afire.

She grabbed his shoulders, prepared to push him away but instead she ended up clinging to him.

He finally ended the kiss, and this only galled her. He ended it. Where was her willpower? She was supposed to be in control, but so far he seemed to be the one in control.

Staring up at him, she realized what a fool she'd been to think she could ever control this man.

He gazed down at her with desire gleaming in his eyes. Her heart stuttered wildly inside her chest. He brushed a thumb over her kiss-bruised lips.

"You can't do this," she whispered, her voice cracking.

"What?"

She moistened her lips and his gaze followed the motion of her tongue. Her belly tightened and she forced hard resolve into her voice. "You can't just kiss me whenever you feel like it."

He smiled slowly and her stomach flipped at the curve of those well-formed lips. "The occasion called for it."

"No." She shook her head. "No more. I can't do this if you continue to kiss me and touch me every time I turn around." As she uttered these words the desire ebbed from his eyes, replaced with cold aloofness. He didn't miss her meaning. He understood.

"That's the way it's to be then? I can't so much as touch you without your express welcome? Will you send me an embossed invitation? Is that how I shall know?" he bit out.

He was angry, but she preferred that to his heated gazes and roaming lips and hands. "I-I-I explained—"

"Yes, I suppose you did. I just did not fully understand until this moment that I was never to so much as put a finger on my wife. Forgive me. Now I comprehend."

My wife. Just those words from his lips sent a bolt of panic through her.

"We're not married," she retorted.

"Indeed. Not yet."

"I don't understand your . . ." she groped for the right word and gave up, reminding him instead what it was he really sought. "You need an heiress. I'm that. You claimed no need for an heir."

One dark eyebrow lifted. "Indeed. I only need the funds that you bring." He looked her up and down, his expression so cold it chilled her heart. "I don't need you."

She flinched even as awareness swam through her that she had incited this.

Turning from her, he stalked across the room.

She watched, a new type of panic rising in

her . . . panic that he'd change his mind and didn't want to marry her at all. Blast it! When had she become such a contrary creature?

"Wait!" she cried. "I still need to speak to you about a matter."

At the door, he turned to look at her. "What might that be?"

"I need your promise."

"Another one?"

She nodded, her misery more than she could understand. She was getting her wish. She'd be saving her family and he wouldn't demand a place in her bed. What more did she require?

"I need your promise that I can use funds to help my family . . . a-and that my siblings can reside with us if need be."

Something flickered in his gaze, a hint of the softness he'd shown her in the library when he comforted her about Bess. Then it was gone. "Of course."

She released a sigh. "Thank you."

He nodded. "Be ready to leave in the morning."

Inexplicable relief rippled through her, easing the tension from her shoulders. He hadn't changed his mind. She'd reached her goal and accomplished exactly what she'd set out to do.

So why did she feel so empty inside?

Chapter Twenty

$\mathcal{A}$t the first sight of McKinney Castle, Cleo felt a mixture of awe and fear. Appropriate, when she considered it. Those were much the same emotions she felt around Logan.

As they trodded along the well-worn road, she peered out the carriage window at what was to become her home—and, hopefully, home to several of her siblings, too. She bit her lip. She still needed to broach the specifics of collecting them with her husband-to-be. Not that they had done much discussing on the journey north. Most of her time had been spent in the company of Jack, Annalise, Marguerite, and her husband, Ash Courtland.

They'd all accompanied her, insisting on attending her wedding. *Wedding*. The word made her stomach twist. She wondered how soon the ceremony would occur now that they had arrived. Apparently the local village had its own church with a Reverend Smythe presiding. And there were Logan's siblings. With the exception of his sister, Fiona, they were all here, and Logan had expressed his wish for them to witness the occasion.

Her stomach plummeted as they rolled along the uneven road, passing a rock structure that she could only surmise was the church from its modest wooden spire struggling to rise up from the rock edifice.

She lifted her gaze, catching sight again of the great, sprawling castle. It was something straight from the Middle Ages. Tarps blew in the wind, covering sections of the left wing, evidently where the rock wall had relented to time and now required renovation.

The nape of her neck prickled and she swung her head around. Her gaze landed on Logan riding alongside the carriage. His shadowed eyes watched her, the dark gray assessing . . . no doubt trying to decipher her reaction to his home—now her home, too.

Jack stuck his head out alongside hers. "That's it?"

Her face burned at his loud question. She

quickly ducked back inside to avoid Logan's watchful gaze.

Jack followed, dropping back against the plush velvet squabs. "Well, I have a fairly good idea what he plans to do with your dowry."

Marguerite smiled encouragingly. "Money well spent, yes? To improve your home, Cleo."

Cleo nodded and returned the smile, knowing it was expected. She was glad for Marguerite's presence. Actually, she was glad for everyone's presence. Even Jack. It felt less daunting—almost like she wasn't doing this all on her own.

The carriage finally rolled into a courtyard, wheels and hooves clacking noisily over the ancient cobblestones. In moments, the carriage door was pulled open. Marguerite nodded at her, indicating she should be the first to descend—the first to greet her new home and all its inhabitants. Contrary to the unease and doubts rolling through her, she vowed to wear a happy countenance.

Logan stood there, hand held out, ready to assist her. She met his eyes as she accepted his hand. Ash stepped in behind him, quick to hand down Marguerite and Annalise, leaving Cleo in the hands of her husband-to-be.

"Welcome home," he murmured, his gray gaze searching her face.

Home. The word coursed through her, warming

her heart. In her mind, she envisioned her little sisters and brothers scampering all over the place, exploring every nook and cranny. "Thank you."

The serene moment was short-lived. A loud screech pierced the air, followed by what sounded like a dozen horses.

Cleo turned toward the sound, gasping as a girl no older than twelve charged from the castle doors, past the half dozen servants—none of whom blinked an eye over her wild display. On her heels were four others: two boys and one other girl, walking at a much more dignified pace.

The girl launched herself into Logan's arms, her carroty-red hair flying around her in a flaming nimbus. He caught her, not staggering in the slightest even though she was a hearty creature.

"Took you long enough! I was about to expire from boredom."

"Ah, sweet Josephine." He peeled her off him and patted her head. She grinned up at him with a face covered in freckles. "You're too busy about your adventures to ever be bored."

Her gaze found Cleo, and Cleo immediately saw that Logan and Josephine shared the same gray eyes. "Who's this?"

Logan responded with a voice full of teasing merriment, quite different from the way he usually spoke, and she realized she was seeing a new side to him. "Oh, just a pretty lass I found on the roadside."

Josephine sent him a chiding look. "You jest!"

"Of course he jests," one of the boys behind her broke in. His chest swelled in what Cleo guessed was an attempt to look manly and worldly all at once.

"Who do you think she is, pet?" Logan asked.

"A wife? You found us a wife then?" She clapped merrily.

He chuckled, his hand coming to rest on Cleo's back. She tried not to shiver at the warm press of it there. "Well, I found myself a wife. She'll be your sister-in-law." Logan stepped back to include everyone. "And this is her family. They've accompanied us home for the wedding."

Logan quickly made the introductions, and Cleo learned the names of his four siblings: Josephine, Abigail, the elder girl, and the boys: Simon and Niall.

"A wedding!" Josephine clapped again. "Here? Oh, splendid! We have so much to do in preparation. We must decorate, plan the menu, fetch flowers—"

Logan interrupted, "We shall do all we can in the time permitting, Josie."

The girl frowned. "Whatever do you mean?"

"We're not taking weeks to plan the affair."

"Well, we can accomplish much in a week—"

"What do you mean 'we'?" Abigail spoke from behind in sobering tones. "This is not your wedding, Josie. Let Logan handle matters."

Josie crossed her arms in a huff. "I only want it to be a grand celebration. Fiona didn't marry here. We've never had a wedding ceremony here before."

"In your thirteen years." Niall pointed out with a smirk.

Josie scowled again, her freckled nose bunching. "You're a mere year older. Don't act as though you're so ancient, Niall."

"We've journeyed far to get here, and I should simply like the matter done." Logan's gaze cut to Cleo. She read the question clearly there. He was trying to see if she concurred. "We can see it done this night. If agreeable, with you."

This night? So soon? She swallowed against the sudden tightness in her throat.

Was he afraid she'd change her mind? She had not come all this way to turn tail and run now. No matter how tempting the notion, she wasn't a coward. She wasn't backing down.

"Tonight suits me." She glanced at her family, as if they might object.

Marguerite, bravest of the bunch, recovered her voice. "If that's what you wish, Cleo."

Cleo nodded.

Marguerite faced Logan, her manner turning brisk and efficient. "If someone would show us to Cleo's room, we can begin preparing."

"Of course. Mrs. Willis will see you settled and take care of any needs you have." He nodded to the apple-cheeked housekeeper. "She's a marvel. This place wouldn't function without her."

Mrs. Willis snorted. "That's putting it mildly. Now that you've married a proper lady, all will be well here, mark my words." She executed a short curtsy for Cleo. "Glad to have you here, m'am. We've needed a lady's touch for years now." The woman's small blue eyes flew over Logan and his siblings with feverish accusation and Cleo gathered the tribe of them had been something of a handful. With her background, she well understood the disorder of a large family. She almost winced at the thought of introducing some of her siblings into the existing fray.

"Thank you," Cleo murmured.

Mrs. Willis bobbed her head happily. "We've kept you dawdling out here long enough. Right this way." She muttered quick instructions to the other lingering maids, indicating they should escort the other guests to their chambers.

Once inside, Cleo could see the house wasn't as outdated as she'd suspected. Gas lights lined the long corridors, so she knew some renovations had been made to at least part of the castle.

In moments, she was inside a vast bedchamber with a daunting four-post bed. A large rock fireplace, huge enough for Cleo to step inside, took up almost one wall.

Marguerite and Annalise remained with her. Annalise rotated in a small circle, limping as she moved. With her hands tucked inside her fur-lined muff, she assessed the room with an open mouth. "I've never seen a chamber such as this one. It's fit for a king."

"Oh, it's slept its fair share of kings," Mrs. Willis admitted. "Generations ago, at least."

"It's a fine room," Cleo murmured, knowing words were expected of her. She struggled with the notion that a chamber so large was to be all hers. Space was not something she'd been granted growing up. Even Jack's Mayfair mansion couldn't boast a room of this size.

"We've been preparing the master chamber for your arrival ever since Master Logan left for Town."

The housekeeper's words settled like stones in the pit of her stomach. She leveled her gaze on the housekeeper, struggling to appear unaffected. "You were so certain he would return with a bride?"

Mrs. Willis smiled. "Well, of course. It was his duty. And for all his wild ways and devilish good looks, the master's always been a good lad and known his duty."

Cleo nodded. *Duty.* Of course. That's all this was to him. All she was. That's why he didn't care about the stipulations she placed on their marriage. A useful reminder.

Mrs. Willis exhaled, her look extremely satisfied as she surveyed the room. "Good to see a new Lord and Lady McKinney in this chamber again. It's been too long. The master's parents would be so proud." She nodded to the colossal bed. "Can't even count how many babes have been born right there in that bed. Does my heart good to know that I'll be here to witness the arrival of the next generation."

Cleo felt the blood drain from her face as she stared at the bed under discussion. She would share this room—that bed—with Logan?

Marguerite must have read the horror writ upon her face. She squeezed Cleo's hand. "That will be all for now, Mrs. Willis. Please send Miss Hadley's trunks up and we'll help ready her."

Mrs. Willis nodded and departed with a quick curtsy of her portly frame. As soon as the door clicked shut, Cleo sank down onto the nearest chair. Her sisters watched her with concern and she forced a wobbly smile, struggling to reclaim her composure. She'd rather not collapse into a fit of vapors in front of them. She was made of sterner stuff than that.

"Well," Marguerite said, her voice loud and jarring in the cavernous room. She clapped her hands together with an air of efficiency. "What gown shall you wear? Something blue? You look very fine in blue."

Cleo nodded and tried to summon her voice. She should at least appear to care. It was her wedding day, after all.

Marguerite and Annalise were soon sifting through Cleo's trunks.

"This is so exciting," Annalise commented. "You're marrying a fine lord." She cast an almost shy glance at Cleo. "He's very handsome, too." Her gaze swept over the room. "And you'll live in a castle."

"A dilapidated castle," Cleo reminded, hating for Annalise to become swept up in the seeming romantic nature of it all.

"Oh, but you'll repair it now."

Marguerite held up a lovely peacock blue gown. "I think this is the one."

Cleo hardly cast it a glance. "Yes. It will do." Her gaze drifted again to the bed. Her face reddened when she caught Marguerite following her gaze. Her half sister cleared her throat. "Annalise, why don't you find your room and freshen up a bit yourself? I'm sure you'll want to change before the ceremony."

Annalise looked from Marguerite to Cleo. For the first time, Cleo noted the keen intelligence in those lovely brown eyes. For all of her naiveté, the girl wasn't a dullard. She nodded and rose. "Of course. Send for me if you need anything."

As the door clicked behind her, Marguerite resumed digging through Cleo's trunk, hunting for the gown's matching slippers.

Cleo rose and approached the fireplace, staring into the writhing orange nest of flames. "I imagine it gets very cold here in the winter."

"I imagine so. But you'll have that fine fireplace . . . and that fine husband to keep you warm."

It was as though Marguerite baited her, knowing precisely what to say to make her want to run and hide like a frightened child.

She snorted indelicately. "I think you know he'll not be keeping me warm. This isn't a love union, Marguerite. It won't be like your marriage."

Marguerite didn't respond for some moments, and Cleo finally looked over her shoulder to find her sister staring at her thoughtfully.

Cleo continued, "I suppose you think that's wretched of me? A wife unwilling to consummate . . ."

Marguerite inclined her head. "I suspected that might be why you were spending so much time with Thrumgoodie. You thought he would be safe." She spread the gown out on the bed, smoothing a hand over the glimmering blue fabric. "You certainly went in the opposite direction in choosing McKinney. I imagine he will be a hard man to resist."

Cleo closed her eyes in a long, pained blink. "You have no idea."

Marguerite smiled a small grin. "I think I might have an idea. I wasn't always eager to wed Ash. But he changed my mind."

Cleo's cheeks heated. "Of course." Her husband was a handsome man with an illicit reputation about Town—at least before he had married Marguerite.

"Let me just say the rewards of the marital bed can be . . . immeasurable." Marguerite's expression took on a dreamy quality that made Cleo decidedly uncomfortable.

"Rewards?" she scoffed. "The rewards the man receives versus the woman seem decidedly unbalanced."

"I've no complaint." Marguerite smiled ever patiently and Cleo bit back her automatic, *not yet.*

"You know"—Marguerite sat down upon the bed, picking at the lace trim of her gown—"there are things to do that don't involve actual consummation. Certain pleasurable acts. For both of you."

Cleo sniffed, striving for disinterest. But it didn't work. She strode forward and sank down beside Marguerite, looking her steadily in the eye. "Such as?"

Marguerite smiled broadly. "It may shock you, but I assure you . . . there's pleasure to be had for both of you, even if you never consummate the marriage."

Cleo studied her sister, noting her wide, solemn eyes. She looked innocent enough. Clearing her throat, she nodded once. "Tell me. Tell me everything we can do. I'm listening."

Chapter Twenty-one

The ceremony moved in a blur. There were words, vows exchanged as they stood before the tall, cadaverously thin Reverend Smythe. Despite his appearance, he managed a jovial air.

Everyone crammed inside the small church beamed good-natured smiles. Josie fairly bounced in her seat in the front pew. Cleo felt an inexplicable stab of guilt. They'd been waiting for this moment a long while, it seemed. The moment their eldest brother finally married. She swallowed thickly and glanced down at the little bouquet of flowers Josie had thrust into her hands. She wondered if the girl—if any of them—would be quite so delighted if they knew the restrictions she'd imposed on their marriage. That this marriage was, in fact, a farce.

Logan faced her, his well-carved features revealing nothing. He'd held himself stoic all through their vows. Lowering his head, his lips didn't so much as soften as he sealed their vows with the obligatory kiss.

The church burst into applause. Cleo supposed none of them thought anything amiss with the brief kiss. She knew, however. Everything was wrong with it. She'd been a recipient of Logan's kisses before. She knew just how long and savoring and delectable they could be.

Turning, he took her arm and led her from the church. A barouche waited, decorated with ribbons and flowers, and Cleo marveled that so much had been accomplished in a few hours.

She settled onto the stiff cushion as Logan took up the reins. With a flick of his wrist, they lurched forward. Villagers lined the road leading up to the castle, waving and cheering, tossing flowers. It was like something out of a fairy tale—and Cleo was caught in the midst of it.

Logan waved and called out greetings. Cleo's cheeks warmed from so much attention. She hadn't expected it—hadn't expected any of this. It was as though Logan ruled over a small kingdom here, so far from the drawing rooms of the *ton*. No wonder he seemed so indifferent to that world. It meant little to him. This was his world.

And he'd just made her a part of it.

Something in her chest tightened at the thought of that. Lifting her hand, she waved to the villagers, fighting back feelings of shyness. They welcomed her with unabashed enthusiasm. They wanted her here. Without even knowing anything about her, they'd embraced her. Because Logan had chosen her.

Amid all the well-wishers, one face stood out. Very likely because she was so beautiful, with her vivid red hair and curvy figure. But more than likely because she was scowling. The only unsmiling face in the crowd. The girl's gaze fastened with stark intensity on Logan. Tears swam in her red-rimmed eyes, shining wetly.

She quickly forgot the woman as they arrived at the castle and were ushered into the great dining hall. Tables laden with food awaited them. One table sat upon a dais, well above the others. Logan guided her into a chair at the center of the table. Jack and her family soon arrived to join them, along with Logan's siblings.

Toasts rang out as they ate and Cleo couldn't help marveling how unlike this was from all the stuffy dinners she'd attended in Town.

And she was glad for that. Voices and laughter whirled around—all save her own. No one seemed aware that she was mostly silent, only answering questions, absorbing her new world—a world in which she was now married to Logan. This reality sank upon her slowly, like pebbles descending in water.

She nibbled on a bite of roasted pheasant, achingly aware of the man next to her. He radiated heat. Life and vitality.

"Are you not hungry?" he asked as Jack was regaling everyone with one of his anecdotes. She nodded just as everyone burst into laughter as he reached the high point of his story. "I've eaten my fill. Everything has been delicious."

"Then perhaps we should retire. It's been a long day."

She gulped, wishing suddenly she'd drawn out her dinner, toying with her food and at least acting like she was eating. Now she had to walk up those winding stairs with him and climb into that big bed.

A bed big enough for an entire regiment. They wouldn't even have to brush toes with each other. With that encouraging thought, she took a fortifying breath and rose to her feet. It wouldn't be awkward. They had an understanding after all.

Logan wrapped his hands around her waist and swung her down from the dais. She stood beside him as he bid good night to everyone, nodding and smiling and praying she appeared happy as any bride ought to be—especially any bride marrying a man like Logan. Most girls only dreamed of such a match. Of course, she wasn't most girls.

His brothers cheered perhaps the loudest and she blushed, guessing at their thoughts. They doubtlessly believed their brother was in store for a vigorous night of passion.

Only she knew better. And so did Logan.

Even so, her nerves were stretched unbearably taut as they walked side by side up the winding stairs. She skimmed her hand along the smooth stone balustrade, trying to ignore the sensation of his hand against the small of her back . . . and deliberately avoiding thinking of the night ahead. Her wedding night.

The sound of a crackling fire greeted them the moment they entered the chamber. A log hissed and crumbled with a sparking pop. Cleo watched this for a moment, holding herself still as the warmer air glided over her.

A dull orange glow suffused the room, reminding her of those sunsets back home, when she'd stand upon the seawall and watch the sun sink into the sea. Logan dropped down upon a velvet-cushioned bench and began tugging off his boots.

She lingered near the door, taking it all in— him, her husband, the bedchamber she was to share with him. It was too much to absorb. She crossed her arms and hugged herself, feeling suddenly small. Like an uncertain girl.

"Are you cold?" One boot hit the floor with a thud. She gave a small jump. Blinking, she looked up from the dark leather boot. She chastised herself for her jumpiness. He wasn't going to pounce on her.

He glanced to the bed. She followed his gaze to the soft fur draped over the bottom half of the bed. "You'll warm up quicker in bed."

She nodded, not bothering to point out that she wasn't cold. On the contrary. Heat swam beneath her skin, hummed through her like a charged current.

His next boot hit the floor. She watched as his hands went to his jacket, the long fingers deftly shedding it with strong, sure movements. Nothing hesitant or nervous. And why should he be? He'd probably done this hundreds, thousands, of times.

The notion that he undressed before countless females filled her with an unjustified sense of outrage. *He's mine!* As quickly as the thought entered her head she banished it.

Of course there'd been others. And there was nothing to say there wouldn't be more. What could she expect? It was only fair. She'd banned him from her bed. She couldn't expect him to lead a life of celibacy. Just because that was what she'd chosen for herself, she could not demand it of him.

Her mind drifted to the stunning redhead from earlier. Had she shared his bed? Was she even right now weeping into her pillow?

Firelight danced off the sculpted flesh of his naked torso.

"Is this necessary?" she blurted.

He froze, looking up at her with an arched eyebrow. "What?"

She motioned in a small circle. "This . . . this chamber. You." Deliciously, temptingly naked. "Me. Sharing a room together."

Something in his expression tightened. The gray of his eyes seemed chillier, frozen ash. "We're married now," he reminded.

"Yes, but not in the truest sense."

His gaze drilled into her, hard as iron. "And you want the world to know that? That you're a wife eschewing her duty? Her responsibility to the marriage bed?"

The skin of her face grew prickly hot. The merry toasts and well wishes of earlier tonight echoed in her head. The faces of the happy villagers flashed through her mind. "No. I don't wish for the nature of our marriage to be public. It's our concern." *Our secret.*

"Agreed." He continued to undress. As if the matter were settled.

"Would you please explain?" she persisted, unable to let the matter drop. Self-preservation forced the words from her. "How would keeping our own rooms alert the world that our marriage is a—" She stopped herself just short of saying *a farce*. Their union wasn't a farce. It meant something. Even without consummation, it was real. It mattered to her.

Moistening her lips, she finished, "Spouses often keep separate rooms."

He sighed deeply, the sound weary. "Life is different here. This isn't the *ton*. Where spouses practically lead separates lives. Both the Lord and Lady McKinney have always occupied this bedchamber. It's tradition. And tradition weighs heavily here."

"Can you not ever break with tradition?"

He stared at her stonily. "I did marry an Englishwoman. That's sending a few ancestors tossing in their graves."

"Well. What's one more?" She attempted for lightness, but the look in his eyes told her he was quite finished with the discussion.

"Everyone knows I would share my wife's bed. Unless there were something wrong with her . . . unless our marriage is a contentious union." He stared at Cleo rather pointedly. "Is that what you prefer everyone conclude?"

She shook her head, shoulders sagging. She had to live here for . . . well, forever. Her siblings, too. She needed Logan's people to see her as one of them so they'd welcome her siblings with open arms. In short, she needed to win them over and not come across as some shrew who barred her husband from their bed.

But isn't that what you are?

She shook her head at the insidious little voice, and searched for the memories that had driven her for so long.

"No," she answered through numb lips. "I don't want them to think our marriage contentious."

"Good." His hands moved to his trousers. She commanded herself to look away, to move. She couldn't just stand here watching him slack-jawed as he removed the last of his clothing. She already knew he preferred to sleep naked, and in the fire's glow, she'd see every bare inch of him. That was more than she could bear.

She swallowed against the sudden thickness in her throat and scanned the room, spotting a wooden screen etched with a hunting scene. Her nightgown already happened to be draped over it—the wisdom of her maid, Berthe, no doubt.

She could change behind that with relative privacy. With luck, Logan would be tucked out of sight beneath the covers by the time she emerged.

Strategy in mind, she strode across the room and positioned herself behind the screen. Within moments of straining her arms behind her back, she realized she could not undress herself unassisted. Blast it! She should have considered this sooner.

Face flaming, she bowed her head in misery for a long moment. Inhaling, she gathered her nerve and stepped out from behind the screen once again. He was in the bed. Just as she'd hoped. And feared. He'd have to rise to assist her and then she'd see every bare inch of him.

She cleared her throat unnecessarily. He was already looking directly at her from where he was propped against the pillows in the bed, the coverlet pooled around his waist, leaving that enticing bare chest of his exposed.

She couldn't help notice that he had positioned himself squarely in the middle of the bed, with no thought, evidently, for granting her any space of her own where she wouldn't brush against him.

"I can't quite manage the buttons on my gown."

"Come here," he said and she didn't think she imagined that his voice was rougher than usual, the burr deeper, more gravelly.

She stepped closer, briskly at first and then

slower, her steps dragging as she neared the bed. He remained where he was. She stopped near the edge, her fingers bunching the skirts of her gown.

"Turn around," he instructed.

She turned, fixing her gaze straight ahead. There was a slight rustling and her pulse kicked against her throat as she imagined him pushing back the covers . . . his naked body moving toward her.

She waited. Nothing happened. She glanced over her shoulder. He loomed behind her, his bare shoulders smooth and vast, the flesh rippling over tightly corded muscle. She quickly faced forward again. But it was too late. The image was permanently branded on her mind. Just as his clean, woodsy scent was fixed in her nostrils.

At the first touch of his fingers, she gasped. Even though she was waiting for it, expecting it, even though he was only actually touching the top button of her dress. Her bodice loosened as he undid more buttons. And then she felt him— his hand inside her dress, the backs of his fingers brushing her back, grazing her spine as he worked free the last of the tiny, satin-covered buttons.

Her dress sagged, only her arms holding it up, covering her breasts. She couldn't command her legs to move. Could only feel his fingers on her back, the spark of heat where their skin connected. The air had ceased to flow in and out of her. He didn't move either and she wondered if she stood there long enough would he move and take the choice away from her? That would make it blessedly simple.

Marguerite's scandalous advice whispered through her head. She'd been shockingly candid, explaining how Cleo might pleasure both herself and Logan without engaging in actual . . . relations.

Even with the advice swimming through her, leaving nothing to the imagination, one question still remained. How did she go about initiating the advice Marguerite had given her?

"There. All done."

Rustling behind her indicated his return to the bed. Clutching her gown to keep it from falling to her feet, she scurried behind the screen. Stepping free of her gown, she flung it over the screen, angered at her cowardice. Her undergarments soon followed. Slipping the nightgown over her head, she emerged again, her gaze immediately flying to the bed. He was still there, square in the middle, naturally.

Only he no longer sat upright with pillows propped behind him as though he were waiting for her. He was lying on his side. She squinted, unable to even make out his face. He appeared to be . . . sleeping.

She lowered onto the stool before the vanity table and quickly removed her hairpins, sending the glossy dark mass tumbling to her shoulders. She quickly ran a brush through her tresses, inspecting herself critically.

Perhaps if she looked more like that curvaceous redhead she'd seen weeping in the village, he'd be more inclined to stay awake.

With decided vigor, she slammed the brush on the table. Now she was just being ridiculous. She'd ordered him to leave her be. That's what he was doing. Even on their wedding night. She wasn't about to nurse some wounded feelings because he took her request seriously. She wasn't that fickle.

She moved to the bed, flinging back the covers, her movements agitated and excessive. In the back of her mind she knew she was trying to deliberately gain his attention. Like a child throwing a tantrum, she wanted to rouse him from sleep. She frowned, recognizing the bad behavior in herself. And yet she couldn't stop.

She glared at the shadowy shape of his broad back peeking out from the covers. Even lying in the middle of the bed, there was plenty of bed left for her to occupy without touching him. She saw that now—and felt a stab of disappointment.

Turning, she beat her pillow loudly, as though getting it in the right condition for her head was of critical importance. At the very least, it was an excellent exercise in frustration.

She flopped back on the pillow with a loud sigh, her hair billowing all around her in a floating dark nimbus. She sent one last baleful look at his back. His shoulder moved the barest amount, a slow rise and fall matching his even breathing. He slept. The cad.

Rolling to her side so she did not have to endure the sight of him, she tucked her hand beneath her cheek. She doubted she would sleep a wink.

This was her last thought before drifting away.

Chapter Twenty-two

$\mathcal{L}$ogan didn't move until he heard her breathing shift into that rasping cadence that marked sleep. Only then did he roll over to observe her, admiring the softness of her features relaxed in sleep.

She'd been spitting mad at his seeming indifference to her. It had taken every ounce of will inside him not to do more than unbutton the back of her gown. He'd had to force himself not to strip her gown all the way off and touch her, caress her as he longed to do. She was his wife now . . . and he couldn't even lay a finger on her. The absurdity of it galled him. It was a situation beyond his imagining a month ago. He had envisioned himself married to a female. Perhaps one he didn't want or crave with the intensity that he wanted Cleo, but a tolerable wife. Someone he could stomach, who could in turn tolerate him. He'd assumed she'd at least be willing to share his bed. That she would even expect it—desire it.

Cleo had moved about in a huff, clearly offended about something, before she succumbed to sleep. What did she expect of him? To attempt seduction after she'd already laid forth the terms of their marriage? No. He hardened his resolve. He'd wait for her to come to him. She was a passionate creature. He had proof of that—memories that left him aching with need.

He had to believe that she couldn't spend night after night in this bed with him and not cave, not surrender to even one kiss. One kiss that could open the door to so much more . . .

He intended to make it as difficult as possible for her. Despite what he told her, he could have taken a chamber down the hall. His staff and siblings would have speculated, but he didn't care. More than likely they would have thought it her English ways . . . a haughty *Sassenach* simply desiring her own chamber. Or they might think he was giving her more time to acclimate to her new role as his wife.

Reaching out, he slid a dark tendril back from her cheek and wrapped it around his finger. Honestly, he didn't give a damn what anyone else thought. He cared only about making Cleo his wife in the truest sense. And he'd use all his cunning to make that happen.

Cleo's eyes opened slowly, and she blinked, trying to shake free her groggy thoughts. The cloudy vestiges of a dream pulled on her consciousness like cobwebs clinging to the skin.

She lifted her head, her unfocused gaze staring into a room of flickering shadows and dying light. For a long moment she could recall none of it. Not what had happened. Not where she was.

Her gaze landed on a large window dominating one stone wall. The drapes were cracked, but no light slipped inside, so she knew it was still dead night. Stillness surrounded her, draping the room in its hush. And yet she knew something had woken her.

And then she saw Logan and it all came back in a burst, in an instant of aching awareness.

He bent before the hearth, adding logs into the dwindling fire. He looked like some mythical man, a creature not of earth. Firelight licked over him, gilding his magnificent form, sliding over the ripple of muscle and sinew as he worked. Her palms tingled, itched to follow the trail of firelight over him.

Everything came back to her. Including Marguerite's lessons. Her breasts tightened beneath her gown and an ache pooled low in her belly.

Determined to gain his notice, she readjusted on the bed in a calculated pose, flinging the covers off her and making certain her nightgown rode higher . . . exposing her legs up to her thighs. Marguerite had convinced her that there were other things to do aside of actual consummation. Pleasurable things. Cleo wanted that. She wanted to experience it for herself . . . and she wanted to please him, too.

Marguerite's voice rolled through her. *The sight of bare skin always puts a man in an amorous mood.*

She only hoped the room's dim lighting hid the flush to her cheeks, and that he wasn't alerted to the fact that she was awake.

At least until she wanted him to be.

Closing her eyes, she arranged herself in what she hoped was an artless pose. And waited.

She heard his approach. The steady fall of his footsteps. Then nothing. He stopped. Was he looking down at her? She struggled to control her breathing, keep it even and deep as though she were believably asleep.

Then the bed dipped with his weight. He scooted closer but she felt nothing. No brush of him against her. She was sprawled in such a way that, she knew, he had to take special care not to touch her. When positioning herself, she'd assumed he'd want to reclaim his spot in the middle of the bed. The spot she now occupied.

She waited several moments, listening, feeling the air. There was an initial shift of the covers and adjustment of his body as he settled down into bed again, and then all fell still. Not the faintest movement. No rustling sheets. She couldn't even hear the fall of his breathing.

She waited several minutes, but the worry that he'd perhaps fallen asleep again prompted her to crack open an eye.

He was beside her, on his back, eyes closed. Sleeping already? Disappointment shot through her yet again, but with it she felt a jolt of determination. He couldn't be sleeping too deeply yet. And what if he was? She knew what would wake him. If Marguerite was to be believed, she knew precisely what might rouse him.

Chapter Twenty-three

He felt her move upon the bed and his every muscle tightened in near pain.

It had been hard enough to return from stirring the fire and find her sprawled so delectably across the bed, her bare limbs curled enticingly, inviting him to touch, caress. His palms sweat just thinking about it. The only thing for him to do was lie down and close his eyes and try to forget the image. Try to pretend a mere inch didn't separate them. That he could stretch out an arm and touch the satiny skin of her thighs. He squeezed his eyes tighter, trying to rid himself of the image. It did nothing, however, to rid him of the memory, the well-remembered sensation of her skin beneath his hands.

Now she was moving. He heard the rustle of

fabric, felt the nudge of her body against him. Was she mindlessly moving in her sleep? Was she one of those who tossed and turned? He envisioned countless torturous nights ahead where she rubbed up against him. How long was he to keep his hands to himself in such a scenario?

Her head found his chest. She snuggled against him like he was a pillow to be cuddled. He ground his teeth, but didn't move as she slid one delicious leg around him. He hardened to aching attention at the feel of her leg draped over him. Skin to skin. Only the merest shift of their bodies, and he'd have her against that part of him that most longed to join with her.

He could imagine her horror if she woke to find herself nuzzling against him in such a manner. It was a tempting notion. Perhaps he should wake her. That would certainly put an end to their proximity—and stop this blissful torment.

But the torment didn't stop. It continued in full assault. Her hand landed on his stomach, dropped there, fingers lightly curled, the tips resting, light as a moth on his quivering flesh. He tensed. Ceased to breathe. Her fingers flattened and spread wide at his navel, burning him like a brand. If he didn't know any better, he would have said it was an experienced move. Deliberate.

An action intended to seduce a man. Absolutely not something Cleo would do.

Then all sane thinking fled as that hand crept down and found him. Everything he thought about her, about this moment, about them, vanished in an instant.

There was only sensation. Only need.

He gasped and arched on the bed as her small fingers wrapped around him. The sensation of her fingers, soft and gentle, exerting just the barest pressure . . . it was bliss. The exquisite feeling only intensified as she began moving her hand, stroking him, working her hand over him in deft strokes.

He looked down and the sight nearly undid him. She stared up at him with heavy-lidded eyes, her midnight hair pooling over his thighs as her hand worked its wonder on him.

It was too much.

He groaned and reached for her arms, determined to pull her up on top of him . . . to end the agony with one deep thrust inside her. He was blind to anything else. Only hot need pumped through him.

She made a sound of protest and dodged him. He propped himself up on his elbows and growled her name, "Cleo . . . I need you."

On her knees, she kept herself out of his reach. Shaking her head at him, she warned in a sultry voice, "We'll do this my way or not at all."

He studied her, wishing he could refuse her terms, but knowing he was totally at her mercy. He could refuse her nothing.

He dropped his hands at his sides on the bed, palms up. His heart seized as he watched her, stunned when she reached for the hem of her nightgown and pulled it over her head in one liquid-smooth move.

Even in the gloom he could detect the faint stain of color on her cheeks—the only telltale sign that she felt any embarrassment to be stark naked on her knees before him.

Serrated breaths fired from his lips as he watched her lower down to both hands on the bed. She crawled toward him, her hair a dark curtain on either side of her face as she positioned herself above him. She watched him from beneath dark lashes, and the look was wholly seductive, a temptress incarnate as she bowed her head over him.

Still watching him, her eyes never leaving his, she tasted him. Sensation shot through him. He hissed a stinging breath.

His gaze fastened on the sight of that tongue as it descended for another taste. He couldn't stop himself. He lifted one hand and ran it through her hair. The need to touch her, feel her, overwhelmed him. His fingers sifted through the dark strands. Her mouth grew more assertive, her tongue more thorough, more sure. He moaned, his hips lifting up as she took all of him in her mouth.

"Cleo," he gasped, choking out, "stop!"

He clasped her shoulders and tried to lift her away.

With her hands braced on each side of his waist, she looked up at him with a thoroughly satisfied grin. "You want me to stop?" she asked in a throaty voice he'd never heard from her.

She trailed a fingertip down the center of his chest. "You see, I've been considering what you said about there being other ways we can satisfy each other . . . without consummation. You gave me a sample of that the other night." Her finger stopped on the hard tip of him. "Now it's my turn." Her eyes looked liquid dark staring up at him. "Let me pleasure you, Logan."

His head dropped back in defeat as she lowered her lips to him again and he let her have her way with him. "As long as you understand, fair is fair. It will be my turn next to pleasure you."

She came up, her hair falling in a seductive inky-dark curtain against his stomach. Her voice purred in a rumble that vibrated along his nerve endings. "Oh, I'm counting on that."

Chapter Twenty-four

Cleo raised the teacup to her lips and took a savoring sip of the warm brew, letting the flavor of bergamot flood her mouth and revive her. Considering how very little she'd slept, she could use a little revitalizing.

"Don't you look satiated," Marguerite murmured for Cleo's ears alone.

Heat crawled up her cheeks as last night replayed in her mind. A quick darting glance around the table revealed that no one else seemed aware of the illicit nature of her thoughts. Her father chatted amiably with Annalise and Logan's sister Abigail.

Logan and his brothers had left at dawn to call upon surrounding farmers and crofters. Ash had opted to join them, too. Cleo couldn't help feeling impatient and itchy at Logan's absence. Especially after last night. She doubted the feeling would go away until she saw him again.

Marguerite watched her expectantly, and she realized she hadn't answered her yet. She set her teacup back down with a soft click. "I slept well, thank you."

Marguerite smiled knowingly. "I didn't say you looked rested. On the contrary. You look rather weary."

Cleo fidgeted with her napkin.

Marguerite continued, "I take it you took my advice."

Cleo's cheeks burned hotter.

Marguerite chuckled. "You needn't say anything. The bright red of your face is answer enough." She leaned in closer, her words hushed. "I must confess my curiosity, however. Did your plan work?"

"My plan?"

"To keep a certain . . . distance?"

"Oh." She cleared her throat lightly, understanding her meaning. She wanted to know if the marriage had been consummated. "Y-yes. It worked."

"Oh." Marguerite looked almost disappointed.

"What's wrong?"

"Nothing. I just imagined that . . ."

"Yes?" Cleo prodded.

Marguerite hesitated, taking a sip of her tea before she explained, "Once intimacy begins and is enjoyed . . . well, it's almost impossible to resist following through."

Cleo stared at her unblinkingly for a long moment, letting that information sink in. It made perfect sense actually. It explained the longing, the itchy impatience thrumming through her. Her desperate need to see him again, touch him . . . and that ache deep in the core of her that begged for satisfaction.

"Oh dear," she murmured, her hand shaking as she toyed with the handle of her teacup.

Marguerite sent her a sympathetic smile and cut into her kipper.

"Why did you not warn me?" Cleo looked at her rather reproachfully.

Marguerite chewed thoughtfully, tilting her head. "You only asked if there were things you could do without . . . you know." She waved her fork, implying the rest of their conversation with the gesture. "And I told you."

"But you know why I wanted to know. What I was hoping to avoid . . ." Hot desperation choked up her throat.

Her voice must have given something away. Jack glanced down the table at her. Cleo took a deep breath and tried to look normal, unaffected.

Marguerite suddenly looked solemn. "I knew that. Yes. I just don't think you truly want that."

"I do," she insisted in a whisper. "I don't wish to consummate my marriage." She suddenly felt trapped, like a lioness caged—her fate out of her hands.

"Cleo." Marguerite reached for her hand.

She stood abruptly, stopping herself just short of running from the dining room. She didn't want her father to think anything was wrong—or Annalise to think she was some flighty, temperamental creature. Even if she did feel overwrought with emotion at this particular moment.

Marguerite had tricked her—or at least omitted certain facts. *It's almost impossible to resist following through.* The words rumbled through her head like ominous thunder.

She roamed the castle, relieved to be alone, not sure where she was going, and not really caring, only trying to make sense of what it was she wanted from her marriage to Logan. Because Marguerite was correct. She had begun something last night with him . . . and she wanted more.

Passing a series of long stained-glass windows that looked generations old, she saw a flash of lightning through the colorful panes. Seconds later, the sound of thunder rumbled in the far distance.

Her heart thumped hard against her chest. She immediately thought of Logan and the others out there in the rain. Would he return now? Her skin warmed at the prospect.

She walked faster, eagerness tripping through her at the prospect of seeing him again and continuing where they'd left off last night. And then panic rose up inside her, warring with the euphoria.

Everything was slipping away. Her long-held fears, everything she'd always believed—everything she'd always told herself she wanted. For the first time since Jack sent for her, she wasn't sure what she wanted anymore.

Slowing her pace, she continued her stroll through endless corridors, taking turn after turn until she knew she was well lost. She snorted at this irony. It was exactly how she felt.

She peered inside various rooms, entering what appeared to be a music room. Several instruments filled the space. None of which was collecting dust. Either Logan and his siblings made good use of them or the staff did an excellent job cleaning in here.

Her eyes alighted upon floor-to-ceiling double doors leading outside. Snatching an afghan off a nearby sofa, she wrapped it around herself and stepped outdoors. The wet cold of the paving stones immediately seeped through the soles of her slippers as she stepped out into the gray morning. She suspected she would be wearing her boots more often in this climate.

She looked skyward. Dark, almost black clouds rolled in from the west, and she wondered what direction Logan had ventured for the day. Shaking her head, she commanded herself to stop thinking about him. That would be the first step toward avoiding Marguerite's prediction that there was only one inevitable conclusion for the two of them.

Lowering her gaze, she stared out at a well-tended garden. One side appeared to be flowery shrubs and rows of juniper trees. The other section was devoted to plants and herbs.

Maids busied themselves, pruning, clipping, edging. They worked quickly, with one eye to the sky. One maid worked amid the herbs. She wore a heavy wool apron and sat on her knees, clipping snippets of herbs for her basket. Cleo's gaze fastened on her, narrowing on the thick plait of red hair snaking out from the wool kerchief covering her head. Cleo admired the glorious red hair for a moment before her gaze drifted to the girl's profile. The creamy complexion. The full, bow-shaped mouth. The lovely, slightly upturned nose. Sudden recognition seized her.

She must have made a sound. The girl swung around on her knees. At the sight of Cleo, she almost lost her balance. One hand came down on the dark soil to balance herself. Her face paled for a moment as she eyed Cleo up and down. Then a fetching shade of red flooded her cheeks.

"My lady," she murmured in a lilting brogue, dipping her head in deference.

"Hello," Cleo returned, feeling suddenly awkward, more aware than ever that she was a stranger in her new home. This girl's place and position here were more natural than her own.

The notion mortified her—especially when she recalled the tears in the girl's eyes on her wedding day . . . and what they perhaps signified about her relationship with Logan.

Were they lovers once? Still?

Her fingers tightened around her blanket. And yet she couldn't move. They simply stared at each other.

"What's your name?" Cleo asked. She had to know—had to know the name of the girl who may or may not have a place in Logan's heart. Perhaps he would even have married her if she'd possessed the requisite dowry.

Cleo's gaze traveled over her lush figure, resting on her chapped, work-roughened hands. Not too long ago her own hands had resembled those.

She was peasant stock—just like Cleo. Only fate and fortune had shone on her.

"Mary," she answered to Cleo's question. "Can I get you anything, my lady?" She clearly wondered why Cleo was lingering out in the chill and wanted her to be gone if the anxious glitter in her blue eyes indicated anything.

"No. Thank you. Just exploring. Don't let me keep you from your task."

With a considering look, Mary nodded and returned to her work, lowering back to the ground. Her movements were stilted though, measured, and Cleo knew she wouldn't relax as long as Cleo stood there . . . pretending not to watch her. Pretending not to care.

Whatever solace she had hoped to find in the garden vanished. Turning, she slipped back inside the music room. Discarding the afghan, she resumed her exploration, eventually stumbling upon a library.

Unlike the music room, this room appeared long neglected. Logan's family's fondness for music evidently didn't translate to reading. As she walked the length of one vast wall of shelves, she swiped a finger along a dusty spine. She browsed the books, noting that the selections were quite dated. She would have to see about acquiring some current titles. No doubt the family tutor would appreciate some of the more current titles to introduce to Logan's siblings.

She found a volume of *Jane Eyre* and settled herself before the fire that someone had started in the room. The rain was falling steadily now, an occasional burst of thunder breaking the patter. For all that, it was a lulling cadence and she snuggled beneath the pashmina blanket draped on the back of the sofa. Soon the words grew blurry and unfocused and she surrendered to the heaviness of her eyelids.

Chapter Twenty-five

$\mathcal{A}$ sharp rattling woke her. Blinking, she propped herself up on one elbow. The book on her chest slid to the floor with a thud.

A maid tending the fire whirled around at the sound. "Oh, apologies, my lady. I didn't mean to wake you. Just wanted to rouse the fire a bit so you didn't grow cold."

"That's fine," she murmured with a croaky voice. Sliding her legs to the floor, she brushed a hand over her mussed hair, wondering how long she'd been asleep. For all she knew, it could be the next day.

She parted her lips, on the verge of inquiring the hour when another figure entered the room.

Instantly, her body sprang alive with awareness. He was wet, she could see, his dark hair molded like a slick helmet to his head. His clothes hung heavy with moisture on his large, muscled frame.

Logan froze as his gaze landed on her. There was worry in his expression that faded away at the sight of her. "I've been looking everywhere for you. No one's seen you since breakfast."

"I'm sorry." An uncomfortable tension rose up between them. She flicked a glance at the maid. Caught staring, the girl's freckled face blushed and she quickly looked away, returning her attention to the fireplace.

Cleo faced her husband again. *Husband.* The word jarred her—nearly as much as his gleaming gaze. Those gray eyes searched her, looking, it seemed, for something.

She fidgeted with the folds of her skirt. "I fell asleep." She motioned to the sofa where the rumpled blanket sat piled in a heap. "I didn't mean to cause alarm."

"The castle is big. I worried you'd lost your way." He motioned to the door. "I'll escort you."

With a glance for the maid who was inordinately focused on stirring the fire, Cleo moved past him and through the door. Hands laced before her, she walked, sliding him a glance as he fell into step beside her.

"You're wet," she announced and winced at the obviousness of her comment.

"The rain cut our work short for the day. I'll have to visit the other crofters another time."

"Perhaps tomorrow," she suggested, feeling unaccountably nervous. Tension swirled on the air between them, even more pronounced now that they were alone, away from the maid's curious gaze.

"Perhaps. I need to oversee some of the renovations on the west wing."

She nodded and slid him another glance. He stopped, looking down at her with that devouring way of his.

An answering tremor racked her.

He spoke her name, quickly, so softly that she barely registered the utterance. His face, the carved lines achingly handsome, the eyes deep with a hunger that she felt echoed deep into the core of her . . .

It undid her.

They moved as one, reaching for each other, coming together in a desperate tangle of arms and lips. His weight pushed her back against the wall, rattling a framed painting near her head. She didn't care, didn't even look up.

Cleo wrapped her arms around his neck and

clung as if some great force might pull her away, separate them. Their mouths consumed each other, kissing, sucking . . .

He groaned her name. "I have to have you, Cleo . . . please . . ."

And this sent none of the usual panic racing through her. It thrilled her, excited her . . . intensifying the ache at her core. Because she felt the same way. She pressed herself against him and moaned when she realized she could get no closer.

His hand came over her breast and she whimpered in frustration, loathing the barrier of her gown. She wanted them back in their room, in that colossal bed that had so terrified her at first. It terrified her no more. Strangely, she was devoid of fear or hesitation or the usual doubts. She wanted him between her thighs. She needed that final closeness—him filling her and taking away the aching emptiness inside.

Then he was gone, wrenched from her arms. She sagged against the wall, panting and aching with disappointment. He stood back from her. She reached a trembling hand for him, but saw that he wasn't even looking at her.

She followed his gaze to his younger brother. Niall's amused expression showed no remorse at interrupting them. "Now I see why you were in such a hurry to get back home. I was sent to fetch you to dinner, but I can see that you both might want to skip dinner and go directly for dessert."

"Niall," he warned in a deeply guttural voice, the cords of his throat working with tension as he took a menacing step toward his young brother.

Niall held up a palm, looking hard-pressed not to laugh. "My apologies." His gaze cut to Cleo. "I didn't mean to embarrass you."

Still fighting for her breath, she nodded, thinking she was less embarrassed and more frustrated at the interruption. Not normal thinking, she was sure. She'd become insatiable. Just as Marguerite had intimated—this could end only one way.

At that disturbing thought, she pushed off from the wall. "Excuse me. I'll freshen up for dinner. I know my way back."

Logan watched her intently as she passed, as a predator studies its prey. She tried not to notice. Tried not to look in his direction. Still, she felt his gaze as she hurried down the corridor. The heat of it followed her. Even when she was out of sight, she felt it. She felt him—the scent of him, the memory of his mouth, his hands . . .

Dear God. Marguerite was right. She'd set out to satisfy them both, thinking it needn't go very far. And now she was enslaved, desperate for it to go much, much farther.

* * *

Dinner was a painstaking affair. Conversation. Laughter. Everyone seemed in fine spirits. Cleo's father was particularly fond of Logan's Scottish whiskey.

"And you make this here?" Jack asked after a deep swallow of the amber liquid.

Logan dragged his gaze from her. "Yes. Ever since the days of my great-grandfather." His gaze returned to her—where it had been ever since they sat down to dinner.

She wasn't certain where he had changed clothing. He hadn't followed her to their bedchamber, but he'd been dressed in fresh clothing, waiting with the others when she joined. She didn't know whether to be relieved or disappointed that he hadn't joined her in their chamber.

His finger tapped the rim of his glass silently. She watched that tapping finger, feeling the anxiousness of that gesture inside her.

"Cleo, where did you disappear today?" Marguerite asked, her voice light, belying the concern in her eyes. Natural, she supposed, considering their last encounter.

"Just explored the castle a bit . . . and then I fell asleep in the library while I was reading."

"I spent the day studying Latin." Josephine pouted and stabbed at her dinner. "Latin! A dead language. What use is it, I would like to know?"

Logan glanced at his sister. "Cruel of me, I know, to see that you receive an education."

Josephine scowled. "Well, I doubt it will serve me on the dance floors of London."

Cleo's lips twitched. The interplay reminded her of her own siblings. She frowned, missing them and wondering how long before she could put her plan in place to bring them here. The oldest of her brothers and sisters might be better served in a school that would provide them the education and polish they'd missed thus far. She'd have to investigate the matter. But the rest, the little ones—she was eager for them to join her here. She wouldn't feel easy until she had them safely in her care. A pain stabbed the area surrounding her heart to know she couldn't save her mother.

After dinner they all moved into the drawing room. Logan escorted her. Leading them at a creeping pace, she quickly grasped that he was deliberately positioning them last. Just as they were about to cross the threshold into the room, he pulled her back and pressed her against the wall outside the drawing-room doors, trapping her with his body.

"Logan? What—"

He smothered her words with a long, rough kiss that turned her knees to liquid. It went on and on. If not for the warm press of his body, she was certain she would slide to the floor in a boneless heap. Which she probably wouldn't even mind as long as he joined her there.

"There." He broke away, breathing fiercely, his broad chest rising and falling. "I've wanted to do that all night."

"I-I . . ." she stammered uselessly as he grabbed her hand and led her back into the drawing room.

She tried to appear composed, unaffected—not as though she'd been kissed senseless seconds ago.

He sat beside her on the chaise, his leg so close that it brushed the skirt of her dress. Heat seemed to reach her from that trouser-clad leg. It drew her gaze again and again, distracting her from everything and everyone.

Her lips tingled. Bruised and sensitive, she brushed her fingers to her mouth, testing the surface, the shape of lips that she had lived with all her life but suddenly felt different.

At one point, she looked up to find Marguerite staring at her with a knowing lift of her eyebrow. The sight of which annoyed her to no end. Cleo dropped her hand from her face and lifted her chin at a defiant angle. Almost to prove that point, she scooted herself as far as possible down the chaise without falling off.

She didn't have long to endure her sister's smug gaze, however. Ash unfolded his long frame and helped his wife to her feet. "Excuse us. It's been a long day, and I'm not entirely certain Marguerite has recovered from the journey."

Marguerite cast her husband a sardonic look, and Cleo well understood that he wasn't concerned with his wife's need for rest. Her cheeks burned knowing precisely the nature of what it was they were retiring for the night to do.

As Jack swept Logan into a conversation on matters of whiskey and agriculture, she stood abruptly. Too abruptly, evidently. Everyone looked at her with sudden curiosity.

"I'm tired, as well."

"Even after your nap?" Josephine asked.

Cleo's cheeks prickled with heat.

Logan started to rise. She held out a hand. "No, no. That's quite all right. I don't want to take you away from everyone. Stay. Enjoy yourself."

His eyes glittered darkly, and she read the message there quite clearly. He was agreeable to leaving everyone and joining her. *He wished* to enjoy her.

With an awkward curtsylike dip, she turned and fled the room, overhearing Logan's sister as she departed the room. "She likes to sleep a lot."

She practically raced up the stairs. Holding her skirts high to make certain she didn't trip, she rushed down the corridor, desperate to be in bed asleep—or rather feigning sleep—before he joined her. Cowardly, she knew, but she could not help herself.

Behind the screen in her chamber, she stripped off her clothes, heedless of the loud rip behind her back. Blasted buttons. She kicked her skirts free, pulled off her undergarments and slid her nightgown over her head, freezing, her heart beating like a wild bird in her chest at the sound of the bedchamber door opening and shutting.

Chapter Twenty-six

She hadn't been quick enough. He'd followed her. She waited a long moment, listening closely as if he might announce himself . . . as if she might somehow disappear altogether and appear somewhere else far from this room.

The silence grew thick and cloying. She squared her shoulders and stepped from behind the screen. She was no coward. She was in absolute control of herself. She needn't fear him . . . or herself. Marguerite's prediction needn't become reality.

He'd yet to move far into the room, but stood just a few feet from the door, still looking crisp and fresh and startlingly attractive in his evening attire. She doubted there would ever be a time when she would see him without feeling a sense of astonishment over his appeal. His utter masculinity, his dangerous beauty. And he was hers. If she would only allow herself to have him.

He pushed off from the door and started toward her, his stride cutting a hard line.

Her heart leapt to her throat. Blood rushed in her ears. She should move. Run! And yet her feet remained planted, rooted to the carpet, her bare toes curling with anticipation.

And then he was reaching for her. Taking her. His hand slid around her neck in one smooth move, pulling her in as his head ducked for her mouth, crashing their lips together.

His mouth tasted of man and heat and the slight flavor of whiskey. Hunger surged inside her, dark and dangerous, as ravenous as a beast released to hunt. She couldn't remember ever feeling this . . . a desire so enveloping it made her forget all her fears.

Cleo clenched her hands and shoved them between their bodies, determined to stop this. It took everything in her to resist flattening her palms against his hard chest and simply feel him, savor the hard press of muscles surrounding her.

She willed her lips to still, willed her body not to respond to the wonder of his mouth on hers, coaxing forth feelings and emotions long denied. New feelings. Terrifying, exciting feelings she had been so careful to kill. Freed from a dark hidden place, they spiraled through her like warmed wine, dizzying, invigorating, feeding her courage—or idiocy. Either way, she was a new woman, drinking from his mouth as though his lips were some intoxicating elixir she could not resist.

His hands slid into her hair, scattering the pins. Her scalp shivered with sensation. Her trembling fingers unfolded, caressing and exploring his unyielding warmth.

With a choking cry, the last of her resistance slid away. She parted her mouth wider, meeting the slick glide of his tongue with her own.

She clenched fistfuls of his shirt and mimicked his kiss, returning it with eagerness, pulling him down over her, sinking back onto the bed.

He growled low in his throat, dragging his mouth over her jaw and down her sensitive neck. Cleo opened her eyes and shut them again, afraid that she would wake from this dream and put a stop to it all.

His hand moved down her nightgown, fumbling for the hem. She set to work on his clothing, shedding him of his jacket and vest, pulling his shirt over his head. Leaning up, she rained kisses over his jaw and neck, skimming her palms over him, scoring her nails lightly over the smooth, muscled chest, stopping to test the small dusky circles of his nipples with her fingertips.

He moaned, breaking away and flinging her nightgown over her head. Then his hands were everywhere, the feverish caressing of his palms exciting her only more.

Naked beside him, not a moment of hesitation seized her. It was as if she were someone else entirely, someone unafraid, someone willing to trust, to give herself over to his strength and virility. To him.

His hand wandered her thighs, the callused fingers and palms rasping the tender flesh. His gray eyes flashed darkly in the firelight as he stared down at her.

"You're beautiful," he murmured, and she believed it—believed that he meant it and wasn't just saying it.

"So are you." Propping herself up on her elbows, her hands sought him. He watched her, his eyes intense and burning, his large body unmoving, still as stone as she unfastened his breeches and shoved them down his lean hips.

Biting her lower lip, she feasted her gaze on that familiar part of him. Heat swirled through her, pooling low in her stomach and she knew this time she wouldn't just touch and taste him there. She had to have him. All of him. Inside her.

Her belly contracted and she fidgeted restlessly in an attempt to ease the throbbing ache between her legs. Her hand reached and closed over him. A tremor rushed over him as she wrapped her fingers around the hard length of him, luxuriating in the feel of him, silk on steel in her hand. Encouraged by the sound of his rough approving growl, knowing what it meant, what he wanted, she stroked him, her fingers gliding over his length, her breath increasing, matching the harsh sound of his that filled her ears.

She watched him, relishing the sight. He swallowed visibly, his throat muscles working. Aroused beyond endurance, every nerve in her body screaming with a desperate urgency, she parted her legs, leaving herself exposed before his searing gaze. She didn't care.

Cool air rushed over her, caressing that most vulnerable part of her. With one hand still holding his throbbing member, she urged him closer, guiding him to her entrance as her thumb rolled leisurely over the velvet tip of him.

Her eyes never strayed from the taut lines of his face, and want twisted deep inside her. She rubbed him against her opening and the ache inside her grew, increased and twisted to a painful need.

"What are you doing to me?" he groaned.

His body pressed closer, beautiful in the firelight. His hips nudged her thighs wider, splaying her open for him.

He eased his member inside her, stretching her slowly. Her breath caught on a gasp. She watched his face hungrily, his eyes dilated with desire.

His chest lifted on a ragged breath. "God," he gasped, eyes burning gray fire. His arms fell on each side of her, caging her in. His gaze held hers, dark and dangerous, feral as a wolf cornering its prey. He pushed his hard heat just the barest amount deeper.

She whimpered and lifted her hips, angling for more. With a cry, he thrust himself deep. A sharp pain tore through her. She lurched against him, shocked at the sudden invasion that stretched her and filled her to capacity. She dug her fingers into his bare shoulder, stunned at the heat of him pulsing deep within her core.

He murmured nonsense, soothing words against her hair as he held himself motionless inside her. Gradually her body acclimated to the feel of him and that ache returned. Deeper. Hotter than before. She wiggled—adjusted to the searing pressure. A sharp gasp ripped from her lips as the lancing pleasure spiked between her legs.

Instinctively her hands smoothed down his

back and she seized the tight mounds of his buttocks, urging him to move, needing more.

It was all the encouragement needed.

He began moving, thrusting and pumping inside her until she couldn't catch her breath. She scored his back with her hands and angled her hips, meeting his every plunge, taking him deeper.

"More. Harder," she gasped in his ear and he increased his thrusts, burying her deeper into the soft bed. She cried out, feeling herself unraveling, coming apart inside from his each and every stroke.

She writhed beneath him, desperate for more, for an end to the torment, an end to the aching emptiness . . .

"Cleo," he gasped, biting down gently on her earlobe.

She arched beneath him, pressing her breasts into his sweat-slick chest. He followed his bite with a kiss, his tongue licking and laving.

She let go then, surrendered, muscles squeezing and tightening in a blinding flash of pleasure and pain.

Her vision grayed at the corners and she wondered if she had perhaps died, the feelings shuddering through her too great, too powerful . . . too much.

Her muscles eased, body liquefying into a puddle as he moved a last time inside her and then removed himself suddenly, spilling himself elsewhere. Her head lolled to the side as a great lethargy stole over her. Even in that moment with her thoughts muddled, she understood what he was doing . . . that he cared about what she wanted enough to take such precautions for her.

The bed eased from his weight and he was gone. Frowning, she lifted her head and searched for his shape, smiling when he soon returned. He settled back down beside her, spooning his body to hers.

She lay utterly still as her body's pleasure ebbed. But still a lingering pleasure remained with his warm chest aligned to her back. *Her husband.*

It felt right. Everything about this felt right. He brushed the hair from her shoulder. His chest lifted with a deep inhalation behind her. He'd be asleep soon.

Slowly, Cleo returned to herself. It had come to pass. She'd surrendered to her passions. Although somehow this didn't frighten her anymore. She wasn't repeating her mother's mistakes. She looked down at his darker hand splayed against her stomach, deciding it was a sight she could grow accustomed to seeing.

Chapter Twenty-seven

Cleo woke sprawled in the middle of an empty bed. Her cheeks warmed and she couldn't help wondering if she'd been in this position all night, naked and tangled up with Logan.

He was missing now, but the bed beside her still radiated his warmth. He couldn't have been gone long. She rolled onto her back. A slow smile curved her mouth as she relived the night. Pleasurable heat suffused her. There was no regret. Only an anxious eagerness to do it again.

The pale light of dawn crept through the crack in the heavy tapestry drapes. In the back of her mind, she mused that those needed updating. Perhaps a lighter color and in damask.

Eager to see Logan again, she hopped from the bed and made short work of dressing herself. Accustomed to doing such things for herself—and her many siblings—she arranged her hair in a loose chignon. Satisfied that she was presentable enough to emerge and face the world, she stepped from the room into the chilly corridor with a buoyancy of spirit she hadn't felt in years. Perhaps ever.

Striding down the corridor, she passed a servant who looked decidedly nervous when she caught sight of Cleo. The woman's gaze skittered from Cleo down to her feet. Cleo hoped she didn't look that intimidating. Certainly in time the household staff would warm to her.

Still focused on her feet, the maid practically raced the last few steps to get past Cleo. Frowning at her odd behavior, Cleo continued down the hall.

The sound of low voices reached her ears just as she rounded the corner. Everything slowed then.

As if she were moving underwater, she stilled, her feet sliding to a stop on the worn-thin runner. Her gaze fastened on her husband standing practically nose-to-nose with the maid, Mary. Each of his large hands gripped her shoulders.

The girl was weeping. Again. With Logan's hands on her, the sight did nothing to stir Cleo's pity. Tears were often used in order to manipulate. If that was Mary's game, it was working. Logan's face was sympathetic, perhaps even apologetic as he murmured words to her. Words of comfort? Regret? She couldn't hear. Perhaps he was making promises to her? Promises that their relationship wouldn't change simply because he'd married.

An ugly feeling swept over her. Anger but something else, something more. A myriad of emotions too deep and complicated to sort.

Mary stroked Logan's cheek as if she had every right to touch another woman's husband. And Logan allowed it. Allowed her fingers to caress his face so tenderly.

Cold rage washed over her. Humiliation so deep and aching she wanted to lash out. At him. At her. He was what she had been running from, after all—the very man she'd wanted to protect herself from. Someone who took what he wanted and then stomped all over her as she were dirt to be trod upon.

He was the type of pain she'd wished to avoid. And still he had found her. The moment she trusted him. The moment she gave herself to him, it had happened. He crushed her.

She pressed the back of her hand to her feverish cheek and inhaled. She'd never be so foolish again. He could have whatever village girl he wanted. He could have every single one of them for all she cared.

But he'd never have her again.

As if to solidify this decision, Cleo held her ground, forcing herself to watch as Mary stood on her tiptoes and pressed her mouth to his.

Despite her vow not to care, she gasped—too loudly to remain undetected.

Logan jerked and pushed Mary's lush figure away. He whirled around, his gaze zeroing in on Cleo, his gray eyes alert as a hawk, intent and alive in that way that always curled her toes and melted her resolve. Now it only left a sour taste in her mouth.

Mary brightened, her tears vanishing as she settled her hands on her curvaceous hips and swayed where she stood, her eyes flashing with triumph as she assessed Cleo.

Logan took a step in her direction, reaching for her. "Cleo—"

She shook her head and stepped back swiftly. "No."

It was just a word but she put everything into it, conveyed all her anger, all her hurt and disappointment with the single utterance.

His eyes flickered with something, an emotion she couldn't identify, and she knew he understood. Whatever they'd had, however close they'd come to something special . . . it was lost.

Turning, she raced back to her bedchamber. He

was there, after her before she could consider a better place to flee. Not that any part of this castle belonged to her. Not that she could escape him or his world.

He caught the door before she could slam it shut. She hurried to the center of the room, hoping to put distance between them. Whirling around, she faced him, feeling as wild and desperate as a cornered animal.

He held up two hands in the air as though to placate her. "It isn't what it looks like—"

"Said the husband to the wife," she mocked bitterly.

"Cleo—"

"No." She swiped a hand through the air. "And you claimed you didn't want everyone to think our union was contentious?" She laughed harshly, dizzy from her furious thoughts. "What an idiot I am! You can't even wait a day before you begin your dalliances. And after last night?" She squared her shoulders. "I want my own room. Either this one or another. I care not. I refuse to share a bed with you again."

His face tightened with frustration . . . and something else she'd never seen before. Something that made her feel a stab of discomfort. As though something were slipping away here, dying for good.

"Cleo, it doesn't have to be—"

"What? As long as I turn a blind eye to your dalliances we can continue our farce of a marriage? I can continue repeating last night with no shame or regret?" She motioned to the bed, her face heating as she recalled everything she'd done last night. The memory mortified her.

"It wasn't like that . . . Mary is an old friend—"

"Stop!" She held up both hands and squeezed her eyes in a tight blink. "Please spare me the details. I don't want to hear about your sordid history."

He grabbed her hands and pulled them down, stepping close, encroaching on her space. "I suppose I should feel flattered you're so jealous."

"Jealous?" She winced at the shrill quality to her voice. Swallowing, she tried again, her tone much more even and controlled as she said, "Hardly that, I can assure you!"

He angled his head and stared down at her, his expression stark. "Don't let this destroy us before we've even had a chance."

"We never had a chance. I see that now."

His face hardened, his eyes darkening so much that they didn't even look gray any more but black instead. "That's what you think?"

She nodded, a painful lump rising in her throat.

Turning, he marched for the door. "Perhaps you're right then."

She flinched as he yanked open the door. She pressed her lips into a thin line, almost as though she didn't trust herself not to call him back. What a terrible contrary creature she was . . . her body in constant battle with her head.

His chest rose and fell on a deep breath. "If we never had a chance, it's because you decided that from the start."

She opened her mouth to argue, but managed only a small squeak when he slammed the door shut again and charged toward her.

She backed up several steps until she collided with one of the bedposts.

"You're a prisoner of your fears. I'm not your father. I'm not your stepfather." His hands came up to seize her arms. "And you're not your mother."

His words flayed her. Tears burned her eyes. Her voice shook unconvincingly. "You don't know . . ."

"I've got a better grasp on what's real than you do." His eyes sparked like shards of ice. "And I know this." Before she could react, he forced a punishing kiss on her, trapping her hands between them. She balled her hands into fists, desperate to strike him, but could not free them.

He came up for air, growling against her mouth, "You know that I didn't betray you out in that corridor . . . not hours after I spent loving you in this bed. You're looking for a reason to run, and I won't let you."

"I know no such thing."

"Stubborn," he rasped and then kissed her again. This time less punishing, but no less consuming.

Heat blossomed where their mouths fused. She didn't know the moment everything changed but it did. Her hands loosened, palms turning outward to splay against his chest. Her mouth softened and opened to him. She kissed him back, her anger releasing itself in this. In passion.

Now she knew what to do. She'd had a taste, a sample, and she couldn't resist what her body craved, needed like air.

He picked her up off her feet and dropped her down on the bed. They came at each other hastily. His hands dove beneath her skirts as he settled between her thighs. She reached for the front of his trousers, fumbling to free him.

Their lips never severed. They kissed hotly, tongues mating. She gasped into his mouth as the hard length of him sprang into her hand, silk on steel, thick and pulsing hard. She wrapped her fingers around him and squeezed. A shudder racked his body.

And then he was there, shoving inside her with one smooth thrust. Her body took him, eager and ready. He moved fast and hard, every stroke slick with their desire.

His fingers dug into her hips, gripping her for his sensual assault. She cried out, whimpering as he increased his pace. He lifted her higher off the bed, and the position did something to her—each plunging thrust ignited her, struck some unidentifiable spot in her clenching core. Sensation ripped through her, sparking each nerve ending.

She arched her spine, anxious to accommodate. The delicious friction grew, became unbearable. She fisted the bed at her sides, a boneless, quivering mass as he worked over her. It was close . . . that place where she'd exploded into a million tiny particles before. She kissed him harder, bit down on his lips.

He moaned and slammed into her, flinging them both over the edge. Cleo shouted, bursting from the inside out. Shivers rippled over her. He came over her, his weight covering her even as he remained lodged inside her.

For a long moment, she reveled in it. The delicious weight of him. His pulsing member inside her. And then horror arrived in full force.

She beat him on the shoulder. "You didn't stop!"

He'd stayed inside her the entire time. Even now she could feel the wetness of his seed between her thighs.

He pulled back to look down at her, his expression slightly dazed. She hit his shoulder again. "Was this your ploy to chain me to you? Get me with child so that you can trap me forever?" she cried.

Comprehension washed over his face. "I didn't intend—"

"Get off me," she choked, having no desire to hear his lies.

He rolled off her.

She scooted to the edge of the bed, her shaking hands tidying her garments. "It won't work. I'm leaving."

"You're my wife—"

"I don't require the reminder." She faced him, shaking from what just happened—from the possibility that she could now be with child. "I never wanted this."

He stared at her, his eyes hard pewter again, all the softness gone.

"I'll return home with my father. I'll simply explain that I can't live here. The marriage will still stand, as does the settlement. You'll get your money. And I'll keep a portion, as promised . . . for my family," she reminded.

His expression twisted bitterly. "And if there's a child?"

Her chest tightened at the notion. "I'll inform you."

He nodded. "How very civil." He pushed off from the bed, his motions jerky as he straightened his clothing. "Have a good life, Cleo," he declared, striding away from the bed, from her, with a suddenness that left her blinking after him.

"Oh. One more thing." He faced her. "Whether you want to hear it or not, I'm going to explain. Mary and I grew up here together. Nothing ever happened." He shrugged. "She looked up to me, may have fancied herself in love with me." His gaze fastened on her. "I never bedded her . . . there was only ever one kiss. Five years ago. At Christmas, under the mistletoe."

A breath shuddered painfully from her lips. This time when he opened the door he didn't look back. He left. He was gone.

And she was all alone.

Precisely what she had asked for—what she wanted from him. Dropping facedown on the bed, she lost herself to ugly, wet sobs that were quite beyond her understanding. *Have a good life.* At this moment, feeling as she did, her heart a twisting, painful mass in her too-tight chest, she didn't see how that was possible.

Chapter Twenty-eight

Logan stormed from the room, his steps hard and jarring. Part of him still wanted to turn around, go back and shake Cleo . . . or kiss her. But that only worked for the duration. He might be able to seduce her, but the moment it was over, she'd still be the same distrustful female—a hard shell he couldn't penetrate.

He passed the spot where he'd stood with Mary and resisted the urge to slam his fist into the wall. They'd been children together. He had no idea she still harbored a yen for him after all these years. Even if he hadn't married Cleo, there would be no future for them. He'd been explaining that to Mary when Cleo stumbled upon them. *Hellfire.*

What he felt for Cleo . . . damn, he didn't know what he felt. He only knew it was real. Frightening and exhilarating and like nothing he'd ever felt for another woman. He didn't want to lose that.

Now what was he going to do? He was married to a woman fully imprisoned by her own demons. He had no doubt she was packing her bag this very moment.

"Logan!" Simon strode down the corridor toward him. "Wasn't sure if you were going to sleep the day away. I thought we were going to work on the north wing with the men, but if you'd like to idle the day away with your bride—"

"No chance of that," he grumbled beneath his breath.

"What? Trouble in paradise already?"

At Logan's look, some of Simon's levity slipped away. "Sorry. I know you're fond of her."

"How do you know that?" he bit out.

His brother blinked. "Aside of the fact that you married her, any fool can see you're enamored with one look."

"I had to marry someone," he replied, even as he knew Cleo was the only female he had ever *wanted* to wed.

Simon lifted an eyebrow. "Right. I'm supposed to believe she's of no account to you."

Logan strode past his brother, in no mood to discuss his feelings for Cleo with him. "Believe whatever you like."

"Och." Simon followed in his steps doggedly. "You're behaving like a lion with the proverbial thorn in his paw."

He stopped and whirled around. "She's leaving, Simon."

His brother stared at him for a moment before asking haltingly, "What do you mean?"

Turning, he continued down the corridor. "She will be returning to Town with her family."

"Why?"

Why. The word reverberated through him. He swung around. "Because she doesn't love me, Simon. I couldn't make her love me."

Logan turned swiftly back around, unable to stomach Simon's astonished expression. His brother was young, but he still recalled their parents' loving marriage. He likely thought every union should be like that. A few moments passed and his brother's footsteps sounded behind him.

"Logan, wait! Where are you going?"

"We've work to do," he called over his shoulder. "This castle won't repair itself."

"Are you certain you know what you're doing, Cleo?"

Cleo walked briskly down the corridor, Marguerite doggedly following in her wake. She worked her gloves onto each finger with an air of efficiency even though inside she felt a wreck. "I'm quite certain of my actions."

Marguerite grasped her shoulder and pulled her around to face her. "Are you really? Because once done, some things are difficult to undo." She angled her head and stared at her intently. "I just don't want you to regret this later."

Cleo moistened her lips, hating that her sister's words held such power over her. She already felt nauseated and heartsick. She had ever since Logan left her this morning. She didn't need Marguerite making her feel any worse. "I already feel regret. What's a little more down the road?"

Cleo slid free of her sister's hold and continued down the corridor until she reached the main foyer. The sound of hammers and men at work grew louder once she stepped outside. The tarp had been removed and several men worked on the west side of the castle. A scaffolding had been erected, along with several ladders. Even across the distance of the front yard, she could make out Logan's shape. He worked alongside other men, without a jacket. Wearing a simple wool shirt and trousers, he looked like any other laborer. Except for his aura of command. His noble bearing. And the way he turned to stare in her direction—with all the alertness of a beast of the woods. It was like he scented her from afar. There was no doubt in her mind that he was staring at her. Another man spoke to him, but he didn't turn to acknowledge him.

She started to hold up a hand to wave goodbye, but that felt so inadequate. How did one say farewell to the husband you were leaving forever? *Forever.* The notion rang like a death knell in her heart. Her eyes burned and she blinked rapidly.

"Cleo?" Jack was at her side, his hand taking her elbow. She sent him a sharp glance. He wore one of his ridiculous jackets. A bright shade of purple that seemed to belie his serious countenance. "Are you certain you want to leave?"

"Yes." Why must everyone ask her that?

Was she certain she must go? *Yes.*

Was she certain she should never see her husband again? *Yes.*

Was she certain she loved him?

Turning, she hurried into the waiting carriage, lest she answer that question in her mind. She nodded a tight greeting for Annalise, who stared at her with sympathy. Cleo looked away, refusing to hazard a guess at what she might be thinking—this girl who believed in fairy tales and happy endings.

Her father joined them inside the carriage. He gave a brisk knock on the ceiling and in moments they were moving. Anxiety rode high in her chest, rising into her throat, making it difficult to breathe.

Jack watched her anxiously as if she might swoon. She pasted a smile on her face that felt as brittle as glass—and told herself she simply had to hold on. Get past this. Put distance between herself and Logan. Soon, she'd be far from here and she'd forget. Common sense would prevail and she'd stop loving him.

From atop the scaffolding high along the wall, Logan watched the two carriages wind their way through the village, his heart clenching at the sight. Cleo was in the first carriage. She'd been standing too far away for him to read her precise expression before she climbed inside. Had she wanted him to say something? To cry out and beg her to stop?

"She's gone," Simon announced needlessly from the scaffolding beside him.

Logan nodded.

Simon followed his gaze, his youthful face reflecting all of his bewilderment. "I don't understand. You like her . . . and I don't care what you say. I know she cares for you, too."

Logan continued to look out at the horizon. The carriages were small, no bigger than his thumb in the distance. Soon they would round the turn and be out of sight. Gone for good.

Simon made a grunt of disgust. In his world, husbands and wives stayed together. The only time his father had left was to fight in the Crimea. Wives never left. "Is she ever coming back?"

Logan watched as the first carriage, the one Cleo occupied, took that final turn. She was gone. "No."

He turned his attention back to the task at hand, stepping off the scaffolding and onto a jutting ledge. "She's not. You coming?" He looked back at his brother.

Simon glanced around the scaffolding. "I forgot my pickax." Shrugging at his forgetfulness, he crouched down and descended the ladder to retrieve the tool he would need for the day's work.

Logan advanced along what was once a thick stone-fortified wall but was now only a crumbling outer shell, offering no protection to the interior room whatsoever. The entire thing needed to come down. Even if it meant removing each and every stone by hand.

Gripping his own ax, he strode inside the cavernous room. Now empty of furniture, it had once been a bedchamber. Flexing his fingers around the ax's handle, he joined the other two laborers already at work, attacking the outer wall and sending stone raining down into the yard.

He worked with a fury, taking solace in the labor. By the end of the day he intended to be aching sore and exhausted—too weary to contemplate Cleo and what precisely he felt within himself.

He lifted his ax and took a healthy whack. Stone sparked and crumbled. He grunted, and repeated the motion. The sound of steel hitting rock filled the air.

Arm pulled back, he was in mid-swing when the earth spit up a growl and rumbled all around him. He dropped his tool, arms reaching, stretching out to hold on to something amid his suddenly shifting, shuddering world. But there was nothing to grab. Only air.

One of the men beside him shouted. The other one dove for the ground.

And then there was nothing. Not even that anymore. The ground opened in a great, hungry maw beneath his feet. The floor gave out, disappearing in a fierce cloud of rock and rubble and debris. Taking him with it.

Chapter Twenty-nine

Cleo watched as her father removed his gloves and slapped them against his hands. The small taproom was crowded at this hour, and he eyed their surroundings impatiently, ostensibly hoping that they might be served by one of the harried-looking servant girls sometime soon.

Jack stood up from the table, his impatience getting the better of him. "I'll go speak with the innkeeper and see when we might expect service."

Cleo watched him stalk away, feeling as miserable as ever. In fact, with every mile they'd traveled, a pore-deep misery had infiltrated every inch of her.

"Are you well?" Annalise asked from beside her, blinking those wide brown eyes of hers with their impossibly long lashes.

Cleo nodded mutely. She should ask Annalise the same question. With her handicap, cooped up in a carriage for hours couldn't be that comfortable. Only Cleo couldn't muster the energy or inclination to talk.

"I'm certain a warm meal will do you good," Marguerite volunteered.

Cleo stared out at her bleakly. "Will it?" She wasn't convinced she'd ever feel well again.

Marguerite cocked her head, her gaze sharpening on Cleo. "Well, no, actually. I'm not convinced you'll ever be fine. You just walked away from your husband. And you may be too foolish to realize it, but you love the man."

"Marguerite," Ash chided.

She glared at her husband. "What? I won't sit silently as she does this. She needs to hear the truth."

Cleo turned to look out at the taproom. She didn't need to hear it. Because she already knew.

Yes. The word had slipped inside her mind before she could stop it. It was the answer she'd been fleeing from when she earlier asked herself if she loved her husband. It was there, inescapable. *Yes.*

She felt as though she'd left a part of herself with Logan. She couldn't recall ever feeling this wretched . . . save for when she buried one of her siblings.

So the remaining question was whether she was protecting herself at all if she was left hurting so much.

She closed her eyes in a tight blink. When she opened them moments later, she found herself staring at a young couple at the table next to her. Two small children crowded around the mother, eating from a single bowl of stew. She brought the spoon to one child's mouth and then the next, taking only an occasional sip for herself. The husband tore a large loaf of bread into pieces, placing the hunks upon a trencher that already held bits of cheese he'd torn up for the family. It wasn't much food for a family of four. But they smiled. They laughed. The mother kissed her children, and when she looked at her husband her eyes glowed.

They loved each other. They were happy. Even with their meager food and their well-worn clothes.

Her hand drifted to her belly. Did a life already grow there? A part of Logan? It dawned on Cleo that she'd like that. She would love that. In fact, she wanted that. She wanted it with Logan.

She stood abruptly. "I-I have to go."

Ash rose without a word and left the inn. Cleo hardly paid him any note. She looked desperately at each of her sisters. "I made a mistake. I have to go back."

Annalise smiled. "Oh, Cleo. You do love him."

Cleo nodded. "Yes, I have to see Jack. We have to go back now. At once."

Marguerite made a shushing sound and guided her back down.

"No," Cleo shook her off. "You don't understand. I left him. He thinks I don't care about him."

"I understand," Marguerite said evenly. "And so does Ash. He went to fetch the driver to ready the carriage."

"He did?"

Marguerite smiled. "We knew you would come to your senses."

"I wish I'd done so sooner." Her shoulders slumped.

Annalise scooted close and patted her back. "At least you did it before reaching London."

Cleo nodded, feeling only a little mollified. She wouldn't feel totally at ease until she saw Logan again. Until she told him how sorry she was. Until she told him how she felt—that the only thing that terrified her any longer was the possibility of losing him.

Hopefully, he'd forgive her for running away. Hopefully, she wasn't too late.

It was well past dark when they arrived back at McKinney Castle. She'd expected a sleeping village, but the lights of countless lanterns glowed through the curtains of her carriage. Every cottage window was lit, almost as though in vigil. Several people walked along the road toward the castle, slowing the progress of the carriages.

"What's happening?" Annalise asked, glancing left and right out the carriage window.

"Something's wrong," Cleo announced, her stomach sinking.

"I'll find out." Jack opened the door and hopped down from the slow-moving carriage.

She lost sight of him as he moved to talk to a villager and their conveyance clambered on, eventually entering into the yard, blazing with the light of dozens of torches and lanterns. Or at least they advanced as far as they could into the yard. People, wagons, and several draft horses blocked them from going any farther.

Unable to wait for her father to arrive with an explanation, she popped open the door and eased herself down, holding her skirts in one hand. Ignoring the sound of Annalise calling her name, she hastened through the crowd, scanning the yard, eager to see Logan. Would his eyes light with joy when he saw that she had returned? Or would they still look as cold and empty as before? Perhaps he'd resigned himself to her leaving . . . perhaps he was even glad to be rid of her.

She banished the thought, refusing to let it deter her from her course.

Shaking her head, she stepped to the side as a wagon loaded with rock and stone rolled past. Was it typical for them to work so late into the night? Ahead, she spotted Simon and cut a direct line for him. He'd know where she could find Logan.

"Simon!" she called out, rushing to reach him.

He swung around, his hair mussed and wild about him—but not nearly as wild as his eyes. She paused, unease taking hold of her as she surveyed him. He was covered in dirt. Even his dark hair was chalky with it.

"Cleo." He took a halting step toward her. There were others around him—a fact that only caught her notice because they all stilled unnaturally.

"Simon." She glanced at the faces watching her. "Where's Logan?"

Behind her, she heard her name being called. A glance over her shoulder revealed Jack, pushing through the crowd, his expression grave and urgent.

She looked back at her brother-in-law. He'd moved closer now. "Cleo . . . you came back . . ." His voice faded as he reached for her.

"Where's Logan?" Her voice rang sharply.

He shook his head at her, his countenance bleak and beyond weary.

Her gaze drifted, lifting over his shoulder. A gasp tore through her throat at the giant pile of rubble where the north-wing wall had once stood. Where she'd last seen Logan.

Her stomach dipped, dropped to her feet as understanding washed over her. She wasn't aware of anything. Not her scream. Not the hands holding her back as she attempted to launch herself at the pile of ancient stones that buried her husband.

Cleo hefted another rock onto the wagon bed, hardly breaking stride before she turned to fetch another one.

"Cleo, take a rest. Here . . . have a drink."

Shaking her head, she strode past Jack. After her initial shock, she'd changed into a pair of Josephine's spare trousers that the girl had been quick to volunteer. Considering that Josie and Abigail had been working alongside everyone else, there was no chance Cleo was going to stand idle.

"Cleo," Marguerite called from the side where she watched everyone work. She stepped out of her husband's way as he dumped two buckets of stones into the back of a wagon. "Please . . . you haven't stopped."

And she wouldn't. She couldn't. Not until she found Logan. Her mind strayed, inched toward that voice whispering through her mind. *He can't be alive. Not in there. Not beneath the crushing weight of those stones.*

"We found someone!"

Cleo dropped her bucket and raced forward at the shout, clambering up the rubble to the spot where several men crowded. Simon and Niall were there, at the head of the group.

"He'd dead!" a voice shouted.

She jerked to a stop, wobbling on the uneven surface, a sob strangling in her throat. *No, no, no.* She couldn't move. Couldn't bring herself to look. It's not Logan. Logan couldn't be dead. She couldn't have lost him just when she learned how much she loved him.

Jack was there, at her side, his fingers wrapping around her arm in support. She looked at him, her chest a twisting mass. "Is it . . ."

Jack shook his head and released her arm. He hurried ahead, climbing toward the body they'd unearthed and taking position beside Logan's younger brothers.

She waited, watched with her heart in her throat as he stared down alongside Logan's brothers. In moments, he whirled around, his gaze locking with hers. "It's not him!"

Relief sagged her shoulders, poured through her in a wash of gratitude—quickly replaced with the familiar fear again. Logan was still buried under all those stones. Bile rose in the back of her throat. She pressed her hand to her lips until the nausea passed.

Becoming ill would accomplish nothing. Without a word, she turned and gathered another stone, hefting it in her arms.

She paused when she caught sight of Simon's face. The defeat there, writ upon the youthful lines and hollows, struck a painful blow. He said something to one of the men, shaking his head.

Had he given up? Logan's own brother?

Fresh determination burned a fiery trail through her. Logan wouldn't give up if that was her down there. Not until he found her. Dropping the stone in her bucket she picked up another one. Stopping wasn't an option.

"Cleo." Jack arrived at her side again.

She faced him, blowing at a strand of hair that dangled before her eyes. "What are you waiting for? Pick up a rock."

She didn't wait to see whether he joined her or not. She simply resumed moving, working quickly, past the point of exhaustion . . . telling herself there was still hope. He was still under there. Still alive. She couldn't let herself believe otherwise.

Opening her mouth, she called his name as she removed stone after stone, convinced he was down there somewhere, and determined that he hear her voice and know help was coming.

Jack spoke her name gently. "Let's go inside and rest. The others will continue to work."

"I want to be here when he comes out."

Jack cleared his throat. She didn't even look up from her task, determined not to lose even a moment more of time. "Cleo, you have to consider . . . he's probably gone."

"No," she barked. "I don't have to consider that. I won't. Not unless I'm staring at his dead body. Until then, I'm digging. We all are. Now cease your prattle and get back to work."

There was only a moment's hesitation before Jack continued, tossing rocks into his bucket with a steady clink of stone on stone.

Opening her mouth, Cleo called out for Logan again, unearthing rocks until she couldn't feel her hands inside her heavy work gloves. She just moved from instinct and memory, her heart driving her.

Chapter Thirty

$\mathcal{L}$ogan winced as another stabbing pain shot up from where his foot was pinned.

He cursed himself for making the movement, the slight adjustment of his body that caused the lancing agony. It was too dark to investigate what trapped his foot.

He couldn't sit up. He splayed his hands flat on the stretch of wood that hovered two to three inches above his chest. It was the bottom of the scaffolding. One of its chains rattled somewhere near his head and he knew without its protection he would have been crushed beneath stone.

Somehow in the collapse, the heavy plank had fallen above him, covering him. The scaffolding was wedged at an angle, creating a small shelter of sorts—a pocket of air and space that wouldn't last forever.

He knew this, and in the endless dark he took careful sips of air, clinging to the hope that his brothers would find him—that they wouldn't stop. That they would be in time.

Cleo. Her face drifted through his mind. He was glad she'd gone. That she wasn't here, up there with the rest of them, suffering all manner of anxiety and grief. He knew she cared for him. That's why she'd left. Ran. Her feelings for him had grown into something real. Too real for her to face.

But he'd let her go anyway, instead of confessing his feelings, baring all for her, everything— and demanding the same from her.

He supposed that made him as much of a coward as she was. And now it might be too late.

He stopped breathing abruptly. The slow, easy cadence he'd established forgotten as his ears strained, listening. And there it was again. A sound. Faint. Far away—as if from the bottom of a well.

Logan!

His name. If he could hear them—perhaps he could be heard, too. Forgetting the need to save his air. He opened his mouth and shouted.

* * *

Cleo moved beyond the point of feeling. Beyond exhaustion. The only thing driving her was sheer faith that Logan lived.

She'd know if he was dead. She'd feel it. Practical or not, this is what she told herself as she dumped another bucket into the waiting wagon and tromped her way back up the mound of depleting stone. They'd find him soon.

She secured her footing on the uneven surface, ignoring how her legs trembled, and resumed working, calling out Logan's name periodically, forcing her voice to ring loudly even as it cracked from overuse.

She'd just tossed another rock into her bucket and was bending down for another one when she heard something.

She stilled, cocking her head to the side. It came again. Directly beneath her. She tossed her rock and began digging furiously, flinging stones aside. It didn't take very long for her to reach something that wasn't stony rubble—a small smooth patch of wood, no more than an inch in diameter, peeked out from where she'd cleared away rocks. She tapped the surface with her fingers.

An answering cry greeted the sound.

She shot up, nearly losing her balance. "Over

here!" she shouted, waving an arm wildly for the others. "I heard someone! Here!"

Men rushed her, crowding all around her, clearing the stones away, revealing more and more of the long stretch of wood. Scaffolding—it was the scaffolding, she realized with burgeoning excitement.

Jack wrapped an arm around her shoulders and moved her off to the side. She let him, knowing the men would all work faster than she could. Her gaze ached as she watched more and more of the plank become exposed.

Suddenly there was a hand—a filthy, dirt-covered hand shooting out from beneath the plank.

She shouted and lunged forward.

Jack pulled her back. "Wait. Let them clear the area and see . . ."

His words faded and she knew the rest of what he was saying: *let them see if he was fit to view.*

She didn't care. She'd seen that hand reaching for help. He was alive and she had to let him know she was here for him. That she'd be here for him no matter what.

She broke free and stumbled forward. She fell, caught herself on her hands and climbed, shoving through bodies, calling for Logan.

"Cleo!"

Simon appeared through the press of figures. He grabbed her hand and pulled her the rest of the way. One arm around her, he held her up as men lifted Logan to freedom.

Her throat constricted. She'd called his name for countless hours but now she could say nothing. Could only stare at his face, dirty and streaked with blood. *Alive.* Her heart squeezed so tightly within her chest she feared it might burst.

And then he saw her. He blinked, shook his head as if he couldn't believe his eyes. As if he were suffering a mirage.

He hobbled toward her, one arm around Niall for support, his eyes fastened on her—feral and alert. Not the eyes of a man trapped for hours beneath a pile of crushing stone.

He winced as he took a jarring step and she realized he couldn't put his weight on his right foot. She hastened forward, slipping her arm around his waist and closing her eyes in one long blink at the solid sensation of him alongside her body. He was whole. Alive.

"You look good in trousers," he murmured near her ear, stirring the hair that hung there loosely.

She snorted. Of all the things she'd imagined him to say, that had not been among them.

"I shall wear them every day for you then."

She smiled up at him as they eased off the rocky ground.

He turned to look at her, his face completely absorbed in the study of her. "Are you making promises?" he asked, bewilderment in his voice.

She swallowed against the sudden lump in her throat. Was he simply stunned that she was here? Or was there something more to his reaction? Did he not want her here?

Emotion swelled through her and her body trembled, the ordeal of the last hours catching up with her.

Hope filled her, eclipsing everything else. She wanted to hold him, talk to him, say all those things that desperately needed to be said. But Mrs. Willis was suddenly there, all efficiency as she took charge, sweeping Logan into the foyer, brushing Cleo aside so that she might assist him up the stairs. Just as well, she supposed. She was so shaky, her legs possessing all the consistency of pudding. She wouldn't want to risk losing her grip on Logan as they ascended the steps.

Cleo followed, letting Mrs. Willis direct. Logan needed tending and she was the best person to see it done. As he was carried up the stairs, he looked back several times, his gaze finding her. She resisted the impulse to rush after him and pour out her soul, confess her fears and proclaim her love.

That was a selfish need. Logan needed to be taken care of first. The needs of her heart could wait.

"Come." Abigail was at her side, taking her by the arm. "Let's get you changed and freshened up. I imagine you could use a bath. When was the last time you ate?"

Cleo looked longingly after Logan, mumbling some inane response.

Abigail followed her gaze. "Mrs. Willis will care for him. Let's take care of you so that you may be there for him when she's finished."

She glanced down at her filthy person and grimaced. Abigail made good sense. And she would like to look her best when she begged his forgiveness and asked for another chance as his wife. With that thought, Cleo permitted Abigail to tug her away, wincing when she grasped her gloved hand.

"What's this?" Abigail pulled her glove free and hissed a breath at the sight of Cleo's ravaged palms. Even with gloves, her palms were raw with broken blisters. "Come. Logan's not the only one requiring some nursing."

As she was pulled away in the direction of Abigail's chamber, she glanced down the length of corridor. Logan was already out of sight and her heart squeezed. As grateful as she was that he lived, this wasn't precisely the sweet reunion she had imagined.

Logan barely withstood Mrs. Willis's examination. He ground his teeth through all her poking and prodding, if for no other reason than to get through her inspection as hastily as possible. The more he complained, the longer she would linger over him, convinced he was mortally wounded. He hadn't lived his entire lifetime at McKinney without coming to know how the woman operated.

"I need to see Cleo. Where'd she go?"

"There now." Mrs. Willis rose from where she'd wrapped his left foot tightly in bandages. "Not broken, I believe. Just sprained and mightily bruised. It will take a while to heal fully, but you've always been a strong lad." She motioned to a crutch propped against the edge of the bed. "When you're fit to rise, you can walk with that. Belonged to my nephew Joseph when he broke his leg. Remember him? Great lumbering ox was always clumsy."

"Good." He began to rise, reaching for the crutch. "Now let me find Cleo."

She pushed him back down by the chest. "You're not going anywhere. Your sister's looking after her. She'll come to you soon enough."

He growled low in his throat, but knew better than to raise a fit with Mrs. Willis. In his present condition, he wouldn't get two feet before she dragged him back to bed by the ear.

Nodding, he forced out the words, "Very well."

She eyed him dubiously, and he wondered if he'd surrendered too soon. "I'm hungry," he volunteered. "I could use some food. The quicker to regain my strength."

Mrs. Willis nodded once, obviously satisfied, as he knew she would be. "That's a good lad. I'll be back with a plate for you. You just rest here and wait."

He nodded, struggling to maintain a neutral expression on his face as she ambled from the chamber.

As soon as the door clicked shut, he slid his legs over the side of the bed and reached for the crutch. Propping it beneath his arm, he began a slow, limping walk from the chamber.

Cleo couldn't be far. He assumed Mrs. Willis meant Abigail was looking after Cleo. Josephine could hardly look after herself much less someone else. In his anxiousness, he simply opened the door to his sister's room.

Abigail spun around, startled. "Logan!" she uttered his name quietly, and he immediately saw why.

Cleo had fallen asleep upon the bed wearing only a robe, her hair still wet from her bath. Dark smudges marred the tender flesh beneath her eyes.

"Leave us, Abbie. We'll stay the night here."

Abigail gathered up the garments Cleo had worn before her bath, pausing to look down at her sleeping sister-in-law. "She just sat down for a moment, and then she was asleep. She's had quite the day." Abigail's gaze slid over him. "You both have."

"She came back," he murmured.

"She never stopped, Logan. She pulled stones alongside the men. She was like a woman possessed."

His gaze devoured Cleo as she slept upon the bed. He wasn't surprised she possessed such tenacity and determination. He'd seen evidence of that since he met her. He was only astonished that he was the recipient of such steadfast resolve . . . that she should care about him that much.

Abigail glanced from him to Cleo upon the bed. "Are you certain you want to sleep in here? I can have someone carry her to your chamber."

"No." He wouldn't stand idle and helpless as someone else carried her for him. No one would hold her but him. Seeing as he was in no condition to do so at this time, they would spend the night here.

"Very well. I'll keep Willis away." Abigail hugged him quickly. "I'm so glad you're safe, brother."

As his sister left the room he snatched a blanket off the nearby chaise and limped the remaining steps to the bed. Lying down beside his wife, he covered them both with the soft fabric.

Sighing, he felt his beaten body finally ease and relax. Draping an arm around her waist and holding her close, he inhaled her clean scent and forgot all of his aches and pains. The elation in his heart eclipsed all else.

"Logan?" she murmured sleepily, lifting her head.

He looked down at her face, brushing a wet strand of hair from her cheek. "I'm here."

"I thought I was dreaming." Her eyes blinked with alertness.

"No dream."

"How . . ."

"Did you think I could stay away from you?"

Emotion brightened her gaze. "You're not angry at me . . . for leaving you?"

He stared into her eyes for a long time, the knowledge seeping into his bones that she was the one. The woman he was born to love. The woman he was meant to live out his life with. And that just maybe . . . she felt the same way. "You came back." His thumb brushed her bottom lip. "That's all that matters to me. That's everything."

A sob choked her throat and her lips quivered. "I never should have left. I was scared. I was running away . . . too scared to give us a chance. To take a risk. When we returned and I learned what happened, that you were buried under that wall, I thought it was my punishment for turning away from you . . . from denying what I felt. I love you."

"No punishment," he muttered fiercely, holding her face in both hands and kissing her roughly. He broke away to rasp against her lips, "I'm still here. I'm not going anywhere. And neither are you. Because if you ever try to leave again, I'll chase you down and drag you back home—here where you belong."

She snuggled closer to him, her face upturned to his. "I'll never leave again."

"I've always wanted you, Cleo. You just had to let go . . . and let me love you."

Her eyes shimmered wetly in the dim room. "I'm letting you."

"And I'm yours. Forever."

"I love you, Logan."

He smiled and kissed her again, long and deep. "It's about time you said it."

Epilogue

One month later . . .

Cleo looked up from her knitting at the sound
of wheels rolling into the courtyard. She was attempting to make Logan a scarf but so far it more
resembled a lopsided belt. She gave it one last
disapproving glance before rising to investigate
the noise outside. She was almost to the window
when the drawing-room doors burst open.

"Stop right there," her husband directed, wag-
ging his finger at her. His handsome grin belied
his commanding tone.

"What? Who's here?"

He seized her hand. "Come and you shall see."

Pulling her behind him, he hastened through the foyer and stepped outside.

Several carriages filled the courtyard. A dog barked anxiously around the wheels. Cleo held up a hand to shield her eyes from the rare brightness of the afternoon.

A carriage door opened. She grew breathless as one groom handed down a small child. And then another. And another. Bedraggled children began to spill out from the other carriages. They were the most beautiful sight she had ever seen.

"Cleo!"

She choked back a sob as the little bodies ran over to her and embraced her so fiercely she nearly lost her balance. Tears blinded her.

She turned to face her husband, blinking through the deluge. "You did this?"

She'd spent the last month writing letters to her family, to Roger, receiving no response. She'd begun to fear that her stepfather had changed his mind.

Logan reached out and wiped the tears from her cheeks. "Yes. I would do anything for you, Cleo."

A sob escaped her then. Logan pulled her into his arms for a long hug, his hands strong and warm on her back. In that moment, she believed this man could do anything. He'd saved her family. *He'd saved her.*

The children clamoring for her attention finally forced her to pull away. "Yes, yes, my loves! Welcome home!"

They clapped gleefully, but in their joy she read the desperate relief on their faces. Down to the youngest one of them, they each knew they were safe now. Everything was going to be fine. Her heart clenched as she thought of her mother, missing her. She should be here, too . . .

Then suddenly Cleo saw her emerge from the last carriage.

"Mama," she whispered hoarsely, unable to believe that she was here. She was free. Her gaze shifted to Logan again, knowing, understanding that somehow he had done this . . . For her.

I love you. She mouthed the words to him over the happy din of her siblings and he nodded, his hand closing around hers, the pulse of his heart fusing to her own, matching the beating rhythm.

"I love you, too, Cleo."

They may argue the precise shade
and design, but London's
finest dressmakers all know . . .

Scandal
Wears Satin

By

New York Times bestselling author

LORETTA
CHASE

On Sale Now
Read on for a sneak peek!

For the last week, the whole of the fashionable world has been in a state of ferment, on account of the elopement of Sir Colquhoun Grant's daughter with Mr. Brinsley Sheridan . . . On Friday afternoon, about five o'clock, the young couple borrowed the carriage of a friend; and . . . set off full speed for the North.

—*The Court Journal*, SATURDAY 23 MAY 1835

London
Thursday 21 May 1835

*W*aving a copy of *Foxe's Morning Spectacle*, Sophy Noirot burst in upon the Duke and Duchess of Clevedon while they were breakfasting in, appropriately enough, the breakfast room of Clevedon House.

"Have you seen this?" she said, throwing down the paper on the table between her sister and new brother-in-law. "The ton is in a frenzy—and isn't it hilarious? They're blaming Sheridan's three sisters. Three sisters plotting wicked plots—and it isn't *us!* Oh, my love, when I saw this, I thought I'd die laughing."

Certain members of Society had more than once in recent days compared the three proprietresses of Maison Noirot—which Sophy would make London's foremost dressmaking establishment if it killed her—to the three witches in

Macbeth. Had they not bewitched the Duke of Clevedon, rumor said, he would never have married a *shopkeeper*.

Their graces' dark heads bent over the barely dry newspaper.

Rumors about the Sheridan-Grant elopement were already traveling the beau monde grapevine, but the *Spectacle*, as usual, was the first to put confirmation in print.

Marcelline looked up. "They say Miss Grant's papa will bring a suit against Sheridan in Chancery," she said. "Exciting stuff, indeed."

At that moment, a footman entered. "Lord Longmore, your grace," he said.

Not now, dammit, Sophy thought. Her sister had the beau monde in an uproar, she'd made a deadly enemy of one of its most powerful women—who happened to be Longmore's mother—customers were deserting in droves, and Sophy had no idea how to repair the damage.

Now *him*.

The Earl of Longmore strolled into the breakfast room, a newspaper under his arm.

Sophy's pulse rate accelerated. It couldn't help itself.

Black hair and glittering black eyes . . . the noble nose that ought to have been broken a dozen times yet remained stubbornly straight and arrogant . . .

the hard, cynical mouth . . . the six-foot-plus frame.

All that manly beauty.

If only he had a brain.

No, better not. In the first place, brains in a man were inconvenient. In the second, and far more important, she didn't have time for him or any man. She had a shop to rescue from Impending Doom.

"I brought you the latest *Spectacle*," he said to the pair at the table. "But I wasn't quick enough off the mark, I see."

"Sophy brought it," said Marcelline.

Longmore's dark gaze came to Sophy. She gave him a cool nod and sauntered to the sideboard. She looked into the chafing dishes and concentrated on filling her plate.

"Miss Noirot," he said. "Up and about early, I see. You weren't at Almack's last night."

"Certainly not," Sophy said. "The Spanish Inquisition couldn't make the patronesses give me a voucher."

"Since when do you wait for permission? I was so disappointed. I was on pins and needles to see what disguise you'd adopt. My favorite so far is the Lancashire maidservant."

That was Sophy's favorite, too.

However, her intrusions at fashionable events to collect gossip for Foxe were supposed to be a deep, dark secret. No one noticed servant girls, and she was a Noirot, as skilled at making herself invisible as she was at getting attention.

But *he* noticed.

He must have developed unusually keen powers of hearing and vision to make up for his very small brain.

She carried her plate to the table and sat next to her sister. "I'm devastated to have spoiled your fun," she said.

"That's all right," he said. "I found something to do later."

"So it seems," Clevedon said, looking him over. "It must have been quite a party. Since you're never up and about this early, I can only conclude you stopped here on your way home."

Like most of his kind, Lord Longmore rarely rose before noon. His rumpled black hair, limp neckcloth, and wrinkled coat, waistcoat, and trousers told Sophy he hadn't yet been to bed—not his own, at any rate.

Her imagination promptly set about picturing his big body naked among tangled sheets. She had never seen him naked, and had better not; but along with owning a superior imagination, she'd seen statues, pictures, and—years ago—certain boastful Parisian boys' personal possessions.

She firmly wiped her mind clean.

One day, she'd marry a respectable man who would not get in the way of her work.

Not only was Longmore far from respectable, but he was a great thickhead who constantly got in one's way—and who happened to be the eldest son of a woman who wanted the Noirot sisters wiped off the face of the earth.

Only a self-destructive moron would get involved with him.

Sophy directed her attention to his clothes. As far as tailoring went, his attire was flawless, the snug fit outlining every muscled inch from his big shoulders and broad chest and his lean waist and narrow hips down, down, down his long, powerful legs . . .

She scrubbed her mind again, reminded herself that clothing was her life, and regarded him objectively, as one professional considering the work of another.

She knew that he usually started an evening elegantly turned out. His valet, Olney, saw to it. But Longmore did not always behave elegantly, and what happened after he left the house Olney could not control.

By the looks of him, a great deal had happened after Olney released his master yesterday.

"You always were the intellectual giant of the family," Longmore said to the duke. "You've deduced correctly. I stopped at Crockford's. And elsewhere. I needed something to drive out the memory of those dreary hours at Almack's."

"You loathe those assemblies," Clevedon said. "One can only assume that a woman lured you there."

"My sister," Longmore said. "She's an idiot about men. My parents complain about it endlessly. Even I noticed what a sorry lot they are, her beaux. A pack of lechers and bankrupts. To discourage them, I hang about Clara and look threatening."

Sophy could easily picture it. No one could loom as menacingly as he, gazing down on the world through half-closed eyes like a great, dark bird of prey.

"How unusually brotherly of you," said Clevedon.

"That numskull Adderley was trying to press his suit with her." Longmore helped himself to coffee and sat down next to Clevedon, opposite Marcelline. "She thinks he's charming. I think he's charmed by her dowry."

"Rumor says he's traveling up the River Tick on a fast current," Clevedon said.

"I don't like his smirk," Longmore said. "And I don't think he even likes Clara much. My parents loathe him on a dozen counts." He waved his coffee cup at the newspaper. "They won't find this coup of Sheridan's reassuring. Still, it's deuced convenient for you, I daresay. An excellent way to divert attention from your exciting nuptials."

His dark gaze moved lazily to Sophy. "The timing couldn't have been better. I don't suppose you had anything to do with this, Miss Noirot?"

"If I had, I should be demanding a bottle of the duke's best champagne and a toast to myself," said Sophy. "I only wish I could have managed something so *perfect*."

Though the three Noirot sisters were equally talented dressmakers, each had special skills. Dark-haired Marcelline, the eldest, was a gifted artist and designer. Redheaded Leonie, the youngest, was the financial genius. Sophy, the blonde, was the saleswoman. She could soften stony hearts and pry large sums from tight fists. She could make people believe black was white. Her sisters often said that Sophy could sell sand to Bedouins.

Had she been able to manufacture a scandal to turn Society's outrage away from her sister's situation, Sophy would have done it. As much as she loved Marcelline and was happy she'd married a man who adored her, Sophy was still reeling from the disruption to their world, which had always revolved around their little family and their business. She wasn't sure Marcelline and Clevedon truly understood the difficulties their recent marriage had created for Maison Noirot, or how much danger the shop was in.

But then, they were newlyweds, and love seemed to muddle the mind even worse than lust did. At present, Sophy couldn't bear to mar their happiness by sharing her and Leonie's anxieties.

The newlyweds exchanged looks. "What do you think?" Clevedon said. "Do you want to take advantage of the diversion and go back to work?"

"I must go back to work, diversion or not," Marcelline said. She looked at Sophy. "Do let's make a speedy departure, *ma chère sœur*. The aunts will be down to breakfast in the next hour or so."

"The aunts," Longmore said. "Still here?"

Clevedon House was large enough to accommodate several families comfortably. When the duke's aunts came to Town on visits too short to warrant opening their own townhouses, they didn't stay in hotels, but in the north wing.

Most recently they'd come to stop the marriage. Originally, Marcelline and Clevedon had planned to wed the day after he'd talked—or seduced—her into marrying him. But Sophy and Leonie's cooler heads had prevailed.

The wedding, they'd pointed out, was going to

cause a spectacular uproar, very possibly fatal to business. But if some of Clevedon's relatives were to attend the ceremony, signaling acceptance of the bride, it would subdue, to some extent, the outrage.

And so Clevedon had invited his aunts, who'd descended en masse to prevent the shocking misalliance. But no great lady, not even the Queen, was a match for three Noirot sisters and their secret weapon, Marcelline's six-year-old daughter, Lucie Cordelia. The aunts had surrendered in a matter of hours.

Now they were trying to find a way to make Marcelline respectable. They actually believed they could present her to the Queen.

Sophy wasn't at all sure that would do Maison Noirot any good. On the contrary, she suspected it would only fan the flames of Lady Warford's hatred.

"Still here," Clevedon said. "They can't seem to tear themselves away."

Marcelline rose, and the others did, too. "I'd better go before they come down," she said. "They're not at all reconciled to my continuing to work."

"Meaning there's a good deal more jawing than you like," Longmore said. "How well I understand." He gave her a wry smile, and bowed.

He was a man who could fill a doorway, and seemed to take over a room. He was disheveled, and disreputable besides, but he bowed with the easy grace of a dandy.

It was annoying of him to be so completely and gracefully at ease in that big brawler's body of his. It was really annoying of him to ooze virility.

Sophy was a Noirot, a breed keenly tuned to animal excitement—and not possessing much in the way of moral principles.

If he ever found out how weak she was in this regard, she was doomed.

She sketched a curtsey and took her sister's arm. "Yes, well, we'd better not dawdle, in any event. I promised Leonie I wouldn't stay above half an hour."

She hurried her sister out of the room.

Longmore watched them go. Actually, he watched Sophy go, a fetching bundle of energy and guile.

"The shop," he said when they were out of earshot. "Meaning no disrespect to your duchess, but—are they insane?"

"That depends on one's point of view," Clevedon said.

"Apparently, I'm not unbalanced enough in the upper storey to understand it," Longmore said. "They might close it and live here. It isn't as though you're short of room. Or money. Why should they want to go on bowing and scraping to women?"

"Passion," Clevedon said. "Their work is their passion."

Longmore wasn't sure what, exactly, passion was. He was reasonably certain he'd never experienced it.

He hadn't even had an infatuation since he was eighteen.

Since Clevedon, his nearest friend, would know this, Longmore said nothing. He only shook his head, and moved to the sideboard. He heaped his plate with eggs, great slabs of bacon and bread, and a thick glob of butter to make it all slide down smoothly. He carried it to the table and began to eat.

He'd always regarded Clevedon's home as his own, and had been told he was to continue regarding it in the same way. The duchess seemed to like him well enough. Her blonde sister, on the other hand would just as soon shoot him, he knew—which made her much more interesting and entertaining.

That was why he'd waited and watched for her. That was why he'd followed her from Maison Noirot to Charing Cross. He'd spotted the newspaper in her hand, and deduced what it was.

By some feat of printing legerdemain—a pact

with the devil, most likely—*Foxe's Morning Spectacle* usually slunk onto the streets of London and into the newspaper sellers' grubby hands not only well in advance of its competitors, but containing fresher scandal. Though many of the beau monde's entertainments didn't start until eleven at night or end before dawn, Foxe contrived to stuff the pages of his titillating rag with details of what everyone had done mere hours earlier.

This was no small achievement, even bearing in mind that "morning," especially among the upper classes, was a flexible unit of time, extending well beyond noonday.

Curious about what was taking her to Clevedon House at this early hour, he'd bought a copy from the urchin hawking it on the next corner, and had dawdled for a time to look it over. By now familiar with Sophy's writing, Longmore knew it wasn't the sort of thing to take on an empty stomach. He'd persevered nonetheless. Though he couldn't see how she could have had a hand in the Sheridan scandal, that was nothing new. She did a great deal he found intriguing—starting with the way she walked: She carried herself like a lady, like the other women of his class, yet the sway of her hips promised something tantalizingly unladylike.

"I married Marcelline knowing she'd never

give up her work," Clevedon was saying. "If she did, she'd be like everyone else. She wouldn't be the woman I fell in love with."

"Love," Longmore said. "Bad idea."

Clevedon smiled. "One day Love will come along and knock you on your arse," he said. "And I'll laugh myself sick, watching."

"Love will have its work cut out for it," Longmore said. "I'm not like you. I'm not *sensitive*. If Love wants to take hold of me, not only will it have to knock me on my arse, it'll have to tie me down and beat to a pulp what some optimistically call my brains."

"Very possibly," Clevedon said. "Which will make it all the more amusing."

"You'll have a wait," Longmore said. "For the moment, Clara's love life is the problem."

"I daresay matters at home haven't been pleasant for either of you, since the wedding," Clevedon said.

Clevedon would know better than most. Lord Warford had been his guardian. He and Longmore had grown up together. They were more like brothers than friends. And Clevedon had doted on Clara since she was a small child. It had always been assumed they'd marry. Then the duke had met his dressmaker—and Clara had reacted with "Good riddance"—much to the shock of her parents, brothers, and sisters—not to mention the entire beau monde.

"My father has resigned himself," Longmore said. "My mother hasn't."

A profound understatement, that.

His mother was beside herself. The slightest reference to the duke or his new wife set her screaming. She quarreled with Clara incessantly. She was driving Clara to distraction, and they constantly dragged Longmore into it. Every day or so a message arrived from his sister, begging him to come and Do Something.

Longmore and Clara had both attended Clevedon's wedding—in effect, giving their blessing to the union. This fact, which had been promptly reported in the *Spectacle,* had turned Warford House into a battlefield.

"I could well understand Clara rejecting me," Clevedon said.

"Don't see how you could fail to understand," Longmore said. "She explained it in detail, in ringing tones, in front of half the ton."

"What I don't understand is why she doesn't send Adderley about his business," Clevedon said.

"Tall, fair, poetic-looking," Longmore said. "He knows what to say to women. Men see him for what he is. Women don't."

"I've no idea what's in Clara's mind," Clevedon

said. "My wife and her sisters will want to get to the bottom of it, though. It's their business to understand their clients, and Clara's special. She's their best customer, and she shows Marcelline's designs to stunning advantage. They won't want her to marry a man with pockets to let."

"Are they in the matchmaking line as well, then?" Longmore said. "If so, I wish they'd find her someone suitable, and spare me these dreary nights at Almack's."

"Leave it to Sophy," Clevedon said. "She's the one who goes to the parties. She'll see what's going on, better than anybody."

"Including a great deal that people would rather she didn't see," Longmore said.

"Hers is an exceptionally keen eye for detail," Clevedon said.

"And an exceptionally busy pen," Longmore said. "It's easy to recognize her work in the *Spectacle*. Streams of words about ribbons and bows and lace and pleats here and gathers there. No thread goes unmentioned."

"She notices gestures and looks as well," Clevedon said. "She listens. No one's stories are like hers."

"No question about that," Longmore said. "She's never met an adjective or adverb she didn't like."

Clevedon smiled. "That's what brings in the customers: the combination of gossip and the intricate detail about the dresses, all related as drama. It has the same effect on women, I'm told, as looking at naked women has on men." He tapped a finger on the *Spectacle*. "I'll ask her to keep an eye on Clara. With two of you on watch, you ought to be able to keep her out of trouble."

Longmore had no objections to any activity involving Sophy Noirot.

On the contrary, he had a number of activities in mind, and joining her in keeping an eye on his sister would give him a fine excuse to be underfoot—and with any luck, under other parts as well.

"Can't think of a better woman for the job," Longmore said. "Miss Noirot misses nothing."

In his mind she was *Sophy*. But she'd never invited him to call her by the name all her family used. And so, even with Clevedon, good manners dictated that Longmore use the correct form of address for the senior unmarried lady of a family.

"With you and Sophy standing guard, the lechers and bankrupts won't stand a chance," Clevedon said. "Argus himself couldn't do better."

Longmore racked his brain. "The dog, you mean?"

"The giant with extra eyes," Clevedon said. " 'And set a watcher upon her, great and strong

Argus, who with four eyes looks every way,'" he quoted from somewhere. "'And the goddess stirred in him unwearying strength: sleep never fell upon his eyes; but he kept sure watch always.'"

"That strikes me as excessive," Longmore said. "But then, you always were romantic."

A week later

"Warford, how *could* you?"

"My dear, you know I cannot command His Majesty—"

"It is not to be borne! That *creature* he married—presented at *Court!*—on the King's birthday!—as though she were visiting royalty!"

Longmore was trapped in a carriage with his mother, father, and Clara, departing St. James's Palace. Though court events bored him witless, he'd attended the King's Birthday Drawing Room, hoping to spot a certain uninvited attendee. But he'd seen only Sophy's sister—the "creature" his mother was in a snit about. Then he'd debated whether to sneak out or to hunt for an equally bored wife or widow. The palace was well supplied with dark corners conducive to a quick bout of fun.

No luck with the females. The sea of plumes

and diamonds held an overabundance of stuffy matrons and virgins. Virgins were what one married. They weren't candidates for fun under a staircase.

"Odd, I agree," Lord Warford said carefully. Though he'd given up being outraged about Clevedon's marriage, he'd also long ago given up trying to reason with his wife.

"Didn't seem odd to me," Longmore said.

"Not odd!" his mother cried. "Not odd! *No one* is presented at the King's Birthday Drawing Room."

"No one but foreign dignitaries," Lord Warford said.

"It was a shocking breach of etiquette even to request an exception," Lady Warford said, conveniently forgetting that she'd told her husband to commit a shocking breach of etiquette by telling the King not to recognize the Duchess of Clevedon.

But it was up to the husband, not the son, to point this out, and years of marriage had taught Lord Warford cowardice.

"I could not believe Her Majesty would do such a thing, even for Lady Adelaide," Mother went on. "But it seems I'm obliged to believe it," she added bitterly. "The Queen dotes on Clevedon's youngest aunt." She glared at her daughter. "Lady Adelaide Ludley might have used her influence on your and your family's behalf. But no, you must be the most ungrateful, undutiful daughter who ever lived. You must jilt the Duke of Clevedon!"

"I didn't jilt him, Mama," Clara said. "One cannot jilt someone to whom one is not engaged."

Longmore had heard this argument too many times to want to be boxed in a closed carriage, hearing it again, his mother's voice going higher and higher, and Clara's climbing along with it. Normally, he would simply call the carriage to a halt and get out, and leave everybody fuming behind him.

Clara could defend herself, he knew. The trouble was, that would only lead to more quarreling and screaming and messages for him to come to Warford House before she committed matricide.

He thought very hard and very fast and said, "It was clear as clear to me that they did it behind the scenes, so to speak, to spare your feelings, ma'am."

There followed the kind of furiously intense silence that typically ensued when his parents were deciding whether he might, against all reason and evidence, have said something worth listening to.

"What with the aunts and all, the Queen would be in a fix," he went on. "She could hardly snub

Clevedon's whole family—which is what she'd be doing, since the aunts had accepted his bride."

"His bride," his mother said bitterly. "His *bride*." She threw Clara the sort of look Caesar must have given Brutus when the knife went in.

"This way at least, the deed was done behind the scenes," Longmore went on, "not in front of the whole blasted ton."

While his mother stirred this idea around in her seething mind, the carriage reached the front of Warford House. The footmen opened the carriage door, and the family emerged, the ladies shaking out their skirts as they stepped out onto the pavement.

Longmore said nothing and Clara said nothing but she shot him a grateful look before she hurried inside after their mother.

His father, however, lingered at the front step with Longmore. "Not coming in?"

"I think not," Longmore said. "Did my best. Tried to pour oil and all that."

"It won't end," his father said in a low voice. "Not for your mother. Shattered dreams and wounded pride and outraged sensibilities and whatnot. You see how it is. We can expect no peace in this family until Clara finds a suitable replacement for Clevedon. That's not going to happen while she keeps encouraging that pack of loose screws." He made a dismissive gesture. "Make them go away, will you, dammit?"

One o'clock in the morning
Saturday 30 May 1835
Countess of Igby's ball

Longmore had been looking for Lord Adderley for some time. The fellow having proven too thick to take a hint, Longmore had decided that the simplest approach was to hit him until he understood that he was to keep off Clara.

The trouble was, Sophy Noirot was at Lady Igby's party, too, and Longmore, unlike Argus, owned only the usual number of eyes.

He'd become distracted, watching Sophy flit hither and yon, no one paying her the slightest heed—except for the usual assortment of dolts who thought maidservants existed for their sport. Since he'd marked her as *his* sport, Longmore had started to move in, more than once, only to find that she didn't need any help with would-be swains.

She'd "accidentally" spilled hot tea on the waistcoat of one gentleman who'd ventured too close. Another had followed her into an antechamber and tripped over something, landing on his face.

A third had followed her down a passage and into a room. He'd come out limping a moment later.

Preoccupied with her adventures, Longmore not only failed to locate Adderley, but lost track of the sister he was supposed to be guarding from lechers and bankrupts. This would have been less of a problem had Sophy been watching her more closely. But Sophy had her own lechers to fend off.

Longmore wasn't thinking about this. Thinking wasn't his favorite thing to do, and thinking about more than one thing at a time upset his equilibrium. At the moment, his mind was on the men trespassing on what he'd decided was his property. Unfortunately, this meant he wasn't aware of his mother losing sight of Clara at the same time. This happened because Lady Warford was carrying on a politely poisonous conversation with her best friend and worst enemy Lady Bartham.

In short, nobody who should have been paying attention was paying attention while Lord Adderley was steering Clara, as they waltzed, toward the other end of the ballroom, toward the doors leading to the terrace. None of those who should have been keeping a sharp eye out saw the wink Adderley sent his friends or the accompanying smirk.

It was the crowd's movement that brought Longmore back, with an unpleasant thud, to his surroundings and his main reason for being here.

The movement wasn't obvious. It wasn't meant to be. Men like Longmore were attuned to it, though. He had no trouble recognizing the sense of something in the air, the shift in the attention in some parts of the room, and the drifting toward a common destination. It was the change in the atmosphere one felt when a fight was about to happen.

The current was sweeping toward the terrace.

His gut told him something was amiss. It didn't say what, but the warning was vehement, and he was a man who acted on instinct. He moved, and quickly.

He didn't have to push his way through the crowd. Those who knew him knew they'd better get out of the way or be thrust out of the way.

He stormed out onto the terrace. A small audience had gathered. They got out of his way, too.

Nothing and nobody obstructed his view.

Wickedly Delightful Romance From

Sophie Jordan

Lessons from a Scandalous Bride
978-0-06-203300-0

Miss Cleopatra Hadley needs a convenient marriage with no complications—especially not love. But then Lord Logan McKinney arrives and changes everything.

Wicked in Your Arms
978-0-06-203299-7

Though she's the illegitimate daughter of London's most disreputable man, Grier Hadley possesses the allure of an elite. And though he's a proper prince expected to marry someone of similar breeding, Sevastian Maksimi can't seem to keep his eyes off of the wild vixen.

Wicked Nights With a Lover
978-0-06-157923-3

When Marguerite Laurent learns that she is to die before year's end, she desires but one thing—passion. Ash Courtland—the wrong man—threatens to give her a taste of the once-in-a-lifetime ardor she so desperately craves.

In Scandal They Wed
978-0-06-157921-9

Chased by scandal, Evelyn Cross long ago sacrificed everything for a chance at love. Bound by honor, Spencer Lockhart returns from war to claim his title and marry the woman his cousin once wronged.

Visit www.AuthorTracker.com for exclusive information on your favorite HarperCollins authors.

Available wherever books are sold or please call 1-800-331-3761 to order.

JOR 0412

Next month, don't miss these exciting new love stories only from Avon Books

A Lady by Midnight by Tessa Dare
When mysterious strangers come looking for Kate Taylor in Spindle Cove, hardened militia commander Samuel Thorne comes to the rescue by posing as Kate's fiancé and guarding her against trouble. The temporary arrangement should be exactly that, so why does Kate find smoldering passion in his kiss? And why can't Samuel get her out of his mind?

The Way to a Duke's Heart by Caroline Linden
Duke-to-be Charles de Lacey is shocked to discover he may be stripped of everything thanks to his father's scandalous past. Having no choice but to find the blackmailer, his only link is Tessa Neville, a beautiful woman who may be part of the plot. With his future at stake, Charles must decide: is Tessa the woman of his dreams or an enemy in disguise?

Chosen by Sable Grace
Finally able to shed her past, Kyana is ready to embrace her new role as the Goddess of the Hunt and her long-deserved union with Ryker. But when evil is resurrected, Kyana must battle her own fierce independence and allow Ryker to help, or risk the fate of the world.

Sins of a Virgin by Anna Randol
Shocking the *ton*, Madeline Valdan plans to auction off her virginity. Gabriel Huntford, determined to find the culprit behind his sister's murder, didn't plan to be involved in Madeline's game. But when the trail leads to one of Madeline's bidders and they must work together to find the truth, the two discover a passion neither one expected.

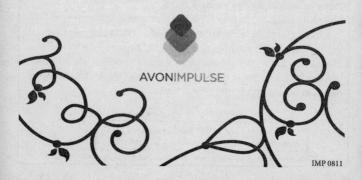